ANOTHER THING TO FALL

When private eye Tess Monaghan finds herself on a collision course with the makers of a TV series, it's not only her introduction to the surreal world of television drama, but also the beginning of a case that only a crazed scriptwriter could have dreamed up for her.

Selene Waites, the sexy, self-centred young star of *Mann of Steel*, has been the victim of a twisted stalker who then committed suicide—just one of a series of mishaps that have dogged the production. Executive producer Flip Tumulty persuades Tess to take on the job of bodyguarding Selene and keeping the lid on further trouble.

At first, Selene seems like a spoiled kook out of central casting and the babysitting job a PR sham, but as Tess gets sucked deeper into the show's labyrinthine web of deceptions and betrayals, she soon finds she's unwittingly become the lead character in a storyline featuring murder, kidnapping and a decades-old obsession.

ANOTHER THING TO FALL

Laura Lippman

WINDSOR
PARAGON

First published 2008
by Orion Books
This Large Print edition published 2008
by BBC Audiobooks Ltd
by arrangement with
The Orion Publishing Group Ltd

Hardcover ISBN: 978 1 408 41427 9
Softcover   ISBN: 978 1 408 41428 6

British Library Cataloguing in Publication Data available

Printed and bound in Great Britain by
CPI Antony Rowe, Chippenham, Wiltshire

In memory of Robert F. Colesberry

'Tis one thing to be tempted, Escalus
Another thing to fall

—*Measure for Measure*

MARCH

First Shot

There she was.

Smaller than he expected. Younger, too. But the primary shock was that she was human, a person just like him. Well, not *just* like him—there was the thirty-plus age difference to start—but flesh and blood, standing on a street in Baltimore, occupying the same latitude and longitude, breathing the same air. Look at her, sipping one of those enormous coffee drinks that all the young people seemed to carry now, as if the entire generation had been weaned too early and never recovered from the shock of it. He imagined a world of twenty-somethings, their mouths puckering around nothingness, lost without something to suck. Figuratively, not literally. Unlike most people, even allegedly educated ones, he used those words with absolute precision and prided himself on the fact, as he prided himself on all his usage, even in the sentences he formed in his head, the endless sentences, the commentary that never stopped, the running voice-over of his life. Which was funny, as he disdained voice-over in film, where it almost never worked.

Yet even as the vision of a suckling nation took shape in his head, he knew it wasn't his exclusively, that it had been influenced by something he had seen. Who? What? A small part of his brain wouldn't rest until he pinned down this fleeting memory. He was as punctilious about the origins of his ideas as he was about the correctness of his speech.

He liked young people, usually, thrived in their company, and they seemed to like him, too. *Crabbed age and youth cannot live together*—whoever wrote that line couldn't have been more wrong. The young people he invited into his home, his life, had given him sustenance, enough so that he didn't mind tolerating the inevitable rumors. *Baltimore bachelor . . . lives by himself in that old house near the park . . . up to strange things with all that camera equipment. People swear he's on the up-and-up, but who can tell?* But those things were said by the neighbors who didn't know him. When he selected the children, he got to know their parents first, went around to the houses, showed them what he did, explained his methods, provided personal references. It got so where parents were calling *him,* begging for a slot for little Johnny or Jill. Gently, tactfully, he would explain that his wasn't just another after-school program, open to any child. It was up to him, and him alone, who would be admitted.

Now that he had this one in his viewfinder—would he have chosen her, glimpsed her potential when she was eight or nine? Possibly, maybe. It was hard to know. Faces coarsened so much after adolescence. Personalities, more so. This one—she was probably sweet, once upon a time. Affection starved, the kind who crawled into your lap and cupped your cheeks with her baby-fat palms. Patted your face and stroked your hair and stared straight into your eyes with no sense of boundaries, much less the concept of personal space. He loved children when they were unself-conscious, but that phase was so swift, so fleeting, and he was left with the paradox of trying to teach

4

them to be as they once were, to return to a time when they didn't understand the concept of embarrassment, much less worry about what others thought. But it was the eternal struggle—once you realize you're in Eden, you have to leave. He watched the teenage years approach with more anguish than any parent, knowing it marked the end.

The lens was a powerful one, purchased years ago. He was no Luddite—there was much new technology on which he doted, and even more for which he yearned—but he could not sacrifice his old Pentax for a digital camera. Besides, the kind of SLR system he would need was out of reach. The Canon he had priced online was $2,500 at discount, and that was for the body alone. No, he would stick with his battered Pentax for now. Come to think of it—how old was this camera? It must be twenty-five, thirty years ago that he had taken the plunge at Cooper's Camera Mart. A memory tickled his nose—what was that wonderful aroma that camera stores once had? Film, it must have been film, or the developing products, all outmoded now. Consider it—in his lifetime, just a little over a half century, he had gone from shooting photos with a Kodak automatic, the kind with a detachable wand of flashbulbs, to shooting movies that he could watch instantly at home, and if anyone thought that was inferior to trying to load an eel-slippery roll of film onto a reel, then they had his sympathy. No, he had no complaints about what technology had wrought. Technology was wonderful. If he had had more technology at his disposal, even fifteen years ago, then things might be very different now.

5

Look up, look up, look up, he urged the image he had captured, and just like that, as if his wish were her command, she lifted her eyes from the paper in front of her, stopped sipping her drink, and stared into the distance. Such an open, innocent face, so guileless and genuine. So everything she wasn't.

Her mouth, free from the straw, puckered in lonely dismay, and he knew in that instant the image that had been tantalizing him—*The Simpsons,* the episode that had managed to parody *The Great Escape* and *The Birds* with just a few deft strokes. He had watched it with his young friends, pointing out the Hitchcock cameo, then screening the real movies for them so they could understand the larger context. (It was the only reason he agreed to watch the cartoon with them, in order to explain all its cinematic allusions.) They had loved both movies, although the explicit horror of killer birds had seemed to affect them far more than the true story behind the men who had escaped from Stalag Luft III, only to be executed upon their capture. He was ten years old when the movie came out—he saw it at the Hippodrome—and World War II, an experience shared by his father and uncles, loomed large in his imagination. Now he found himself surrounded by young people who thought Vietnam was ancient history. They had reeled when they learned he was old enough to have been in the draft. This one—she, too, considered him old, and therefore a person she was free to ignore. She probably didn't even remember the Persian Gulf War. She might not know there was a war going on even now, given how insular she was. Insular and insolent.

He watched the rosebud of her mouth return to the straw and decided that the image that had been teasing him, literally and figuratively, was Lolita. The movie version, of course. No heart-shaped sunglasses, but she didn't need them, did she? *You'll be the death of me,* he lamented, clicking the shutter. *You'll be the death of me.*

Literally and figuratively.

PART ONE

KISS KISS
BANG BANG

Fall came early to Mount Vernon this October—
much to the neighborhood's disgust. According to
Mandy Stewart, vice president of the Mount Vernon
Neighborhood Association, workers for Mann of
Steel *stripped leaves from the trees in order to create*
the late-autumn atmosphere required for the
miniseries, which is being produced by Philip 'Flip'
Tumulty Jr.

'They just came through in late September and
ripped the leaves from the trees, then put up a few
fake brown ones in their place,' Stewart told the
Beacon-Light. *'They stole our fall out from under*
us! And they've made parking a nightmare.'

Steelworkers are equally peeved with Mann of
Steel, *which they say has shown a marked*
indifference to portraying the industry with accuracy.
'These guys couldn't find Sparrows Point on a map,'
said Peter Bellamy of Local 9477. 'They're just using
us for cheap laughs.'

He said retired steelworkers are considering
informational pickets at the series' various locations
around the city, but he disavowed any connection to
the series of mishaps that have befallen the
production, as detailed previously by the Beacon-
Light.

The Maryland Film Commission and the city's
film liaison both said they had received no
complaints, insisting the production had been an
exemplary, polite presence in the city. Tumulty,
through his assistant, refused repeated requests for
comment.

Tumulty is the son of the Baltimore filmmaker
Philip Tumulty Sr., who first attracted attention with

11

lovingly detailed movies about Baltimore's Highlandtown neighborhood in the 1960s and early 1970s, such as Pit Beef *and* The Last Pagoda. *But he turned his attention to more conventional—and far more lucrative—Hollywood blockbusters, including* The Beast, Piano Man, *and* Gunsmoke, *the last a reworking of the long-running television show. The younger Tumulty, after a much-heralded independent film, written with childhood friend Ben Marcus, has worked exclusively in television.*

His latest project, Mann of Steel, *has extended the city's long run with Hollywood, which has been an almost constant presence in Baltimore over the last fifteen years. However, although this series centers on Bethlehem Steel and nineteenth-century Baltimore belle Betsy Patterson, Maryland almost lost the production to Philadelphia, which has more architecture dating from the early 1800s. Special tax incentives helped to lure the show to Maryland.*

Unlike previous productions, Mann of Steel *has had a rocky relationship with the city from the start. Complaints from neighbors and steelworkers are only part of the problems they have faced. There have been a series of small fires set near some of the locations and rumors of bad behavior by up-and-coming actress Selene Waites, 20, who keeps popping up in local bars.*

'We are grateful to Baltimore and Maryland for all they've done to make this film possible,' said co-executive producer Charlotte MacKenzie when asked for comment. 'We just wish others were grateful for the $25 million we're spending, half of which will go directly into the local economy.'

Community activist Stewart is not about to be mollified: 'The economic benefits of film production

12

are wildly exaggerated, based on the stars' salaries, which may or may not be taxed by local authorities,' she said. *'The bottom line is that* Mann of Steel *is a pain in the butt.'*

—THE BEACON-LIGHT,
OCT. 15

MONDAY

Chapter 1

The headphones were a mistake. She realized this only in hindsight, but then—what other vision is available to a person heading backward into the world?

True, they were good old-fashioned headphones, which didn't seal tightly to the ear, not *earbuds,* which she loathed on principle, the principle being that she was thirty-four going on seventy. Furthermore, she had dialed down the volume on her Sony Walkman—yes, a Sony Walkman, sturdy and battered and taxicab yellow, not a sleek little iPod in a more modern or electric shade. Still, for all her precautions, she could hear very little. And even Tess Monaghan would admit that it's important to be attuned to the world when one is charging into it backward, gliding along the middle branch of the Patapsco in a scull and passing through channels that are seldom without traffic, even in the predawn hours.

But Tess had painstakingly rationalized her way into trouble, which, she decided later, is pretty much how everyone gets into trouble, one small rationalization at a time. She wanted to row, yet she felt obligated to listen to her boyfriend on a local radio show, promoting the Oktoberfest lineup at her father's bar. Besides, he planned to play some songs by Brave Combo, a nuclear polka band that Tess quite liked. She would row a path that was familiar to her, and trust the coxswains for the fours and eights to watch her back, a courtesy offered to all scullers.

It did not occur to Tess to row a little later, or skip the workout altogether. The rowing season traditionally ended after Thanksgiving, a mere month away. She had to take advantage of every waning day, especially now that Baltimore was in its full autumnal glory. If aliens had landed in Baltimore on this particular October morning, they would have concluded that it was the most perfect city on the globe they were about to conquer, truly the Charm City it claimed to be. The trees were tinged with gold and scarlet, the breeze was light, the sky was slowly deepening into the kind of brilliant blue that reminded Tess that she once knew the word *cerulean,* if only because it had been on the vocabulary lists for the SATs.

She set out for Fort McHenry, at the distant tip of Locust Point, rationalizing every stroke of the way: She knew the route so well, it was so early, the sun not even up. She had beaten the other rowers to the water, arriving in darkness and pushing off from the dock at first light. She wouldn't wear the headphones on the way back. She just needed to hear Crow on WTMD, listen to him play a few snippets of Brave Combo, then she would turn off the Walkman and—

That's when the police boat, bullhorn blaring, crossed into her line of vision and came charging toward her. By the time she registered everything that was happening—the approaching boat, the screams and shouts coming from all directions, the fact that someone was very keen that she stop or change course—the motorboat had stopped, setting up an enormous, choppy wake that was going to hit her sideways. Tess, trying frantically to slow and steady her scull, had a bona fide moment

18

of prescience. Granted, her vision extended only two or three seconds into the future, but it was uncannily exact: She was going to go ass over teakettle into the Patapsco, a body of water that even conquering aliens from a water-deprived planet would find less than desirable. She closed her eyes and shut her mouth as tightly as possible, grateful she had no cuts or scratches into which microbes could swim.

At least the water held some leftover summer warmth. She broke the surface quickly, orienting herself by locating the star-shaped fort just to the north, then the wide channel into the bay to the east of the fort, toward which her vessel was now drifting. 'Get my shell,' she spluttered to the police boat, whose occupants stared back at her, blank faced. 'My shell! My scull! MY GODDAMN BOAT.' Comprehension dawning, the cops reached out and steadied her orphaned scull alongside the starboard side of their boat. Tess began to swim toward them, but a second motorboat cut her off.

A man sat in the stern of this one, his face obscured by a baseball cap, his arms crossed over a fleece vest emblazoned with a curious logo, *Mann of Steel*. He continued to hug his arms close to his chest, a modern-day Washington crossing the Delaware, even as two young people put down their clipboards and reached out to Tess, boosting her into the boat.

'Congratulations,' said the male of the pair. 'You just ruined a shot that we've been trying to get for three days.'

Tess glanced around, taking in everything her back had failed to see. This usually quiet strip around Fort McHenry was ringed with boats. There was an outer periphery of police launches, set up to protect an inner circle, which included this boat and another nearby, with what appeared to be a mounted camera and another fleece-jacketed man. There were people onshore, too, and some part of Tess's mind registered that this was odd, given that Fort McHenry didn't open its gates to the public until 9 A.M. Farther up the fort's grassy slopes, she could see large white trailers and vans, some of them with blue writing that she could just make out: HADDAD'S RENTALS. She squeezed her ponytail and tried to wring some water from her T-shirt, but the standing man frowned, as if it were bad form to introduce water into a boat.

'The sun's up now,' said the young woman who had helped Tess into the boat, her tone dire, as if this daily fact of life, the sun rising, was the most horrible thing imaginable. 'We lost all the rose tones you wanted.'

The doubly stern man threw his Natty Boh cap down in the boat, revealing a headful of brown curls, at which he literally tore. He was younger than Tess had realized, not much older than she, no more than thirty-five. 'Three days,' he said. 'Three days of trying to get this shot and some *stupid* rower has to come along at the exact wrong moment—'

'Tess Monaghan,' she said, offering a damp, sticky hand. He didn't take it. 'And I'm sorry about the accident, but *you* almost killed *me*.'

'No offense,' said Natty Boh, 'but that might have been cheaper for us in the long run.'

Chapter 2

Are you sure you want to wait for your clothes to go through the wash?' asked the girl from the boat, the brunette with the clipboard. 'We could dress you from the underwear up with things in the wardrobe trailer. What are you? Size twelve? Fourteen?'

Tess was seldom nonplussed, but she found this offer—and eerily on-target assessment of her size, which was usually a twelve, but had been known to flirt with fourteen after a Goldenberg Peanut Chew fling—disorienting to say the least. *Surreal* was an overused word in Tess's experience, but it suited the events of the morning so far. Now that she was on land, her Hollywood rescuers were behaving more like captors, making sure she was never out of their sight. Were they worried about a lawsuit? She covered her confusion by bending down and toweling her hair, checking to see if it still carried a whiff of river water beneath the green apple scent of the shampoo. They had been kind enough to let her shower in one of the trailers, which they kept calling bangers, much to Tess's confusion. Was the jargon some sort of sexual allusion? There also had been mention of a honey wagon and repeated offers to bring her something from craft services, but she wasn't sure what that meant. Macramé?

'No, I'll wait, if you don't mind,' she said. 'My Under Armour tights and jog bra will dry really fast, even on a low-heat cycle, and I don't mind if the T-shirt is a little damp.'

21

'Everything we have is *clean,*' the young woman said, her tone huffy, as if she were personally offended by Tess's refusal of laundered-but-possibly-used underwear. 'And we'd put you in modern clothes, from the present-day sequences, not the nineteenth-century stuff.' Again, that cool appraising look, unnerving in an otherwise sweet-faced young woman, not even twenty-five by Tess's estimation. 'You probably wouldn't fit into those, anyway. They're quite small.'

Tess cinched the belt of the bathrobe they had loaned her. The garment was Pepto-Bismol pink and made of a fluffy chenille-like material that seemed to expand the longer she wore it, so she felt quite lost and shapeless within it. Still, she did have a waist and a respectably solid body somewhere inside this pink mass.

The man in the Natty Boh cap, who had been on his cell phone almost constantly since they arrived at the trailer—*banger*—suddenly barked: 'Arrange for her clothes to go to the nearest coin laundry, Greer.' Then, to Tess, picking up a conversation that he had started perhaps twenty minutes earlier, during one of the lulls between phone calls: 'You see the irony, right? During the Civil War, Francis Scott Key's descendant was held as a prisoner here, in the very fort where Key was kept when he wrote "The Star-Spangled Banner."?'

'Well, Key was on a British ship, stationed in the harbor. But I guess I—'

'Key was on a ship?' He looked dubious. 'Greer, check that out, will you? I think we have a reference to it in one-oh-three. We may have to save that with looping.'

22

His girl Friday dutifully jotted some notes on her clipboard. 'Should I use the Internet or—'

'Just check it out. And do something about her clothes, okay?' Greer scurried away, even as Tess marveled at the man's ability to switch from bossy-brittle to seductive-supplicant and back again without missing a beat. She wondered if he ever got confused, used the imperious tone on those he was trying to impress, then spoke beguilingly to those he meant to dominate. 'On the boat or on the shore, it's the larger irony that concerns me. "Everything connects," like it says in *Howards End*.'

Tess didn't have the heart to tell him that the epigraph for E. M. Forster's novel was *only* connect. Everyone made mistakes. She just wished the man would stop trying so hard to impress her and perhaps do something as rudimentary as introduce himself.

Mr. Natty Boh's cell phone rang for what Tess estimated was the seventy-fifth time since they had left the boat. The ring tone was the *brrrrrrring-brrrrrrring* of an old-fashioned desk phone, something black and solid. It was a ring tone that Tess particularly hated, even more than the one on her friend Whitney's phone, which played 'Ride of the Valkyries.'

'What? WHAT? You're breaking up, let me go outside.'

Greer returned as soon as her boss left. They seemed determined to keep an eye on Tess at all times, although they had let her shower alone. 'I sent your clothes off with the P.A., Brad.'

'P.A. ?'

'The production assistant from the boat. And I

23

realized some-thing—I know you.' The rounded *O* sound—knOOOOOOHw—marked her as a native Baltimorean, although one who seemed to be trying to control her *o*s and keep her *r*s where they belonged.

'I don't think so,' Tess countered.

'I've *seen* you,' she insisted, eyes narrowed until they almost disappeared in her apple-cheeked face. 'You've been in the paper.'

'Oh, well, who hasn't? I'm sure you've ended up in the paper yourself, a time or two. Engagement announcement, perhaps?' The girl wore a simple, pear-shaped diamond on a gold band, and she reached for it instinctively at Tess's mention, but not with the expected tenderness or pride. She twisted it, so the stone faced inward, the way a woman might wear a ring on public transportation, or in a dangerous neighborhood.

Tess babbled on: 'Like Andy Warhol said—in the future, everyone will be famous for fifteen minutes. Actually, he didn't *say* it, he wrote that, in the notes on a gallery exhibit at the University of Maryland of all places. And most people get it wrong, refer to so-and-so's fifteen minutes of fame, which isn't the same, not at all. . . .'

She hoped her prattling might derail the woman's chain of thought, but this Greer had a pointer's fixity of purpose.

'You weren't in the paper in a *normal* way,' Greer said. 'It was something odd, kind of notorious.'

'One of my favorite Hitchcock films,' her boss said, returning to the trailer. 'Written by Ben Hecht, with uncredited dialogue by Odets.'

'No, *she's* notorious.' Greer used her clipboard

24

to indicate Tess. 'She's been in the paper.'

'The local paper?' asked Mr. Natty Boh, suddenly all bright interest.

'Yes,' Greer said.

'No,' Tess said. 'I mean, not really, not often. I started out as a reporter at the old *Star,* and I've worked for the *Beacon-Light* as a consultant, nothing more. Maybe that's why she thinks I've been in the newspaper.'

A lie, but an expedient one, one she assumed would dull the man's interest. Besides, how could a Hollywood director, assuming he was that, care who had been mentioned in a Baltimore newspaper?

But now he seemed even more focused on impressing her, extending his hand, something he hadn't done even while she was treading water. 'I'm Flip Tumulty.'

'Oh, right, the son of—'

At this near mention of his famous father, Flip's features seemed to frost over, while Greer clutched her clipboard to her chest, as if to flatten the squeak of a gasp that escaped from her mouth. Tess was forced to correct her course for the second time that morning. 'I had assumed you were the director on this project, but you're a writer, right? Ben Hecht, Odets—those are the kinds of details a writer would know. Now that I think about it, I remember a Shouts and Murmur piece you wrote for the *New Yorker* a few years back. Very droll.'

That puffed him up with pride. 'I *am* a writer, but here I'm the executive producer. That's how it works in television, the writer is the boss. And you're a rower who reads the *New Yorker*?'

25

Now it was Tess's turn to be offended. 'Rowing is my hobby, not my profession. Besides, rowers tend to be pretty intelligent.'

'Really? I don't recall that from my days at Brown.' Oh, how Tess hated that kind of ploy, this seemingly casual mention of an Ivy League education. Shouldn't the son of Phil Tumulty be a little more confident? Or did having a famous father make him more insecure than the average person?

'Well, *Brown*,' she said, trying to make it sound as if that school's rowers were famously subpar.

'What do you do, when you're not rowing or consulting for newspapers?'

It was a question that Tess had come to hate, because the answer prompted either a surfeit of curiosity or the same set of tired jokes, many of them centering on wordplay involving 'female dick.' She hesitated, tempted to lie, but the opportunity was lost when Greer blurted out: 'She's a private investigator. *That's* it. She shot a state senator who happened to be a killer, or something like that.'

'Something like that,' Tess said, almost relieved to see how the details of her life continued to morph and mutate in the public imagination. She had shot a man, once. He wasn't a politician. If he had been, she probably would have been less haunted by the experience.

'Really?' Tumulty, who had been pacing restlessly, dropped in the makeup chair opposite Tess. 'Do you do security work?'

'Sometimes. Preventive stuff, advising people about their . . . vulnerabilities.' Tess, naked inside the expanding pink robe, became acutely aware of her own vulnerabilities and checked to make sure that the belt was cinched. But the tighter she pulled the belt, the more the cloth seemed to expand. She was turning into a pouf of cotton candy. Or—worse—one of those Hostess Sno Balls, with the dyed coconut frosting.

'And you have an ongoing relationship with the local newspaper? Could you get them to back off us, cut us some slack?'

Tess smiled with half her mouth. 'The *Beacon-Light's* sort of like one of my ex-boyfriends. We're civil to each other, but I'm not in a position to ask for any favors right now.'

'What about bodyguard work?'

'What about it?'

'Do you do it?'

'I've had enough trouble safeguarding my own body over the years.' If she could have found her hands within the robe's voluminous sleeves, she might have snaked the left one down to her knee, fingered the scar she always stroked when reminded of her own mortality.

'Well, it wouldn't be bodyguard work, per se. More like . . . babysitting.'

'You can get a nice college student to do that for ten dollars an hour.'

'Here's the thing.' Tess was beginning to notice something odd about Flip: He paused during a conversation and allowed others to speak, but he didn't necessarily hear anything that was said to him. Perhaps even his face-to-face exchanges were beset by the static and dropped words of a cell phone conversation. 'We have this young actor, Selene Waites. Beautiful. And the real thing, as a talent, but very raw. Young, just twenty. She's

27

playing Betsy Patterson Bonaparte, one of the leads.'

'You're making a historical miniseries about Betsy Patterson?'

'Not a miniseries—a short-order series, eight episodes that will be used midseason on Zylon, that new cable network. And *Mann of Steel* isn't a biopic at all. It's about a young steelworker who gets knocked unconscious at work, in present-day Baltimore, and wakes up in Betsy Patterson's era. He knows just enough about history to realize that she's going to make a terrible personal mistake, marrying Napoleon's brother Jerome, but he's not sure what will happen if he dissuades her, how it will affect the larger course of history, if at all. Meanwhile, he has to get back to the present, because there's a key vote coming up for the union, and he's a shop steward.'

As he outlined his story, Tumulty spoke with the flushed, excited air of a little boy enchanted with his own ideas, preposterous as they seemed to Tess. It wasn't the concept of time travel via head injury that seemed most problematic to Tess, but the idea of a story centered on a steelworker in twenty-first-century Baltimore. Hadn't these guys driven past the ghost town that was Sparrows Point? Didn't they know that Bethlehem Steel had been sold and scavenged for its parts, leaving its retirees without so much as medical benefits or adequate pensions?

'Sounds like *Quantum Leap* meets *Red Baker* by way of *The Dancing Cavalier*,' she offered.

'I know *Quantum Leap*,' Tumulty said, his manner stiff, as if she had insulted him. 'This is *nothing* like that. The other things you mentioned . . .'

He paused, and she realized that he would not admit not knowing something, but he would leave a space if she wanted to fill in the gaps in his knowledge.

'Red Baker is one of the seminal works of Baltimore fiction. It's about a laid-off steelworker. Back in the 80s.'

Tumulty turned to the young woman. 'Make a note on that, Greer. We might want to option it, if it's available.'

Greer promptly began to scribble on her clipboard. Short and a little top-heavy, she was a pretty girl, although she seemed to be playing down her looks. Her dark hair was slicked back in a tight, unbecoming ponytail, her clothes frumpier than they needed to be. She had lovely hands, though, with a perfect French manicure, a fitting showcase for the ring, which she had turned back around at some point.

Tess asked: 'You mean you'd make *Red Baker,* too?'

'No, but we like to hold the options on similar projects, so they don't beat us out of the gate.'

'That seems a little . . . unsporting.'

'Common practice. What's the other one you mentioned?'

'*The Dancing Cavalier?*' Tess could forgive Tumulty's ignorance of literature, but shouldn't this son of a famous director, born and bred in Los Angeles, recognize a reference to one of the greatest movie musicals ever made? 'It's the film within the film of *Singin' in the Rain.* Remember? They salvage the footage from the disastrous attempt at a talkie and recast it as a musical in

29

which a young man travels back in time.'

'Right. Of course. Well, ours is much more *meta*. It's sort of like what Sofia was going for.'

'Sofia?'

'Coppola. When she made *Marie Antoinette*. We've known each other since childhood, of course. I met her on vacations and summers up in Napa, with my dad.'

'Of course.' *My, don't you like to have it both ways, at once denying and invoking your credentials as a second-generation Hollywood insider, while wearing a Natty Boh cap, as if you were a real Baltimore boy.* Of course, a real Baltimore boy would know that National Bohemian had pulled up stakes long ago. Tourists could buy the gear at a Fells Point shop and see the mustachioed mascot winking from a neon sign in Brewers Hill, but the beer itself was brewed out of state. Tess actively boycotted it.

'At any rate, even though she's second on the call sheet, Selene has more than her share of downtime. And she gets . . . bored. Rather easily.'

'She wasn't there for pickup this morning,' Greer put in. Her face was bland, but Tess thought she caught a flicker of spiteful enjoyment in the timid voice.

'What? Why didn't you tell me this before?'

'I just found out. I got a cell call that Selene had shown up in makeup. Two hours late, but she's there.'

'Where was she? How did she get to set if she missed her driver?'

Greer raised one shoulder, a timid halfhearted shrug. 'Taxi, I think. Meanwhile, there was another one of those . . . incidents. A trash can fire on Fort

30

Avenue, which closed the street down when firefighters responded, which is part of the reason she was so late. Or so she said. Apparently, it didn't occur to Selene that she could get out of the cab and walk the last block here.'

'Oh, for fuck's sake.' He grabbed his phone from an interior pocket of his fleece vest even as it started to ring again. 'I'm losing you, you're breaking up,' he shouted as he ran from the trailer.

'Tough gig,' Tess said.

'Oh, he loves what he does.'

'No, I mean for you, being his assistant.'

'Are you kidding?' Greer's eyes widened for once, and they turned out to be quite pretty, a vivid pale blue set off by dark lashes and brows. 'I'm really lucky. I started off as an intern during the preproduction phase for the pilot, opening mail and doing other odd jobs, then got promoted to the writer's office assistant when the network picked up the show. I *jumped* at the chance to be Mr. Tumulty's assistant when the job opened up.'

'What happened to his last assistant?'

'She left. She was a local.' The latter said with great derision.

'Aren't you from here?'

'How could you tell?' She seemed at once insulted and shocked.

Tess considered what would be the kindest way to reply. 'Because I am. Like knows like, right?'

'Well, I may have been born here, but I'm not going to be stuck here,' Greer said.

'What about—' Tess gestured at the ring.

'Everything can be negotiated. That's one of the first things I learned, working for Fli—Mr. Tumulty. If you know what you want, you can get

31

it. The trick is you have to know what you want.' She gave Tess an appraising look, and it was disconcerting to see that calculated, pragmatic gaze in such a young face. 'And I know that—'

The door to the trailer opened, and Greer let the conversation drop.

'Don't you think you should check to see if Miss Monaghan's clothes are ready?' Flip asked, and Greer rushed out before Tess could say that nothing, not even Under Armour, could possibly dry that fast. Scurried, actually. She reminded Tess of a mouse, one of the animated ones that had been so devoted to Cinderella. Tess had always wondered what was in it for the mice. Did they really think they were going to get to live in the palace once all was said and done?

'I wanted a moment with you in private,' Flip said.

Tess nodded. The monstrous pink bathrobe had now risen up to her jawline, so her chin disappeared for a moment, catching in the collar.

'The thing about Selene—Greer doesn't know this—only the other producers and I are aware of this, but . . . there was an incident when we returned here to film this summer. A suicide.'

'Selene attempted suicide?'

'No, no, no. It was a local man, Wilbur Grace, with no known connection to the production. He hung himself in his kitchen. Hung? Hanged?' Tess let Flip work out the grammatical possibilities for himself. 'Hung,' he decided. 'Police came to me, the other exec producer, Ben Marcus, and my unit production manager, Lottie MacKenzie. The man had some things in his possession, things that appeared to come from digging through the trash

32

at the production office. He also had multiple photographs of Selene, taken during location shooting on the pilot, last winter.'

'A stalker?'

'Possibly. And a bit of a creep, based on some other things police found.'

'Creep?'

'Let's just say he had an eye for the kiddies. As I said, no one knew him, and we hadn't been aware of a problem. The problems started *after* he died. Small fires, set near our locations. A power outage, the result of someone vandalizing a transformer. Then there are the complaints from neighbors, who had been delighted to have us when the production was first announced. And now the steelworkers caterwauling. I'm not worried about Selene from a public relations standpoint. I'm worried that she's vulnerable, when she's out in public.'

'But you just said the man was dead, a suicide.'

'Right. Yet all this strangeness now.'

'Maybe he's haunting you.'

Famously smart-alecky Flip Tumulty didn't seem to enjoy flippancy in others.

'We have an order to film eight episodes of *Mann of Steel* in Baltimore, budgeted for three point two million per ep. If we get a pickup for a full second season, we'll be here almost forty weeks out of the year, pumping money into the local economy. But if these petty annoyances continue, we're going to have to rethink our commitment to the city.'

'But you want me to watch Selene, not your set?' Tess had an unerring instinct for when a story didn't quite hang together, but she couldn't pinpoint the logical flaw here, the missing link. She knew only that there was a lie lurking somewhere.

'Yes. Because wherever we film, whatever happens, Selene is the linchpin, our star. She'll make or break us.'

'The show is called *Mann of Steel*.'

Flip glanced around, as if to be sure there was no one else who could hear him. 'The program was built around Johnny Tampa, originally.'

He paused, as if waiting for Tess to squeal with excitement, but she could not bear to admit that she did know Johnny Tampa. She was, in fact, far more familiar than she wished with the entire cast of the long-ago teen nighttime soap opera *The Boom Boom Room,* in which Tampa had starred. In her defense, she had been an actual teenager when the show was in its heyday, which wasn't true of Tampa, playing a high school senior with a receding hairline and crow's-feet.

'He must be pretty long in the tooth now.'

'Only in his forties, and Tampa is actually a good actor,' Flip said. 'Great comic timing. He worked with Ben and me on our first show, *No Human Involved.*' Again, there was a pause, as if waiting for a gasp of recognition, but Tess didn't have to fake her ignorance this time. She remembered a terrific novel by that name, but not a television show.

'It ran for only two seasons, and it never got the ratings it deserved, but the critics loved us. Loved. Ahead of its time, a one-camera show done with voice-over. And Johnny won an Emmy for his guest shot. He was our first choice to play Mann. Like I said, he's really good. But Selene—Selene's got all the heat since *Baby Jane*.'

34

'A remake of the Bette Davis movie?'

'No, this was really gritty, done in the style of *Requiem for a Dream,* about a fourteen-year-old prostitute. The studio that bought it at Sundance had decided it was a stinker and they dumped it in theaters on Memorial Day weekend last year, a sacrificial lamb opposite *X-Men.* It almost disappeared, but then she got nominated for a Golden Globe. Did you see it?'

Tess decided not to volunteer that she had been part of the rabble flocking to *X-Men* with her boyfriend, instead of dutifully paying eight dollars to watch yet another young actress prove her Serious Thespian Chops by pretending to be a prostitute. The only cinematic cliché that bothered her more was high-spirited white guys, à la Ferris Bueller or the Blues Brothers, proving their innate soulfulness by inspiring black people to dance.

'It's in my Netflix queue,' she lied.

'Well, she's great in it. And she's ours, for now. The future of this show depends far more on Selene Waites than it does on Johnny Tampa, and that's all there is to it. I can't risk having anything happen to her.'

'I'm a one-woman agency. I don't have the manpower—womanpower, if you will—to provide the kind of services you want.'

'We just need someone to be with her while she's off set. When she's filming, our security provides all the coverage we need. But away from work, she needs someone, and it has to be a woman.'

'Why?'

'Men are . . . helpless around Selene. Any male between eight and eighty, she can twist to her will.'

'Including you?'

Flip pulled out a wallet and showed Tess a photograph of what appeared to be Philip Tumulty III. Same brown curls, same puckish expression—and probably the same Freudian issues in a decade or so. 'My son, just turned five. He's back in Los Angeles with his mom. Now that he's in school, they can't travel to locations with me, although if we get a full order for *Mann of Steel,* we'll move east. Which would be a godsend, having a chance to raise him some place other than Los Angeles. You know my dad?'

Tess, remembering how upset Flip had been when she almost invoked his father's name, shrugged vaguely to indicate that she might—possibly, maybe—have heard of someone named Phil Tumulty.

'It's okay. I know he's the big man, that I can make television shows the rest of my life and win a hundred thirty-seven Emmys and probably never equal the two movies he made in the '80s. Anyway, my dad is a great director and a brilliant writer. *Was,* before he started doing big-budget crap. He wins on that score. But he was and is a shitty father, and I can beat him at that game. I'm not saying that I'm made of stone, that I can't see how beautiful Selene is. I'm saying that I resist temptation for this little guy's sake.'

'That's great,' Tess said, meaning it, but also wondering at his vehemence. Flip's little speech carried the whiff of addiction, a junkie at his first 12-step meeting, saying the right things, but not yet feeling them. 'I get that you need a woman. But I'm not the right woman for the job.'

'We'll see,' Flip said, putting his wallet away. His

36

cell phone reprised its eerie imitation of a real phone, and he departed abruptly, leaving Tess alone for the first time. A sneeze overtook her, and Tess realized that the pink chenille had spread, like kudzu, almost to her nose. She hoped someone returned with her clothes before the bathrobe swallowed her completely. *Killer Bathrobe*—now that was a promising concept for a horror film. She would rather see that than a hundred Oscar-worthy films about beautiful underage prostitutes.

Chapter 3

What time was it?

The hotel's blackout curtains were drawn, which always disoriented him, made him feel as if he were in a sensory deprivation tank. Going on two months in Baltimore, and he still couldn't get on local time. Couldn't get on anything local, if you didn't count the local girls, and he didn't. He was through with them, anyway.

Ben looked at the empty spot next to him. Had Selene really been there, just a few hours ago? She hadn't left so much as a dent in the pillow. Maybe she didn't weigh enough to make an impression. She was thin even by actress standards, almost fragile. It had been disturbing how young she looked, undressed. He wasn't a pedophile, for fuck's sake. And while a lifetime spent more or less in Los Angeles had inured him to bony women, at least most of those had gone out and bought a pair of tits along the way. But then,

37

Selene liked to say she was 100 percent certified organic, one of those throwback freaks *born* gorgeous. He could never work out whether such women had increased or decreased in value as plastic surgery became mainstream. If anyone could buy a face and a body, then was it so special to have one bestowed on you by nature? The law of supply and demand would seem to suggest that natural beauty was less important than it had once been. But that *face*. With a face like that, he could forgive Selene for not having any tits.

He glanced at his Treo. Several messages from Flip, including a text, which said in its entirety: 'Fucking Selene.' For one paranoid second, Ben imagined a question mark at the end of that flat phrase, and his empty stomach lurched. Flip would not be Mr. Happy if he found out that Ben had bedded Selene. In fact, Flip had expressly forbidden him to fuck Selene, which was when Ben decided he pretty much had to do it. Who was Flip to tell him anything? Other than the boss and executive producer. But Ben was an executive producer on this project as well—finally—because he had brought the concept to Flip. He had been screwed out of the created-by credit, but he was going to have sole teleplay and story credit on four of the episodes and, as always, he would stick a spoon in Flip's mush, make it work. *Flip isn't the boss of me.* Only he was, kind of.

Fucking Selene. Had he made her late for her set call? No, his conscience was pretty clear on that score. He had not only gone downstairs with her at 4 A.M., but had gotten in her cab as well, accompanying her back to her condo, watching her pass through the glass doors. He wanted to kiss her

38

on the front steps, act like the teenager he once was and she had so recently been, at least chronologically, but they couldn't risk that, not even at 4 A.M. in Baltimore, with only a stoned cabdriver to see. Fact was, his little act of gallantry, riding in the cab, had been a big enough risk.

The irony was Ben didn't even sleep with actors anymore, not for years. He had had enough of that kind of crazy to last him the rest of his life. And Selene really was on the bubble, age-wise, fifteen years younger than he was. How old had Jerry Seinfeld been when he dated that huge-breasted seventeen-year-old? Were the rules different for the Jerry Seinfelds of the world than they were for the Ben Marcuses? Probably. Almost certainly. Fuck Flip for telling him not to touch her. Now he had, three times so far, and she was trouble. He should have stuck to Baltimore waitresses, girls for whom a night at the Tremont Hotel counted as an upgrade. Whereas Selene had pointed out to him tonight—twice—that it was relative slumming for her. When she was told she would have to be in Baltimore for almost four months, she had rejected every hotel in Baltimore and Washington, finally agreeing to stay in a furnished, four-bedroom waterfront condo that was costing the production four thousand dollars a week. A week! You could buy most of Baltimore for less. And she had stipulated that it was four bedrooms or nothing, saying she intended to bring her family in from Utah, but none of them had shown yet, thank God. He sometimes wondered if the family—the happy, well-adjusted Mormons who had let their youngest daughter head off to Hollywood at fourteen—were even real, or the creation of some

39

slick publicist.

The budget wasn't Ben's problem, but he found Selene's demands outrageous on principle. 'What a dinky little suite,' Selene had said last night, all but inserting her entire head in the minibar, and he had experienced a clutch of fear for his per diem. Lottie was watching his expenses like a hawk, eager to catch him in any kind of impropriety of the fiscal variety. He wasn't supposed to know it—Lottie had told Flip not to tell—but she had argued against his installation as an executive producer, said they could keep him at story editor, which meant a lower salary. Pretty ballsy, considering that the network had forced Lottie on them, insisted they needed someone with a track record for running a tight set. *And Mussolini made the trains run on time,* Ben wanted to say, but that comparison was decidedly unfair. To Mussolini.

What Lottie didn't know was that it was useless to ask Flip to keep anything from Ben. Their friendship trumped all other alliances. Flip trusted Ben more than anyone, even his old man, especially his old man. Ben, after all, hadn't dumped Flip's mother, moved to fucking Taos, and started a second family. A second family that enjoyed the true big money, while Flip and his mom had struggled to get by on a mere fifty thousand a month.

Ben scrolled through the other messages stacked up on his Treo. Morning had been second-unit stuff, so he had been within his rights to sleep in, yet Flip was out there, raring to go. He probably just wanted to pull a head trip on Wes, the director on this episode, one of the eight hacks that the network had foisted on them, the same way they had shoved Lottie down their throats. 'You two guys know words, these guys know visuals,' the network types had said. You couldn't call them suits anymore because most of these losers didn't wear suits, with the exception of the lone female executive, who looked as if she should be playing the male lead in some Edwardian-era drama. The network, Zylon, aka Plan-Z—God help them, their wizened corporate owner thought the name was hip, as opposed to a ready-made punch line for television critics everywhere—was struggling, trying to find a toehold among the other not-quite networks, the FXs and USAs and Spikes of the nonpremium cable world. The buzz was that Plan-Z was a vanity project, that its billionaire owner would become disenchanted with the money drain, and the network would probably disappear before a single one of its shows even aired. But hadn't they said the same thing about Fox once upon a time?

Then again, Fox had come along before all the buzz about platforms, before it was possible to download a television show on your phone, before iTunes and, worst of all, YouTube, which had convinced half the sentient world that they, too, were filmmakers because they could point and shoot. Ben and Flip were only thirty-five, way too young to be playing the 'back in my day' game, but that's how he felt, the Ancient Producer, with the albatross of new technology and old expectations weighing him down. In fact, his back hurt and his knees creaked a little as he got out of bed, but he blamed that on the subpar hotel mattress.

Selene had a Tempur-Pedic bed in her rental

apartment. She had Tempur-Pedic beds in every room, for the phantom family that never showed up. Lottie had shared that with Ben in a rare burst of camaraderie, assuming he resented Selene as much as everyone else. He had before he slept with her, but he supposed it would be hypocritical now. Instead he resented her for not sharing the pent-house-condo-Tempur-Pedic wealth with him.

Not that he had ever lost too much sleep over being a hypocrite. That was Flip's side of the street, being all earnest and lovable. Ben had no problem smiling in someone's face, taking his money, all the while raking him over the coals behind his back. Even Flip.

He pulled on last night's clothes, but he wasn't a pig enough to stomach yesterday's smells, which carried a faint whiff of Selene, so he rooted around for something fresher to wear. Eau de Selene wasn't the light flowery fragrance that one might expect, more like cigarettes and Red Bull and Kahlúa. In fact, the whole room smelled of her. He'd go out, instead of having his usual room service breakfast, which was pretty ordinary fare anyway, although he enjoyed torturing the kitchen with special requests, such as fresh chives on his omelet. They had tried to get away with dried once and he had sent it back, if only to keep them on their toes.

But today—which, now that he had the curtains open, looked pretty nice—he was going to venture into the city, and not just his usual Starbucks. He was going to find some cool little diner, eat whatever people ate in Baltimore. Pancakes? Scrapple? Flip kept encouraging him to try scrapple, swore by the stuff, but Ben sensed he was

42

being punked. Whatever he ended up eating, he was going to sit at the counter and inhale all the cholesterol and trans fats and scorched caffeine that the city had to offer, read the local sports page, pretend to care about the Ravens, and if Lottie bitched about him being MIA, he'd call it research. Mann of Steel was a man of the people. How could Ben write him convincingly if he didn't get out there, mingle with the Real Folks?

Out in the crisp air, his head clearing even as his feet stumbled a bit, he thought to wonder if Selene really understood that they had to keep their thing a secret. Then he wondered if they had a thing, after three times. He didn't really care if they slept together again. Unless she didn't want to, in which case he would definitely be keen for it. But he cared desperately that she tell no one, because if anyone else knew, it would get back to Lottie, and if Lottie had this morsel of gossip, it would get back to Flip, who would consider it a betrayal. And as much as Ben resented Flip sometimes—for the name that opened doors, for the anticharisma that drew people to him—Ben never wanted to hurt him. Flip was his best friend.

He stopped for a second, physically and mentally centering himself. He was good at understanding people, their desires and motivations. It was, in the end, what he brought to his partnership with Flip—not just a thirty-year friendship cemented on the first day of nursery school, but a genuine curiosity about people. Flip was too used to people being curious about *him*— more correctly, curious about his father, and his various stepmoms. Line for line, Flip wrote terrific dialogue, but it was Ben who gave it depth, because Ben had actually spent some time thinking about other people. The joke on *No Human Involved* was that it would have been the show's modus operandi if Ben hadn't been hired. Flip was kind of a robot—at work. But Ben still remembered the kid he knew all those years at Harvard-Westlake, the one whose dad almost never showed for anything, the one who had cried when the debate team had been trounced at regionals. Sometimes, he had to remind himself that *that* Flip was still somewhere inside the increasingly priggish guy who showed up on set every day, wearing another goddamn local ball cap.

Now, standing on a corner somewhere in downtown Baltimore, Ben turned his knowledge of people on himself. If he had slept with Selene just because Flip told him not to, why was he so fearful of discovery? Wasn't the point of disobeying a friend's high-handed order to remind the friend that he wasn't the boss, that he couldn't control everything? What would Flip *do,* anyway? Wasn't there an argument to be made that Selene would be much easier to handle if she were having an affair with one of the producers? They had actually hoped, for a day or two, that she might get attached to her costar, but for all the chemistry she and Johnny Tampa generated on-screen, their hostility toward each other was palpable. Those two really hated each other. Rumor was that Tampa was gay, but in Ben's opinion, no gay man would have allowed himself to go that much to seed at forty-two. Wardrobe was going nuts, trying to keep up with the expanding ass of Johnny Tampa, and the DP was forced to shoot him above

44

the waist most of the time, a waste of a great DP. Lottie rationalized that they were lucky that Tampa put on his weight below the belt, but wouldn't they be luckier if they could just keep the fat fuck from going facedown into craft services like there was no tomorrow?

Ben popped a Nexium, which would help the reflux, but not the emotions beneath it. What was weighing him down? It wasn't Selene, Ben decided. She was just another secret.

He found a diner tucked into a side street near the courthouse, but his appetite was gone. He drank black coffee and read *USA Today,* going over and over the weather info for California. Where, in fact, it was raining and there were mud slides, but he still would rather be there. Only four more weeks of shooting, and then he could go home. He didn't belong here, and neither did Flip, much as he pretended to love it. If they got the pickup for a second season, Ben was going to actively lobby for Los Angeles or Vancouver. They could reproduce Baltimore on a soundstage. Hell, based on what he had seen, they could make a better one.

Chapter 4

He stopped at the mock-retro diner on Eastern Avenue, the one he had come to think of as his base camp, a term he had picked up from one of the call sheets he had actually seen. They were on the soundstage later today, with the second unit on the water, which would make it difficult to get to

45

her. But then, except for that one brief encounter, it had proven impossible to get to her, and he was beginning to suspect this was no mere coincidence. They were keeping her from him. If he could just get her alone, he was sure she would be understanding, even sympathetic. But he needed her alone.

Perhaps he should hire a pro, someone detached, but that was exactly the reason he didn't want a pro. A pro had nothing on line but his fee. Besides, the pros used so far had done nothing but collect their fat checks. They hadn't even bothered to apologize for their failures, their incompetence.

The diner, with its aluminum siding and leatherette booths, reminded him of *Diner,* although he knew this one was shiny new, a fake on many levels, its booths harboring video games instead of miniature jukeboxes. The real diner from *Diner* had been moved downtown after the movie wrapped, and staffed with juvenile delinquents as part of a training program. Funny to think how desolate East Baltimore and the waterfront had been then, how easy it was to create the illusion that a diner sat on a lonely little forkful of land in the middle of the old industrial base. That had been his first visit to a movie set, more than twenty-five years ago. No—wait, his memory was playing tricks on him. It was only *after* seeing *Diner* in the theater that he realized that a movie had been made here, in Baltimore. He had been almost sick over it. What were the odds that Hollywood would ever return? But Levinson had come back, several times over, and Phil Tumulty had followed with *his* version of Baltimore. Although he thought Tumulty the better

46

filmmaker, he felt closer to Levinson's world. He remembered the day that they closed Howard Street to film the collision outside the old Anderson Cadillac—that was Levinson's *Tin Men*—and the balloon festival in Patterson Park, staged expressly for *Pit Beef,* the first in Tumulty's trilogy about growing up in Highlandtown.

He reached into his briefcase and, after taking care to make sure there was nothing on the tabletop, opened his scrapbook. There were photographs and articles about every production that had ever come to Baltimore—not just Levinson's and Tumulty's films, but *And Justice for All* and *Homicide* and *The Wire* and *Ladder 49* and *Red Dragon* and *The Replacements* and *Step Up* and, almost every year, like the groundhog, another John Waters film. He visited Waters's sets because he felt he had a duty to completeness, to see them all, but he didn't really care for the movies because they so seldom had real stars. What had Gloria Swanson said? She stayed big, the movies got small. He didn't get Waters, his insistence on making things look the way they actually were. Who needed movies for *that*?

He flipped through the pages, stopping at the one instance when a newspaper photographer had caught the both of them, standing on the edge of everything. Their own mothers probably couldn't pick them out of the shot, but he knew they had been there, so he could identify the backs of their heads, then thick with hair. There they were down in Fells Point, the night the big fire scene in *Avalon* was filmed. That had been fascinating. And Levinson's people had been *nice*. When it came down to it, he might have preferred Tumulty's movies, but his people—Tumulty made very bad choices in his people, and now he had foisted those choices onto his son. Tumulty had forgotten where he came from, living out there . . . wherever. Tahoe? Santa Fe? Some suspect place, neither here nor Hollywood.

His breakfast arrived—how did they do it so fast? He was almost skeptical at the speed with which diner food arrived. Given the time, past eleven, he had opted for a grilled cheese and french fries with gravy. Had he put gravy on his french fries before he saw *Diner*, or had the movie persuaded him that this was what people in Baltimore did? He could no longer remember. It wasn't that he had any trouble distinguishing between fantasy and reality. He was as sane as the next guy, and had the tests to prove it, as the old joke went. They had made him talk to a psychiatrist as part of the exit interview, but that had been to cover their own asses. He had been in HRD; he knew the drill. He propped the local section of the *Beacon-Light* against the old-fashioned sugar dispenser, and read the latest litany of complaints about *Mann of Steel. You reap what you sow, you reap what you sow.* He wondered if Mandy Stewart could be of any use to him, but decided that she had been too open in her hostility. She probably couldn't get any closer to Tumulty Jr. and his minions than he could at this point. The steelworkers, too, were of little use. Besides, he didn't know any steelworkers.

His cell phone rang, and he debated not answering. The french fries were at that divine, fleeting moment of perfect hotness. But ignoring Marie was never a good idea, under any

48

circumstances, and she had been especially needy the past few months.

'Where are you?' she said.

'Having an early lunch.'

'Why aren't you at work?'

'Holiday.'

'What holiday?'

'Columbus Day.' The lies were coming so easily now. The mark of an artist, he decided.

'Isn't that the Monday that falls the same week as the twelfth?'

'Used to be,' he said agreeably. 'But they had to start switching it around because people complained about the Italians getting their own holiday. So the federal holiday was last week, but the state-city holiday is today.'

'What does that have to do with the date? And why would they have more Columbus Days if people are angry about the one?' He could imagine her face—forehead creased, mouth turned down—panicking a little at this information, more proof that the world outside the house was going on without her. For some reason, she seemed to think that the world should have halted when she stopped participating in it.

Then again, he *was* lying to her. He should factor that in. But it was out of consideration. Everything he did, he did for her.

'No, there's only one, and it's today.'

'Oh . . .' Her voice trailed off.

'Marie?'

'Hmmmmm?'

'Why did you call?'

'Can't remember. I wanted you to bring me something from the grocery store . . . a magazine?

Candy? Hey—if there's no work today, why did you put on your suit and everything, leave the house at the normal time?'

Good question. He had to remind himself sometimes that while Marie may be odd, an ever-growing bundle of tics and neuroses, she wasn't simpleminded or unobservant. Given how little of the world she could see from her perch on the sofa, she tended to be extremely sharp-eyed about what was within her view.

'Force of habit,' he said. 'It's kind of embarrassing, but—I didn't remember about the holiday until I showed up at North Avenue. Once I was all the way downtown, I thought I could do some work on my own, play catch-up. But there's no heat in the building.'

'Isn't it warm today?'

'You'd think so, looking at the temperature.' She was probably doing that just now, he calculated, pulling the draperies aside and squinting at the thermometer next to the bay window, or quickly punching through the channels on the remote to the Weather Channel. Stand-up comics were always making jokes about men and remote controls, but Marie wielded hers like a light saber. He didn't dare try to take it from her. 'The nights have been getting cooler, and that old pile just holds in the cold, with all that marble and all. And the heat was off all weekend.'

'They never ought to have renovated that old school for the administration headquarters. They just love throwing the taxpayers' money away, don't they? But I guess I shouldn't complain, since that includes paying you.' She made a funny sound, and he knew she had brought her fist up to her mouth. 'I don't mean paying you is a waste.'

'I know,' he said. 'Look, Marie, I have to go. Our minutes—'

'Then why do you tell me to call your cell instead of the office phone?'

'They're sticklers about personal calls,' he began, trying to talk over her, but she was hurtling down her own track of thought: 'You always—Mounds bars! That's what I want. Mounds bars. I was watching television, and there was some commercial, and it reminded me of the old commercial, sometimes you feel like a nut, sometimes you don't. Well, I don't, so I want Mounds, okay?'

Trust me, Marie. You feel like a nut every day. Then he felt bad, as he always did, for his sour interior monologue. Marie couldn't help how she was. 'Mounds bars, got it.'

'The little ones. But not the ones in the bag. The ones that they line up in a row, on the cardboard.'

'You've got it, my sweet tooth Marie.'

He opened his wallet, and looked at the ATM slip from that morning's withdrawal: $17,922 in his account. There was another $55,000 in the IRAs, but they couldn't touch it for another five years. He had their regular expenses down to less than $2,500 a month, so they had a year before the money ran out, and then there was always a second mortgage, although that would require Marie's signature. But he didn't need a year. All he needed was to get that girl's attention, get her to fulfill the promises she had made, even if she acted as if she had never heard of him.

The french fries had passed their peak, but he

51

ate them anyway. Why was that? Why did fries lose their perfection so quickly, and why did people keep eating them once they had turned cold and mushy? If he were an inventor, he would come up with a way to produce ever-crisp, ever-hot french fries. Or maybe a restaurant that served only french fries, and not just the Thrasher's-in-a cup-on-the-boardwalk thing. He'd have french fries with gravy and hollandaise and mayonnaise and all kinds of sauces. That's what he would do, if he were an inventor. But he was a dreamer, in the best sense of the word. His head was filled with beautiful stories, stories that unfolded the way that *How the West Was Won* had raced across the screen at the Hillendale, back when he and Bob were no more than eleven, and you could see the lines on the print, breaking the picture into thirds, because the theater wasn't set up for the Cinerama technique.

He remembered, too, how ancient Jimmy Stewart had looked to them, how they had cringed at the idea of that bony codger pitching woo to Carroll Baker, who made them feel vaguely strange inside, although they didn't want to admit it to each other, and didn't have the vocabulary to explain what they felt, not even to themselves.

Now he was older than Jimmy Stewart was then. How had that happened?

Chapter 5

Tess's day was thrown off course much as her scull had been, and she never quite caught up, running late for every appointment, five in all. Autumn was turning into a reliably busy season, almost as good as February. It was as if back-to-school fever carried over into every aspect of people's lives. Summer gone, people got serious about their messy legal claims. Tess also had a booming business in background checks on nannies. She had told Flip Tumulty the truth: She had more business than she could handle.

Besides, Tess, too, had gone back to school in a fashion, teaching a course through Johns Hopkins' noncredit division, the Odyssey program. To her amazement, there were a dozen people in Baltimore who thought they might want to be private investigators. More shockingly, they believed Tess Monaghan was the woman who could show them how. She had scoffed at the idea when the program's director first proposed it—her own career path had been highly unorthodox, perhaps even mildly illegal—but her network of PI friends had been so openly covetous of the offer that she had been forced to reconsider. The only downside was that it made for a very long Monday, and today's disruptions meant she barely had time to fortify herself with a Luna bar before the three-hour session started at 6:30.

For this, the fourth meeting in the ten-week course, the students had been asked to bring laptops with wireless access. Eleven of her Charles

Street Irregulars, as she had begun to think of them, had their computers open and ready to go. The twelfth, Felicia Blossom, had a cell phone on her desk, a cell phone so ancient and relatively massive that it could be a candidate for a Smithsonian exhibit on early mobile telecommunications.

'Do you not have a laptop, Mrs. Blossom?' The woman was in her sixties and given, perhaps inevitably, to wearing flowery dresses. Had she dressed that way after she became Mrs. Blossom, or had her riotous prints of peonies and cabbage roses attracted Mr. Blossom to her?

She nodded, brandishing the phone.

'That's a phone,' Tess said, trying to mask her irritation.

'Yes, but don't phones have all the same geegaws as computers?'

'Geegaws?'

'You know, the bells and whistles? Whatever. My son's phone can take pictures and send e-mails—he sends me photos of my grandbabies from Phoenix—so I figure mine could, too, if someone showed me how. I couldn't find the instruction booklet.'

Tess was aware of the rest of the class's simmering impatience, an almost Colosseum-like lust for a little Blossom blood on the floor. The woman was never prepared, and she had a habit of asking questions that were achingly off point. But Tess wanted to believe that she would never be one of those teachers who won over the majority by exploiting the class pariah.

True, Mrs. Blossom was never going to be a private investigator—but then, neither were the others in the class. She was simply the only one who was honest about it, writing on her orientation form, under 'What do you hope to achieve through this class?' *Something to do on Monday nights until NBC stops running those weird shows I don't understand.* In some ways, Tess even preferred Mrs. Blossom to the three wannabe crime novelists, who believed themselves undercover in the class. They thought they were so stealthy, but they didn't know that Odyssey provided teachers with all the students' previous coursework in the program, and this trio of thirty-something men had taken two semesters of creative writing and one survey, Writing Wrongs: The Crime Novel in the Twenty-first Century. But even if Tess hadn't seen their records, she would be onto them by now, with their endless questions about the quotidian details of an investigator's life. One had even asked what she ate for breakfast.

'I'm afraid I'm not much good with phones, either,' Tess said to Mrs. Blossom. 'I know how to use mine, but not others. Why don't you come up front and sit next to me, as I talk the class through public record searches, online and off-line?'

Beaming as if she had been anointed teacher's pet, Mrs. Blossom bustled up front and pulled her chair so close that Tess was overwhelmed by her perfume, a sickly sweet gardenia.

'Let's start with land records,' Tess said, trying to reach past Mrs. Blossom and type. The lyrics from the old Police song 'Don't Stand So Close to Me' popped into her head, and she had to lose herself in the byways of the Maryland Department of Assessments and Taxation to stifle her giggles. This woman had paid six hundred dollars because

NBC's Monday night lineup had failed her. She deserved the pretense of respect at the very least. 'In Maryland, you can research the history of ownership with just the address, using the assessor's Web site, but you still might have to go to the courthouse for additional information. Your address, Mrs. Blossom?'

The woman looked around the class, then whispered into Tess's ear. 'University One, at the corner of St. Paul. But only for six months. Before that, we lived on Hawthorne.'

'Let's use the house on Hawthorne,' Tess said. 'Apartments are tricky, and you haven't been there a year.'

'It's a condo,' Mrs. Blossom said, 'and the house on Hawthorne isn't mine anymore.'

There was a world of sorrow in that sentence, but Tess couldn't stop for it. She had eleven Encyclopedia Browns chomping at the bit.

*   *   *

Although the Hopkins campus was not even a mile from where Tess lived, it was almost ten before she disentangled herself from the last student, one of the undercover writers, who kept trying to inveigle her to go to the Charles Village Pub. Her body was so divided between fatigue and hunger that it was her plan to eat dinner while lying down, the prescribed Passover posture, but Crow was on the sofa with Lloyd Jupiter. How could she have forgotten Monday was movie night?

A seventeen-year-old West Baltimore kid, Lloyd was fast becoming Crow's ward, the young Dick Grayson to Crow's Bruce Wayne of semistately

Monaghan manor. But had Batman and Robin's relationship flourished after Robin had tried repeatedly to rip Batman off, con him, and inadvertently almost get him killed? Tess thought not. Still, the always forgiving Crow had taken a serious interest in every facet of the young dropout's education, supervising not only his peripatetic march toward a GED but also his exposure to serious cinema. To-night's selection was *Once Upon a Time in the West,* clearly chosen to counterbalance last week's *Children of Paradise,* which had received one finger up from Lloyd Jupiter, but not a very nice one.

Crow had paused the movie for a talking point, as was his habit. 'You see, throughout his career Henry Fonda always played good guys—hey, Tess—so Sergio Leone really messed with people's heads when he cast him in this part.'

Tess sank to the rug, relieved to see that there was plenty of homemade guacamole left. Crow was trying to broaden Lloyd's palate, too, but that was a much tougher battle.

'That other guy—he was the Tunnel King, right, from *The Great Escape*?'

'Right!' Crow's enthusiastic affirmation reminded Tess of her own cheerleading for Mrs. Blossom's timid trek across the steppes of the Internet. 'He also starred in a series of vigilante films in the 1970s, which were very politically divisive—'

Just out of Crow's eye line, Tess pretended to slump in catatonia at this pedantic discussion of *Death Wish,* and Lloyd began giggling, a high-pitched bubble of sound that reminded Tess he was at once a very young and very old seventeen.

Crow, catching on to their mockery, threw a pillow at her head.

'While you've been here, communing with the end product of Hollywood, I had an encounter with the real thing,' Tess said, regaling them with the story of her accidental set visit, although it was slightly changed now, with her saying out loud many of the things she had merely thought.

'Tumulty?' Crow said. 'That might explain the series of phone messages we've been getting tonight, which I've been trying to ignore. The phone had been ringing every half hour, to the minute, but I didn't recognize the caller ID so I didn't pick up. After the fifth message or so, I checked, and the messages were identical. "This is Greer Sadowski, calling Tess Monaghan for Mr. Tumulty. Are you there? Will you pick up? Please call me back at your convenience."'

Crow was a good mimic, catching the young woman's not quite suppressed *o* sounds, the mechanical flatness of her voice.

'He wants me to work for him.'

'Really?' Lloyd's eyes lit up. It was, quite possibly, the only time that Tess had ever managed to impress Lloyd, who was consistently underwhelmed by the mundaneness of her life as a private investigator. That, and the fact that she didn't know tae kwon do, or how to use nunchakus.

'Yeah, but it's not my sort of gig, Lloyd. More security than investigation or paper trails, and I'm a one-woman agency. I simply don't have the personnel.'

'But you would be working on a *movie*. A movie made by the son of Philip Tumulty, the guy who made *The Beast*.'

Given his youth, Lloyd had no use for the gentle, nostalgic—and, truth be told, very, very white—comedies made by Tumulty senior. Tess wondered how Tumulty would feel to learn that there were, in fact, some Baltimoreans who preferred the special effects epics that had made him rich while destroying his artistic cred.

'I wouldn't be working on the movie, Lloyd. I'd be babysitting a spoiled actress.'

'Still . . .' He groaned in frustration at her stupidity, her obtuseness at rejecting this golden ticket into a rarefied world.

'Lloyd, buddy, why don't you get a head start on the dishes?' Crow asked. Lloyd slumped back in a sullen teen pout, and Crow added: 'You *promised*. I said you could bunk here tonight, and you said you would clean up the kitchen. Remember?'

*   *   *

'He has his own apartment,' Tess said, waiting until Lloyd was in the kitchen and out of earshot, where odds were that one in ten pieces of crockery wouldn't make it out alive. 'You went to a lot of trouble to set him up, get him to establish some independence, but he seems to be here more and more.'

'He *had* his own apartment,' Crow said. 'That didn't work out so well.'

'Don't tell me . . .'

In the six months since Lloyd Jupiter had invaded their lives—and Tess could not help thinking of it as a criminal act, given that it had begun with a series of misdemeanors and felonies—Crow had done everything he could to help the teenager stand on his own two feet, but it was proving far more difficult than even Tess had anticipated.

'He started letting some old friends flop there. Drugs followed, although I'm pretty sure that Lloyd's not using. He's content with smoking a blunt now and then, and I'm not a big enough hypocrite to lecture him on that. But when the landlord got wind of what was happening, he evicted him.'

'You can't evict someone just because you suspect illegal acti-vity.'

'You can if your tenant is an inexperienced seventeen-year-old who doesn't know his rights. Anyway, Lloyd tried going back to his mom's. That lasted all of a week.'

'His stepfather?'

'Yeah, there's no bridging that gap. Lloyd called me today, asked for bus fare, thought he could go back to the Delaware shore and stay with the friends he made there over the summer. But there's not enough work to keep him busy off-season, and an idle Lloyd is a dangerous Lloyd, at least to himself.'

'So he's staying with us—and you're heading out of town tomorrow to scout polka bands. Wow, I just gave birth to a seventeen-year-old and I didn't even know I was knocked up.'

'It's only temporary. And you know money's not the issue.' Lloyd did have a small trust, controlled by Crow, who doled out living expenses while trying to goad him into getting ready for college. 'Finding a way to fill his days is. He's *bored*, Tess. As long as he's bored, he's going to be in trouble.'

60

The phone rang. 'Ten-thirty,' Crow said. 'You could set your watch by this woman.'

'I'll tell her no tomorrow,' Tess said. 'I don't have the energy to talk to her tonight.'

'You know, if you said yes—well, it's my understanding that a film crew is kind of elastic. There's always some place where they could use an extra body.'

It took her a moment to get it, but then—it had been a long day. Tess had risen before the sun, more than seventeen hours ago.

'You're suggesting I make it a twofer? *I'll do whatever you want, if you find a spot for my young friend?* That would be double the stress, Crow. I'd be doing a job I didn't want to do, while worrying about what havoc Lloyd was wreaking.'

'Lloyd would be so thrilled to work on a set that he would be on his best behavior.'

'Lloyd's best behavior isn't exactly the gold standard.' Tess fell back on the rug. She was having her second psychic episode of the day, seeing the next hour in vivid detail. She could argue with Crow, eventually giving in, and he would rub her back as a reward. Or she could give in now and cut straight to the back rub.

'I'll call tomorrow,' she said. 'I'll have to inflate my usual price, to make it worth farming out some of the other gigs I have lined up, but if they agree to my price and a place for Lloyd, I'll do it.'

'I owe you,' Crow said, leaving the sofa to lie next to her, working his fingers into her hair.

'I lost track of who owed whom in our relationship long ago,' Tess said.

Actually, she hadn't. But it *sounded* healthy.

61

Chapter 6

Greer put the phone back in its cradle and looked at the clock on her computer, which she knew to be accurate to the second. That was one of her jobs, making sure that every time device in the office—the wall clocks, the phones, the computers—was synced. Ten-thirty. Flip had told her to continue trying to reach Tess Monaghan every half hour until the news came on. *Until the news came on*—those had been his very words. She had puzzled over those instructions. If the news came on at eleven and she was to call exactly on the half hour, did that mean she wasn't to call at eleven? Did Flip know that Baltimore had a ten o'clock newscast? Didn't most cities have ten o'clock newscasts? And then, in those cities on midwestern time, or whatever it was called, Greer believed they had nine o'clock newscasts. Not that the Midwest was relevant to this situation, but it was interesting to think about, how even seemingly precise instructions can end up being pretty vague. Yet Greer's attention to detail was almost irrelevant, given how scattered Flip could be.

When Lottie had talked to Greer about her desire to move into the job as Flip's assistant—interrogated her, really, in that skeptical, suspicious way she had—she had told Greer that the biggest challenge would be knowing what Flip wanted. 'Even when he doesn't. And that's often.' Greer had chalked the warning up to jealousy. Lottie, who had 'discovered' Greer, couldn't get over the fact that Greer wanted to stay in the writers' office instead of training to be an assistant director. Lottie, like most would-be mentors, needed her protégée to mirror her exactly.

But Greer had no intention of leaving the writers' office, despite Lottie's assertion that a job as Flip's assistant was more of a cul-de-sac than a promotion. Writers were the bosses in television. And here she was in only her second industry job, working for one of the best, Flip Tumulty, the kind of person that others deferred to, sucked up to. People all over Hollywood, people whose names left Greer a little breathless, were constantly checking in with him, sending him gifts, currying favor.

'Aw, the old Tumulty charisma,' Ben had said, when she tried to feel him out on this topic, discover why people yearned for Flip's approval. She didn't think that was the whole story, not quite. You could argue that Ben had more charm, while there was a hint of the—what was the word Ben had used in a different context? A hint of the nebbish about Flip, that was it, and it served him well. Disorganized as he was when it came to his life, he never lost sight of the tiniest detail in the work. He also put in longer hours than anyone else, a trial for Greer, given that she was trying to impress Flip by being the first to arrive and the last to leave every day. Not that he noticed. There were moments where Greer stood silently in the office, assuming Flip was deep in thought, waiting for him to acknowledge her and what she had just said, only to realize that it hadn't occurred to him that her presence required any acknowledgment whatsoever.

He wasn't mean, though. Greer knew from

mean. When she had gone to California right after college, Greer had worked for the King of Mean, an entertainment lawyer-slash-manager-slash-thrower, specializing in tantrums and staplers. He had burned through golden boys and girls with better alma maters and more sterling connections, but Greer was tougher. She quickly developed a way of coping, a strategy drawn, as most of her strategies were, from the movies. She imagined that the lawyer was the Stay Puft marshmallow man from *Ghostbusters,* marching down the streets of New York. He could grimace, he could wave his big puffy arms, he could threaten all sorts of things, but what could a man made of sugar and water really do to her, ultimately? She developed her own stoic marshmallow-ness, an outward manner so soft and placid that he couldn't find a hold or a weak spot, and it wasn't for lack of trying. She hadn't returned to Baltimore because she couldn't cut it out there. Her father had gotten ill, and her parents had insisted that it was a daughter's responsibility to help out at home, even though she had two brothers closer by, one in Pennsylvania, the other in Delaware.

As it turned out, her father had died in less than two months, so her mother hadn't really needed her at all. Greer had been twenty-three and, in her mind, washed up. She couldn't ask for her old job back, and she couldn't get a new one without a good reference from Stay Puft. Sucked back into life in Arbutus, she worked at a small law firm, dating her high school boyfriend. When JJ had asked her to marry him, she had said yes because she was too beaten down to remember that she had the right to say no. She was one of the unlucky ones, who had better take what life offered, meager as it might be.

When it was announced that the *Mann of Steel* pilot would film in Baltimore—through an online service that kept Greer apprised of television and movie deals—she felt like a prisoner glimpsing sunlight for the first time in years. She bluffed her way into a gig as an unpaid intern, given the make-work job of cata-loging Flip's and Ben's papers in case their alma maters wanted them one day. From there, it hadn't taken long to persuade Ben that she should be the writers' office assistant. And when the job as Flip's assistant suddenly became available, she *knew* the gods were finally smiling on her. So what if Flip sometimes failed to notice that a breathing, heart-beating human was in the room? She had lived through the rain of staplers, through the drought of her father's illness. There was nothing she couldn't endure, as long as she was moving up.

'That's it?' Ben had said, when she asked him to put in a word for her, back her for the job as Flip's assistant. 'That's all you want, is to work for Flip?' He seemed at once relieved and disappointed. 'It's not a guarantee, you know. Of anything.'

'Well, I want to write,' she said. 'What better teacher could I have?'

She knew that had been a twist of the knife, suggesting that Flip had more to teach her about writing than Ben did. But all Ben had said was, 'There's a difference, between wanting to write and writing. What are you working on? Show it to me and I'll critique it.' Sensing her hesitation, he had added: 'Honest, I'll give you a fair read. And you know I don't offer my services to just anyone.'

'I'm not ready yet. I'm studying scripts, getting ready. *You* know that.'

'Yeah,' Ben had said. 'You've zipped through the collected works of Ben Marcus and Flip Tumulty, reading our rough drafts, following our stunning trajectory from *No Human Involved* to *Ottoman's Empire* to *Mildred, Pierced*. You might aim a little higher, you know. Billy Shakespeare. Chekhov. Hell, at the very least try Robert Towne or William Goldman.'

She had dutifully recorded those names in her notebook—Towne and Goldman, that is. She wasn't so ignorant that she needed Ben to tell her about Shakespeare. But she also wasn't so naïve that she thought she would learn to write television by studying *playwrights*.

Yet Ben had hit close to an uncomfortable truth without even trying, his peculiar talent. So far, Greer *hadn't* been able to bridge the gap between wanting to write and writing. For one thing, there was never any time. But when she did find a free hour to sit in front of her computer, she froze. Staring at a blank screen almost made her feel sorry for Ben, something she *never* felt. Filling up that emptiness with her own ideas and stories—it seemed as unfathomable as contemplating one's own death. *Where did a story begin? What kind of story should she tell?* In the early days, when Ben still sort of liked her—or, more correctly, didn't actively dislike her—he would offer advice. 'Take one idea—for example, the house-bound private investigator, à la Nero Wolfe. Add something new—a female Archie Goodwin. That's all we had when we started *Ottoman's Empire* and everyone loved it.'

Everyone but the viewers, she had amended silently.

Idea number one: A girl wants to work in the movies. Idea number two: She gets a job, through hard work, and keeps her eyes open. But that was just her life, and she could not imagine her life becoming a movie or a television show. If her life had been rich enough to be the stuff of fiction, she wouldn't be so desperate to flee it.

What she could imagine was *success,* the end result, at once vague and specific. She had—yes, why not, it wasn't wrong to dream, quite the opposite—she had even imagined herself in a gown—floor length, gold, assuming gold was a favored trend, with a high waist to make the most of her top-heavy figure, although she would probably be thinner by the time she won a big award, having found the time and money for a personal trainer. In her fantasy, the statue was an Oscar, which made no sense relative to her own ambitions, but the Oscar looked to be a far more satisfactory object to clutch than the Emmy, with its sharp, pointy wings.

She had held an Emmy, secretly. Flip had won one, awarded for a spec script written for a long-running comedy. Just twenty-three at the time—younger than she was now—he had written it as a calling card, determined to break into the business without using the connections that his father could have provided. Flip had never expected to sell it, but the producers had loved it and used it, revising only a third of it. Greer knew this story because Flip had told it often, in almost every interview. 'I was so depressed to find out that they had rewritten some of my pages. I didn't know that first-timers often see their scripts rewritten from top to bottom, much less that spec scripts seldom become episodes, much less that they go on to be submitted for awards.' Greer was skeptical of that story. Could Phil Tumulty's son really be that naïve about the television business?

She glanced again at the clock, realized she had forgotten to send the backup electronic copies of the call sheet and quickly fired it off to the mailing list. Lottie would chew her out for that, even though the paper copies had been distributed hours earlier. The call sheet shouldn't fall to the show runner's assistant, but Lottie had somehow finagled that. Greer assumed it was punishment for wanting to work for Flip instead of Lottie, but then Alicia had been forced to do it, too, when she was Flip's assistant. She debated once more whether to call the detective again. Flip had to know it was wrong to call people past 10:59. Greer's mother still jumped when the phone rang that late, her flutter of panic running through the house. God, it had been good to get out of that sad little house, even if it had meant moving in with JJ. What would Flip say tomorrow, when Greer admitted that she hadn't been able to get the Monaghan woman on the phone? He would sigh, disappointed. Or he might have forgotten already why he had wanted Greer to call her. That happened sometimes. Monday's whim was forgotten by Tuesday's call time. But the problems with Selene weren't going to go away. And the next time she caused a disruption, Flip would turn to Greer and say: 'Whatever happened with that private detective, the one I wanted you to hire?'

Greer turned out the lights in the office, after

making sure all the equipment was turned off. Ever since Flip had seen *An Inconvenient Truth,* he was insane on the topic of electricity. He had issued a memo, through Greer, that computers and other electronics were to be unplugged every night, and that the production offices were to use fluorescent bulbs everywhere—except in Flip's private office, because he hated the quality of the light. The night was really too warm for her jacket, but she pulled it on anyway, eager for autumn. She had missed fall in L.A. It was about the only thing that she had missed about Baltimore.

Tomorrow's start was civilized, 10 A.M., and they were on the soundstage, which meant that fewer variables would be thrown into the mix. No troublesome bystanders, no sirens going off during quiet moments, no worries about weather, no stupid rowers crashing their perfect sunrise. Today had been a mere nineteen hours, 4 A.M. to 11 P.M.

She rode the elevator down to the lobby of the deserted office building. The production had the top floor, and while the building claimed other tenants, Greer had seen scant evidence of them. Flip and Ben had wanted something flashier for their headquarters—sweeping water views, good restaurants—but Lottie had prevailed on this decision, insisting they take this cheaper suite of offices in a development on Locust Point, a boomtime project that had never actually boomed. Well, it had a water view, it was just from the other side of the harbor. There were perfectly good restaurants, too, although Ben bitched and moaned, even as he hit Popeyes three days out of four. Greer had seen the buckets in his trash. Even before she had known, for a fact, that Ben could

69

not be trusted, she had plenty of reasons to believe that he was a phony and a liar.

As she reached for the outer door, she was aware of a movement in the parking lot, a skittering figure in the corner of her eye. A rat, she tried to tell herself, or a dog. But while both species could be exceptionally large in South Baltimore, neither one walked upright. She fell back behind the glass door, wondering what to do. She had her cell. She could call the police. And say what? 'I want to report a shadow in the parking lot at Tide Point.' *He's more scared of you than you are of him,* she told herself. *He dislikes conflict just as much. More.* Maybe it was a ghost, after all.

'I'm within my rights,' she announced to the empty parking lot. 'Stop bothering me. I don't have to give it back, under the circumstances.'

It was, she realized, an all-purpose pronouncement, one that could work for all the problematic people in her life. She waited, watching for that hint of movement again, then decided she had imagined it. Even so, she ran toward her car, unlocking it with the remote and leaving the parking lot gate open behind her, too scared to get out of her car and close it. She would have to make a point of being the first at work tomorrow, so it wouldn't get back to Lottie that she had left the gate up.

TUESDAY

Chapter 7

'The lamb,' Tess decided. 'And—no, yes, no—yes, a glass of wine, whatever you think best.'

Flip Tumulty, who had ordered a salad and sparkling water, gave her a hard look. Tess wasn't sure what shocked him more, the food or the beverage. Perhaps Hollywood had only two channels on its dial—abstemious self-denial and wretched excess.

'And what can I get for you, young lady?' the waiter asked.

The third member of their party—definitely young, not so obviously a lady, not to Tess's eyes—peered over enormous sunglasses, very Jackie O, circa Ron Galella. The glasses weren't exactly the best way to travel incognito. She was attracting a lot of attention—or would have been, if there had been more people in Martick's for late-afternoon lunch. Tess had chosen this determinedly obscure restaurant on the grounds that Selene Waites would be charmed by what looked like a private club. From the outside, Martick's didn't even appear to be open for business. There was no sign, no way of knowing it existed, and one had to buzz for entry. Of course, anyone who buzzed was promptly admitted, but Selene didn't know that. Tess thought Selene might at least take off her sunglasses to inspect the black pressed-tin ceiling, the sturdy old bar, the stained-glass windows, all dating back to Martick's life as a speakeasy. But Selene kept staring fixedly at her spoon. Was it dirty?

She said in a wispy monotone: 'Venti half-caf frappuccino, please.'

'We don't make cold coffee drinks here, but I could do just about anything else—cappuccino, latte, Americano, even a good old-fashioned cup of joe.'

'Who's Captain Joe?' Selene asked, pursing her lips, eyes still trained on the spoon. *She's using it as a little mirror,* Tess realized. Selene even bared her teeth to check if there was lipstick on them.

'Cup of joe,' Tess said. 'It's slang for coffee.'

'Why?'

It was a reasonable question, albeit one more appropriate to a two-year-old. But then, Tess was quickly discovering that Selene Waites was not that far removed from toddlerhood—a mercurial being who was all id, focused on satisfying her desires as she experienced them, determined to control anything she could, because, on some level, she sensed that she controlled nothing. This explained why Flip had warned Tess to play out the charade of letting Selene believe that it was ultimately her decision to hire Tess as her bodyguard.

Five seconds passed and Selene forgot her own question, or else grew bored with it. Her threshold for boredom was shockingly low. To call it attention deficit disorder would be inaccurate, because it wasn't clear that Selene was attentive enough to achieve a deficit in that area. In the ten minutes they had been in the restaurant, she had already arranged her hair three different ways and applied her lipstick twice, using two different colors.

'Your order, miss?' This waiter was working hard for his tip.

'The mussels to start,' she said, her voice continuing thin and flat. Perhaps she only used inflections when she was being paid. 'And the pâté, and the steak frites, with rolls. And a Bloody Mary, please. Do you have Effen?'

The waiter, a Baltimore hipster—that is, an art student at MICA—was pretty quick on the uptake. 'No, we've got something much better, beat all the other vodkas in a taste test, very smooth, hard to find. I can't even pronounce it.'

Selene nodded, and the waiter, aware that she wasn't looking at him, took the chance to mouth 'Smirnoff' over her oblivious head. Tess enjoyed the joke, but their conspiratorial moment gave Flip a spasm of panic.

'I admire your appetite,' Tess said to Selene. 'It's rare that I meet a woman who can match mine.'

'Well, I have a great metabolism,' Selene said, stroking her hair, styled in a side ponytail. The motion seemed to soothe her, in the manner of a child clutching the remnant of a beloved blanket. 'I eat all the time, constantly. That eating disorder stuff in the tabloids is bullshit. I'm naturally thin. I mean, if I blew up to a size six or eight, then maybe I would worry about it, but as long as I can maintain this weight—'

Her cell phone rang, a mildly surreal moment, as Selene's ring was her own voice, doing a cover of Blondie's 'Call Me.'

The waiter, slightly less relaxed, rushed back to the table. 'We don't allow cell phones here, miss.'

'It's an iPhone,' Selene said with elaborate patience. 'Bill Gates gave it to me personally.'

'Do you mean Steve Jobs?' Tess asked.

'Of course he has a job,' Selene said. 'I mean, he's pretty successful.'

The waiter persisted: 'We don't let people talk on wireless devices here, and we ask that all patrons turn those devices to silent or vibrate.'

'Well, then,' Selene said, 'how am I going to take calls?'

'You're not,' Flip said, his voice kind yet authoritative, as he closed his hand over her iPhone. 'You're here to talk to Miss Monaghan about your safety concerns.'

'Okay,' she said, falling back into an abstracted silence, stroking her hair so long that her first course arrived before she spoke again.

'I wanted mussels,' she said, wrinkling her nose. She had amazing control over her features, Tess noted; the movement was contained to the nostrils alone. The result of acting for film? Botox? But surely she was too young for such things.

'These are mussels,' the waiter said. Now he, too, had taken on the patient tone that Selene inspired in others. *The whole world is her enabler,* Tess thought.

'No, mussels have, like, little legs and you suck their heads. It's fun.'

Tess counted very slowly to ten—not because she was angry, but because ridiculing a potential client was a bad business practice. Luckily, it turned out that Selene really didn't need anyone to participate in her conversations. 'I know what mussels are. I was supposed to shoot a film in New Orleans, but it never happened. Stupid hurricane.'

'That's crawfish you're thinking of,' the waiter said.

'Oh. Well, can I have some of those?'

'We don't have crawfish on the menu. We have mussels. They're quite good, especially prepared this way. And easier to eat than crawfish. Use the bread to sop up the sauce.'

'Could we have more bread? I'm ravenous.'

The waiter brought them more rolls, but Selene had already lost interest. For all her talk about her famous appetite and penchant for head sucking, Selene simply sniffed at the bread, leaving a whitish smear of flour beneath her nose. It looked rather natural to Tess. How strange Selene's world must be, where spoons were used for mirrors, and mirrors were used for—

'The thing is, I don't feel, like, I need a bodyguard.' Selene spoke as if she were picking up a thread that had been discussed at some length, when the topic had yet to be broached. 'Nothing's happened to me, not even close. I don't think I'm the issue. I think the production is. It's jinxed.'

'You're part of the production,' Flip said, 'and if anything were to happen to you. . . .'

'You could write Betsy out, easy,' Selene said. 'The show is called *Mann of Steel,* after all. It's Johnny's show.'

Tess didn't know much about actors, but she didn't think it was common for them to argue against the primacy of their roles.

'Yes, well, the man who died didn't have photographs of Johnny in his house,' Flip said. 'He had photographs of *you.*'

She preened a little, as if she had been complimented.

'If I'm going to have a bodyguard, shouldn't it be a guy, like in the movie?' Selene asked. 'Nobody has a *girl* bodyguard.'

77

'You'll be the first,' Flip said. 'After you do it, everyone will want to do it.'

Selene stroked her hair a little faster, clearly excited by the notion of setting a trend. 'Could we design an outfit for her, a uniform, something like Angelina Jolie in the Lara Croft movies, only by Prada?' She regarded Tess. 'You would look a little like Angelina if you had longer hair with a completely different face. And if you dropped some weight, of course, and got your lips plumped up.'

'Of course,' said Tess, feeling a pang for the long braid she had worn most of her life. Her hair fell to her shoulders now, and she kept it loose most of the time, or pulled back in a ponytail when rowing. She realized these styles were more suitable, perhaps even more flattering, to a woman in her thirties. But she missed her braid. 'Only this isn't a part, and I'm not going to lose weight for it, or wear a uniform, or do my hair a certain way. I'm going to be *working* for you, and I take my work seriously.'

'As do I,' Selene said, a little heatedly.

'Then you both should get along great,' Flip said. 'No fights, no feuds, no egos.'

'Amigos!' Selene sang, although Tess was pretty sure that Flip had slightly mangled the lyrics to the old show tune. 'I was Baby June at summer camp, which is funny that I then became Baby Jane. I wanted to be Louise, though. Stupid old June, she disappears by act two.'

Now that was more what Tess expected in an actress.

'Well, Betsy has plenty to do in our production, more than we planned,' Flip said, buttering a piece

78

of bread and actually trying to press it into Selene's hand, as if he were her mother. Or nanny. 'You know we've been rewriting the last three episodes of the season, because that was the only note the network gave us—more Selene, keep her story open-ended. More, more, more. They love you, and they're willing to spend extra money to keep you safe.'

Flip might seem overly solicitous of Selene, Tess realized, but he was smooth, too, steering her toward what he wanted. Was he manipulating Tess in the same way? But no, she had decided to take the job only for Lloyd's sake, and Flip couldn't have foreseen that. She was calling her own shots.

The main courses arrived and Tess dug in, happy for the cover of chewing. Selene sliced and cut her steak into ever smaller pieces, spread pâté on the saltines provided, and twirled her frites in the mayonnaise she had demanded that the waiter bring, much to his barely concealed disgust. But Tess never observed a morsel of food going *in*.

Meanwhile, Flip was studying Tess, and less covertly.

'I've never seen a woman eat like that,' he said, caught staring at her quickly cleaned plate. 'It's . . . impressive.'

'I eat like that,' Selene said. 'I have a really high metabolism.'

'Of course you do,' Flip said, buttering another roll and handing it to the young woman, who placed it on the bread plate with the other roll she had ignored.

What kind of weird family am I joining? Tess decided to focus on the money she was going to be paid, twice her usual rate. In the fine tradition of

79

private detectives, she told herself that she would believe the money, not the story.

She then spent the rest of lunch trying to forget the kind of terms used for those who did things just for the money.

*   *   *

'You a midget?' the homeless man asked Lottie MacKenzie. Or maybe he was a vagrant. She couldn't know that he was homeless, just that he was dirty. Lottie MacKenzie always tried to stick to the facts, things that could be quantified, even in her private thoughts.

'No,' she said. 'I'm not a midget.'

'Then you a dwarf? There's a difference, ain't there? Whatever you are, you probably prefer to be called a *little person,* right?'

'What I am,' Lottie said, 'is *short*. That's all. Just short. If you must put a word to it, that's the one.'

'Sheeeeeeeeeeeit. *Short* don't cover it. You pocket-size.'

'Depends on the pocket, I suppose.'

He laughed and used her rejoinder as a cue to pull his own pocket inside out, showing that it was empty—and filthy.

Although she usually stiffed panhandlers, especially those who so much as alluded to her height, Lottie gave the man a dollar, rationalizing that it balanced her indulgence in a three-dollar latte from the Daily Grind, not to mention the five-dollar éclair from Bonaparte Bread across the street. Lottie had grown up listening to a lot of people lay a proprietary claim to guilt—Jews, Catholics—but she couldn't imagine that anyone

80

felt the clutch of anxiety she did at the thought of her Scottish father finding out that she had spent three dollars on coffee and milk.

But such extravagance was preferable to making the production pay for every goddamn beverage she bought herself during the course of a working day. That would make her no different from Ben, the moocher, the schnorrer—a word she had embraced since learning it from Flip, although he laughed at how it sounded in her mouth. Her family had arrived in California when Lottie was five, and she didn't have anything resembling a Scottish accent. But there was something clipped about her voice, an inability to wrap her mouth around the Yiddish terms so common to Hollywood and movie-making. Schnorrer. Ben was such a rip-off artist that he had tried to submit receipts for the music he downloaded from iTunes, claiming he listened to music while he wrote, so it was a production-related expense. 'Try that shit on the tax man, not me,' Lottie had snapped at him.

In Lottie's experience—and she had almost twenty years of working in television, far more than the Wonder Boys; she was second generation like Flip, although her father had been a propmaster—there were two ways of looking at a production. You could treat it like carrion and pick its bones clean, or you could give it the respect of a small but solid nest egg that would keep producing income as long as people didn't get greedy. Movies were carrion. *Mann of Steel* had the potential to be a nest egg production, something that could provide them all steady work for three or four years if people didn't lose their heads. She had lectured Ben on this concept just last week, thinking she might actually convert him to being a team player.

'Jesus, Lottie,' he had said. 'Why do you think so small?' There was an awkward pause, and he had apologized, but with a smirk that made it clear his words had been chosen in order to create that awkwardness. Here she was, going on forty, and still dealing with stupid jokes about her height. Four feet ten, she should have told the homeless man, singing the words out loud and clear. *Four feet fucking ten, which is not a midget or a dwarf or a little person, just short, according to the clinical definition.* Four feet ten, a full foot shorter than her father, and almost six inches shorter than her mother, for no reason that anyone had ever discerned. Her mother blamed the postwar shortages, but how could her father's poor nutrition have stunted Lottie's growth when it hadn't affected his? And her mother, an American studying abroad when she met Lottie's father, had never known any dietary lack greater than decent peanut butter. Certainly, food had been abundant for all of Lottie's life, especially after they moved to Los Angeles. Her new schoolmates, incapable of understanding the difference between Scotland and Ireland, had called her Lottie the leprechaun, mocked her size and her vowel sounds. The accent was vanquished quickly, but her small stature was one of the few things that remained beyond her control.

Behind the wheel of her car—a midsize rental, because a small car made her feel doll-like and an SUV would seem so compensatory—she fastened on her headset and began running through her calls with furious efficiency. A long lunch in the

82

middle of a brutal day, what was Flip thinking? He would be logy and cranky for much of the afternoon. Ben wasn't answering his phone, per usual. They may have been hailed as geniuses, but Flip had trouble seeing the bigger picture outside the script, while Ben . . . *Ben*! He was simply one of the most undisciplined men she had ever worked with, and she had known some real fuckups in her time. He procrastinated, got behind, ended up with too much on his plate, and then went into hiding, like a little kid late on his homework. So many people mistook speed for urgency. Lottie was slow and methodical in her movements and her speech, but she almost never had to redo anything. She got things right the first time.

Of course, the most frustrating thing about Ben was that the work, once done, was stellar. Not that Lottie had any intention of letting him know that.

Besides, she had bigger worries. Something was rotten in the city of Baltimore. Throughout her career, Lottie had battled government interference, various actors' addictions, and nepotism. She had weathered weather, gone toe-to-toe with God and won the argument. But this production was off in a way that Lottie couldn't define, and it troubled her. They were making their days more often than not, Flip was dealing pretty well with the network demands for more Selene, and no one in the cast had been arrested. Yet.

Still, there was someone in the production who couldn't be trusted, although she wasn't sure who it was. Lottie had never worked with any of these bozos before—not Flip or Ben, but also not the string of second-rate directors that the network had foisted on them, and definitely none of the union locals here in Baltimore. The last, at least, had been a pleasant surprise. The crew was disciplined and professional, honed by years of steady work. Even the Teamsters were a joy, relatively. But no spring ran forever, and *Mann of Steel* was now the city's only shot at getting something up and running for a few years. Movies spent more by the day, but a successful television series spent it longer. Even a two-season run for *Mann of Steel* would be a godsend for the city, make its little slice of *Diehard 4* look anemic.

So why did it feel as if someone was actively rooting against the project, orchestrating its problems? Ever since that night in August, when the police had come to them with those photographs and the story of that poor man, hanging from his ceiling fan, Lottie had felt a sickening thump in her stomach, the sense that the production was somehow outside her control, an unfamiliar sensation for her.

And she had been right—that was the beginning of their troubles, more or less, although Johnny Tampa had been whining from almost day one. Flip had his theories, but Lottie thought he was cracked. Take Mandy Stewart, the so-called community activist who was always spouting off to the newspapers. Lottie knew exactly why Mandy Stewart had become such a vocal critic, and it didn't have shit to do with the neighborhood. A local baker, she had approached Lottie about getting the production to use her goods. Lottie would have worked it out, too, if the woman had been even semireasonable, but she had quintupled her normal prices. Lottie knew this for a fact, because she had asked her assistant to call and pretend he was looking for pastries for an event at the local library, and gotten the real quote. Then there were the retired steelworkers, who had nothing better to do than drum up bad press. Again, they would go away if Lottie would hire one of them as a consultant, but she refused to be bullied that way. Why did locals try to kill the goose that laid the golden egg? Well, not kill it exactly. No, it was more like fattening a goose for pâté, only in this case, they squeezed everything *out*. Everyone seemed to think that Hollywood minted its own money, that it produced currency the same way it produced stories.

One thing she knew for sure: This Theresa Esther Monaghan of Keyes Investigations was crazy if she thought she could bid a security job so high. They could get twenty-four-hour rent-a-cops for not much more. Flip could promise anything he liked, but all the paper moved through Lottie's office, and she had the final say on expenditures. She would knock Monaghan's price down and insist that the kid, the one she was forcing on them, take an unpaid internship. The specter of that small victory lifted her spirits and carried over to her conversation with the locations manager, whom she proceeded to ream with the quiet, no-nonsense tone that everyone on the crew had learned to fear. Flip yelled, Ben blustered, but it was Lottie's quiet voice that got things done.

Chapter 8

'Man, isn't this something?'

Lloyd stood in the middle of what looked to Tess to be a relatively ordinary suite of offices, indistinguishable from any other in the city, aside from the fact that this one featured posters from several film and television projects she had never heard of—*No Human Involved; Ottoman's Empire; Mildred, Pierced.*

'It's *something*,' she managed.

'And look in there.' Lloyd dashed through the open door of the corner office before Tess could admonish him, emerging with a winged statue.

'This thing is *heavy*,' he said, hoisting it in two hands. 'I want to thank the members of the Academy and my mama—'

'Don't forget God. He's big this year.'

The dark-haired man slouching in the doorway was tall and thin, with the type of sharp-featured face that Tess usually found attractive. But there was something a little mocking in his eyes, unkind. Lloyd was only seventeen, and his life had been sheltered in a lot of ways. Besides, he couldn't be the first person to play this game. Tess bet almost everyone who saw the Emmy grabbed it instinctively, delivering a mock acceptance speech. The cleaning lady had probably done it.

'I'm sorry,' Lloyd said.

'Oh, I don't mind,' the man said. 'And I doubt that Flip would care. Greer—now Greer is another thing. She just had it all shined up, special for the boss man. But then, Greer is always buffing Flip's Emmy, in one sense or another.'

Was that supposed to be a double entendre? It didn't fit the dynamic that Tess had observed between Flip and Greer. Besides, the girl had a fiancé.

'How do they get your name on it?' Lloyd said, puzzling over the inscribed base. 'Wouldn't that give away who won, ahead of time? They always make a big deal of it being a secret.'

'You get them blank, then they send you a band that's fitted over the base. Or so I've *heard*.' There was a lot of topspin on the last word, but Tess decided to make nice, anyway.

'Tess Monaghan. I'm coming on board as security for Selene Waites, and Flip agreed that the production would find a space for Lloyd here in the writers' office, as an intern, doing whatever you need.'

She was a little bitter about Lottie MacKenzie, whom she had yet to meet, shortchanging Lloyd that way. It had been bad enough, agreeing to a cut in her own fee, but the truth was that Tess had jacked it up quite a bit, testing the limits, and even the renegotiated price was far better than what she usually got. Denying minimum wage to Lloyd was downright mean-spirited—not to mention detrimental to Crow's hope of instilling a work ethic in the kid.

'Can you type?' the man asked Lloyd.

'Sorta . . . ,' Lloyd said, an honest enough answer. Tess had seen him on a computer keyboard. He used the two-finger method, and his speed was admirable, his accuracy and spelling less so.

'Work a photocopier? Answer phones? Get a lunch order right? The last is really the most important. A writers' office, like an army, travels on its stomach.'

Tess thought that Lloyd would bristle at this list of less-than-illustrious tasks, but he nodded earnestly.

'Whatever you want, Mr. Marcus.'

'Ben,' the man said, then on a delayed double take: 'How do you know my name?'

'When I learned I was going to work here, her boyfriend, Crow'—he jerked a thumb at Tess—'sat me down with the computer, and we went over everybody's credits on IMDb, then I matched the names to images on Google.'

'Were you familiar with our work before you did that little exercise?' Tess couldn't decide if the question was supercilious, or merely insecure. Of course, it was possible to be both, to use the former as a cover for the latter.

'I seen *The Beast* twelve times,' Lloyd said. 'It's one of my favorite movies.'

Ben Marcus looked pained. 'That's Tumulty, and Tumulty Senior at that. We don't give points for that around here.'

'Yeah, I know, but that's what I like. Horror. You wrote one of my favorite episodes on my favorite show ever, *Freak Fest*. I mean, I admit, I didn't know who wrote it before we looked it up, but when I did, I remembered it and *shit*. There was some righteous evil in that.'

Shamed out of his sardonic smile, Ben Marcus looked awkward, even naked.

'I'd almost forgotten about *Freak Fest*.' He turned to Tess. 'It was an attempt to update the old anthology shows, like *Night Gallery,* and one of the few things I ever wrote on my own.'

'I liked it when those strange little men chanted, "One of us, one of us, one of us."' Lloyd squatted down and began hopping around in the fashion of a demented chicken. Perhaps Crow should have spent less time on the Internet, more time briefing Lloyd on acceptable office behavior.

'Yeah,' Ben said, his tone moving back into its naturally arch range. 'Well, there's a reason for that.'

Lloyd, still in chicken mode, nodded. 'I know, Tod Browning's *Freaks,* 1932. Johnny Eck, the Baltimore screen painter, was in it. You know, one of them guys with no legs. Crow 'n' me watched it a couple of weeks ago. I love those pinhead ladies.'

If the life I see on my deathbed is more a series of greatest hits than unfiltered memories, Tess thought, *then this moment will be part of that final slide show*: Achingly Hip Screenwriter Dude shot down by a seventeen-year-old street kid, left nonplussed by Baltimore arcana. Johnny Eck! Screen painting! Oh, it was lovely.

'Yeah,' Ben said at last. 'Unfortunately, *Freak Fest* was more of a *Weak Fest.* No one can make an anthology show work anymore.'

'Why is that?' Tess asked. She had zero interest in the answer, but she didn't want Ben to resent Lloyd, and appealing to Ben's insider knowledge might restore the equilibrium, allow him to play the expert he clearly prided himself on being.

'I haven't a clue. William Goldman gets credit for saying "Nobody knows anything" in the movie business. I'm just the rare soul who admits it. Okay—Lloyd, was it? Welcome to writers' world.

Flip and I are actually doing all the writing this first season, and Flip has a personal assistant, so you'll be fetching and carrying for me, mainly, but also doing anything that Greer tells you to. Or the script supervisor, Bonnie. Or Lottie MacKenzie, especially Lottie MacKenzie. She may not even come up to your shoulder, but she's the one person you never want to disappoint on this set. Lottie fires people.'

'He's not getting paid,' Tess pointed out.

'That won't stop Lottie. Where's Greer? Never mind, I'll show you the computer basics, and the phones. Lottie has mad-anal systems for everything here, from the phones to e-mail. With phone messages, you have to log everything in by hand and by computer. When you send an e-mail, always blind-copy it to yourself. And make sure you have a list of all the restaurants we like for lunch, along with their menus. But you'll also have to call them to check the specials every day.'

Tess felt a little like a mom, watching the kindergarten teacher lead her son to his cubbyhole. Lloyd, however, had no separation anxiety whatsoever. He couldn't have been more enthusiastic about the mundane tasks that Ben was outlining.

She gave it three days.

*   *   *

Greer tried to wrap her arms around the slippery dry-cleaning bags, but there was too much to carry in one trip, and one of the bags ended up slipping to the pavement. How did someone who seemed to dress exclusively in T-shirts and blue jeans generate so much dry cleaning? When Flip had interviewed her for the job of his assistant, he had cited dry cleaning as the type of errand she would *never* be asked to do. No dry cleaning, no child or pet care, Flip had promised. *Nothing demeaning.* The problem was that Flip, who had been sucked up to most of his life, had no idea what demeaning was. He had kept his promises about children and pets, but that was probably because his son was on the West Coast, along with whatever animals the family kept.

Still, there was no end to the trivial shit she was asked to do. Last week, Greer had spent her workday trying to find out if the cable system in Flip's rented house could be reconfigured so he could get a different menu of pay-per-view options on the sports channels. She had then spent the better part of an afternoon with one of the electricians, setting up the DVR, and writing a sort of 'TiVo for dummies' shortcut guide for Flip.

And now Greer was supposed to be shopping for a bigger house, in case the series got a pickup and Flip had to relocate to Baltimore. This meant endless and exhausting conversations with Mrs. Flip, whose singular obsession seemed to be kitchen countertops. Mrs. Flip had decreed that *granite was over,* that her Baltimore kitchen, should it come to pass, must have cement or slate surfaces, a hard-to-find decor element in a Baltimore rental, where granite was considered pretty high-end.

Mrs. Flip also had endless questions about the quality of life in Baltimore, which she seemed to think was one rank above a Third World country. Were there mangoes in the grocery stores? Bottled water? *Good* bottled water? Gluten-free products? What was the local version of Fred Segal? She prefaced every conversation by saying, 'You know me, Greer, I really don't want to be any trouble,' then proceeded to outline a list of demands, questions, and needs so extreme that she was right, they weren't any trouble. They were way beyond that.

Mrs. Flip's most offensive moment, however, had come when Greer was offered the assistant job. Mrs. Flip had e-mailed Flip, asking that he send a photograph of the prospective employee. After seeing the JPEG, she had replied: 'So not a temptress. Approved.' Greer knew this because she was the one who had sent the photo—attachments were beyond Flip's computer capabilities—and she opened Flip's in-box every morning, per his instructions, and 'previewed' his mail, assigning each communication a priority code. But then, Mrs. Flip must have known that, too.

The dry cleaning, even halved, was still too much to handle, and another bag slid to the street just steps from her car, a pair of khakis brushing the pavement. Would Flip even notice, much less care? If he did, she could always blame the dry cleaner. Greer had quickly learned that it was always easier to blame someone else, then promise to handle the problem as if she hadn't caused it. Things had a way of working out. The detective lady had come to work on the production, after all, just as Flip wanted, and as far as he was concerned, Greer got the credit for that. And she would be happy to take it, as long as everyone was happy.

Of course, Tess Monaghan had made it a package deal, which bothered Greer far more than it did anyone else. She had insisted on installing some inner-city kid in the writers' office, and Greer had worried for a moment that he might turn out to be a spy or, worse, someone as ambitious as herself. But when she came into the office, her arms full of plastic, and saw how young the kid was, she decided that she had nothing to fear from him.

'You the new intern?' she asked, and he nodded eagerly. 'Go to my car and get the rest of Mr. Tumulty's dry cleaning, then hang it in his office.' He all but ran from the office, happy to have something to do. Later, she would blame him for the dirt on the khakis.

'Don't abuse him, Greer,' Ben said, popping out of nowhere. He was a sneaky one, although not quite as sneaky as he thought. 'There's enough scut work. You don't have to create more for him.'

'He works for the writers' office and Flip is one of the writers, is he not?' She had a troubling thought. 'Hey, will he get a credit?'

Ben sighed. 'Jesus, Greer. You worry about the tiniest things.'

'Well, I could worry about some pretty big things, but I think you would prefer that I not do that.'

'Flip wants you on set,' Ben said. 'He wants you to give the lady dick a tour, show her where the magic happens, give her the lay of the land. More clichés to come, as they occur to me. In fact, I think I'll just plug that in the minipub for episode seven—more clichés TK. She's going to meet you over there in an hour.'

93

'Are you heading over to the soundstage eventually?' she asked. 'I'll drive you.'

'I was going to check in later, see how the new scenes are working.'

'We should go together,' she said. 'Then we can . . . catch up.'

'Yeah,' he said, rubbing his chin. Flip liked to tease Ben that the mannerism was a holdover from their college days, when Ben had sported a Vandyke for a while. *Ben rubs his chin like that to apologize to it for the years of pretentious stupidity.* Flip could tease Ben, and Ben could tease Flip, but no one else was allowed to speak about them the way they spoke of each other. 'Okay, if that's what you want to do.'

'Yes, it is what I want to do. Let the new kid answer the phones.'

'He's barely been briefed on Lottie's system—'

'It's not exactly rocket science.'

'Speaking of clichés.'

She shot him a look. 'I'm going to set. Flip likes to have me around. Do you want to come or not?'

She could tell that Ben longed to say something snarky, but he remained silent, bobbing his head slightly. Greer felt a strange surge of emotion—a rush of blood to her cheeks, a flip in her stomach. She wasn't sure what to call it, but *power* was as good a word as any.

Chapter 9

He stopped at an ATM, making sure it was affiliated with his own bank to save the two-dollar user fee. Even before his money worries had become chronic, he had kept track of such fees, calling the bank each month to argue over ATM charges and point-of-service fees. The bank always backed down, too, refunding him the ten or twenty dollars on his statement. More things could be negotiated than people realized. The key was to have the stamina, the willingness to fight, and that was one thing he did have.

The drawback to using his own bank was that it always showed him the balance in his account, a number he preferred not to see, much less think about. He took out twenty dollars. How much time did he have to resolve things? Six months? Nine? It was the COBRA that was killing him, an apt bureaucratic acronym if ever there was one. He was being poisoned, oh so slowly, by that monthly nut for medical insurance, a breathtaking two thousand dollars, as much as all their other bills combined, even the mortgage, which was five years from being paid off. But the only thing worse than making COBRA payments for eighteen months would be *not* making them, because no other medical plan would touch them if they had to go through an underwriting period. If they exhausted COBRA, then someone would have to take them. That was the law, the very rules and policies he had explained to so many others, over the years, with patience and, in his opinion, compassion. Yet people had yelled at him, and cursed, as if he were the arbitrary power denying them what they needed. In hindsight, he had to admit that he was a bad fit for human resources. He was a scientist by nature. He never should have left the classroom for a job in administration.

Was there any way he could save money? He could pack a bag lunch, but Marie would find that odd. When he started working at North Avenue, he had always maintained that eating lunch out was the one reward in his dull gray day. Perhaps he could say he was putting himself on a diet? But she would find that strange, too, possibly suspicious. Sometimes, when her moods sunk to their lowest, Marie would accuse him of having an affair. No, *accuse* wasn't the right word. It was more like an invitation, a concession. She would enumerate all her inadequacies and issues, making the case for him to find another woman, and he would be forced to argue the other side—death till do us part, for better for worse, in sickness and in health. Secretly, he had wondered over the last few months whether he was still obligated to stay with her. Whose enmity would he risk if he left? Who would care now?

He had hated that glimpse into himself, however. He hadn't married Marie because she was his best friend's sister, and he wasn't staying with her for that reason, either. He remained because he loved her, strange and surprising as that fact might be to everyone, including Marie. Marie needed him. He wouldn't let her down. He was going to make sure they were set for life.

Let's see—according to his source, they were on the set today. Of course, that didn't mean *she* would be on the set. She wasn't, not every day. Still, he decided to drive over there, take his position, as he thought of it. He never parked in the part of the lot directly in front of the soundstage. That might be noticed. Instead, he chose the far end, near a run-down Chinese takeout. The people who owned the restaurant were wonderfully incurious, indifferent to his on-again, off-again presence. Only once, when he had been writing in his notebook, had anyone approached him. The owner, Mr. Chen, had questioned him nervously, and he realized that he had been mistaken for some sort of official, probably from immigration. He had shown Mr. Chen his legal pad, and said the first thing that came into his mind: 'Poetry. I'm a poet and I find this a peaceful place to write.'

Mr. Chen had been happy to accept the idea that the parking lot of a derelict strip center on Eastern Avenue was a suitable place to write poetry. But then, people often were quick to hear what they wanted to hear. Wasn't he the same way himself?

He glanced toward the far end of the parking lot. He wished he could buy some expensive surveillance equipment, but he was stuck with the old camcorder, which he didn't dare bring up to his eye here. From this distance, it wasn't really possible to make out the people coming and going. Of course, she was somewhat distinctive, and he knew her vehicle, too, but she had a way of slipping in and out that made her easy to miss. Not that he could always stay until the end—the later they started, the later they went—which was frustrating. It was very hard for him to come up with plausible cover stories for any late-night shenanigans, although he sometimes found a way to sneak out after Marie was asleep, especially if she had been hitting the Xanax a little harder than usual. But there was almost no way he could justify being out regularly between the hours of eight and twelve, not without sending her into shrill lamentations about how she would wander, too, if placed in his situation.

He saw a car pull in, not the usual one, and he wondered if they were onto him, trying to trip him up. He watched the driver help her out of the car, as if she were fragile. Ah, she was anything but, he was sure of that. If only he could get to her, talk to her. Then she would be on his side, he was sure of it. Once they met, face-to-face, she would be his.

Chapter 10

Places in Baltimore often have many lives. Tess recognized the soundstage on Eastern Avenue as a former department store, one of the better ones—Hochschild Kohn, she thought, but maybe Hecht's—that had then been demoted to bargain chain status before settling into life as a members-only big lots store. It anchored the end of a sad and lonely strip mall, where at least half the stores were vacant. A small band of protesters—ah, the disgruntled steelworkers—marched along a grassy strip, earning a few halfhearted honks of support for their cause, but they looked pretty harmless to Tess. She parked and walked the perimeter of the freestanding building, noting the entrances. There was a fire door in the rear, but otherwise no way in and out of the building. That was good.

The front, however, had no security—no lock on the door, no one sitting at the front desk just inside the doors. A worker tried to wave her in the direction of a sign that said extras holding, even as Tess insisted she was here to meet with Greer. The young woman arrived just in time to save Tess from being shunted off to a wardrobe fitting.

'Isn't that a little slipshod?' Tess asked. 'Anyone could get in, under the guise of being an extra.'

'Oh, you wouldn't get far,' Greer said. 'Strangers are noticed pretty quickly.'

'Still, it's a risk, and I'm here to assess weaknesses. Remember, I'm watching Selene only during her nonwork hours. It's up to the production to make the workplace as secure as possible. And most of the problems have happened at work, right?'

Greer was turning out to be one of those people who simply didn't answer questions not to her liking. 'I suppose you want a tour of the set,' she said. 'Flip said I should take you around, if that's what you want.'

Tess didn't really care about a tour, but Greer sounded grudging, as if she resented being given this task, and her attitude made Tess perverse.

'Love to.'

The former store had been more or less stripped down to its concrete floors, with a labyrinth of plywood now taking up half of the space. Vast and high ceilinged, the building held the morning's chill and then some.

'I'll take you to the sets we're *not* using, first.' Greer headed toward the maze, and Tess had one brief paranoid fear that Greer was planning to lose her in it, that Tess would end up wandering for days among artificial rooms.

'This is the Mann row-house,' Greer said, stopping in front of a living room that played to every stereotype of how blue-collar workers lived, replete with shag carpeting, velvet paintings, and a plaid La-Z-Boy. 'We're not using it in the current episode, because that's set almost entirely in the nineteenth century.'

'It looks a little wide,' Tess murmured. 'But then, that's the problem, isn't it? Film isn't very good at conveying narrow spaces like eleven-foot rowhouses.'

'What do you mean?' Greer appeared to be offended by the mere suggestion that a film could fail to emulate real life.

'My boyfriend and I went to New York this summer, and we toured this amazing museum in a former tenement, the Lower East Side Tenement Museum, the kind of place you saw in *The Godfather, Part II,* or *Once Upon a Time in America*.' Tess didn't bother to add that she had been motivated to visit the museum because of memories of books like *A Tree Grows in Brooklyn* or the *All-of-a-Kind Family* series. Film was the only language spoken here, the only cultural reference that anyone seemed to get. 'And the thing is, the real tenements were so tiny, so claustrophobic and dark. Even in the best films, the tenement sets are too big, too filled with light. I'm guessing it's going to be the same for this row-house.'

'We have a very good DP,' Greer said, still haughty.

100

'DP?'

'Director of photography.'

'Oh.' Tess decided not to suggest that Francis Ford Coppola and Sergio Leone might have had good directors of photography as well. *DPs*. She was a quick study. She would learn to talk the talk, if that's what it took.

The next set was a run-down meeting room. 'The union hall.' Tess stepped into the room, marveling at the level of detail—the newspaper splayed across the Formica-topped table, the mismatched chairs, the faded memos tacked to the bulletin board, the coffee cups. There was even a fake coffee stain on one table. Tess couldn't help but approve of such conscientiousness.

She was taken aback, however, by the view through the 'window'—an extremely realistic photographic backdrop of the waterfront, with cranes rising in the distance, the blue smear of the harbor just beyond.

'So the things we see through the windows in a movie or television show—they're not real?'

Greer looked amused, superior—Tess's intent. People tend to reveal more to those they consider ignorant.

'Of course not. Think about the lighting and continuity issues created by a real window.'

'But it looks so *real*. I mean, on film. Here, it looks like a photograph, but on a screen, you can't tell.'

'The camera has no depth perception,' Greer said. 'And, of course, sometimes they cut in a shot of the real view—say a character had to look out the window and see something in particular. You edit that shot in, and it heightens the illusion. But look up and you can see the lights hanging from the ceiling, which allows us to light the view for day or night.'

It was an intriguing insight, but Tess wasn't sure she *liked* this behind-the-scenes view of things. While movies weren't as magical to her as they had been, back in her late teens and twenties, she still wanted to be able to suspend belief, not think about all the ways she was being fooled. She didn't share these thoughts with Greer, however. Instead, she continued to inspect the set with pretended awe, as she assumed most people did.

'You said they were filming today?'

'They are, but it's way off in another corner of the set, where we've created Betsy's world.' We, we, we. To hear Greer tell it, she was part of everything that happened on *Mann of Steel*. 'I'll take you there.'

Tess had not necessarily wanted to watch filming, but she figured she should. Observing Selene at work might give her a sense of what her charge would be like at rest. Restless, she supposed.

They wound their way through the maze, stepping over endless rivers of coiled cords and cables, until they finally found themselves in a thriving hive of activity, where young men and women—and they were overwhelmingly young, Tess noticed—rushed around with ferocious certainty. She was shocked at how many people there were working—twenty, thirty, maybe even forty. It was hard to keep track, given how they kept moving. Maybe *Mann of Steel* could be a good little economic engine for Baltimore, assuming these technical folks were locals, not imports.

'Last looks,' someone called out, and Tess watched as makeup and hair people swarmed Selene and a puffy middle-aged man—oh dear, it was Johnny Tampa, seriously gone to seed. 'Last looks' turned out to be a flurry of pampering— makeup was tweaked, hair smoothed and coaxed into position. One woman produced a camera and shot Polaroids of both actors, instructing them to hold up their hands.

'Continuity, again,' Greer said, as if sensing what Tess was about to ask. 'We have to keep careful records, so if there are reshoots, or other scenes in this time frame, everything matches up. If Selene's wearing a ring, we can't have it disappear later.'

A round-shouldered man lumbered over to Selene and Johnny, mumbled something inaudible to them. Selene, stroking her much-amplified mane of hair, nodded absently while Johnny Tampa looked confused, not unlike an animal that had just been poleaxed. The round-shouldered man shuffled away. Whoever he was, his posture made him quite the saddest sack that Tess had ever seen.

'The director,' Greer said. 'Wes Stark. Flip calls him Willie Stark, but I'm not sure why.' Tess thought about explaining *All the King's Men* to Greer but knew she would be depressed if Greer's only point of reference was Broderick Crawford. Or even worse, Sean Penn.

'But I thought the woman, the one who's been running the crew, calling out some of the orders—'

'First AD. Assistant director, Nicole. She's really good, and Stark's smart enough to cede a lot of power to her. Smart or lazy—he doesn't like to

103

leave the video village if he can help it. At any rate, she's pulling his bacon out of the fire on this ep.'

Something in the phrase, the bit about pulling Stark's bacon, didn't ring true to Tess. She didn't doubt its veracity, having no basis to judge his performance. But she didn't believe it was Greer's unique opinion. Someone must have told her that, or Greer had overheard that scrap of phrase and decided to appropriate it.

'You need to watch from the village,' Greer said. 'Where the director is.'

'Oh, I'm fine here,' Tess said.

'You may be fine, but Johnny's not. You're in his eye line, and he freaks out when there are strangers watching him.'

Tess decided not to point out that someone who freaked out when strangers were watching was a bad fit for the acting profession.

Greer led her to an encampment of director's chairs, some of which did have names on their backs. Here was Flip, along with the tiniest adult woman that Tess had ever seen, her chair fitted with a wooden footrest higher than the others, so her legs didn't swing free. The back of her chair identified her as Charlotte MacKenzie. So that was the bean counter who had cut her fee and reduced Lloyd to an intern. Ben wasn't in his chair. He was several feet away, standing next to a cart piled high with food. Flip glanced up, caught Tess's eye, greeted her with a curt, professional nod. Ah, she had segued into the category of 'help,' alongside Greer. She no longer qualified for the thick charm Flip had piled on when trying to hire her. As long as his checks cleared, she didn't give a damn.

'Here you go,' Greer said. 'If you want to watch,

you can take Ben's chair and I'll get you a headset.'

'Oh, I—' But Greer was off, catching a man by the sleeve and bringing Tess back what looked like a small battery pack with headphones.

'Just remember to give it back to me, okay? Don't walk off with it, whatever you do.'

'I wouldn't—'

'Do you want sides?'

'You mean like french fries?'

Greer gave an exaggerated sigh and thrust some pages into Tess's hand—not a script, proper, but just a few pages, including the scene in question—then rushed away again, returning to her natural orbit at Flip's elbow. She considered Tess a waste of time, and Greer clearly didn't value people unless she felt they could do something for her. She wanted to be around those with power, and Flip was the power source here.

'Rolling . . . action . . . *fuck*.' The camera, a two-headed behemoth set on a wheeled cart, had snagged on its track. Workers rushed to it, not even waiting for instruction, already aware of what they had to do to fix the problem.

Ben wandered over to Tess, having snagged a handful of miniature candy bars, but waved Tess back into his seat when she tried to surrender it to him.

'Exciting, isn't it?'

'I suppose so,' Tess said.

'I was being sarcastic. The most exciting thing on a movie set is craft services. The food,' he added helpfully, brandishing a Snickers. 'Movie sets are lousy with free food.'

'Isn't that hard on the actors?'

'Harder on those of us who have no incentive to maintain our boyish figures.' More sarcasm, she figured, as Ben still had the beanpole skinniness of an adolescent who had grown six inches in the past year. Tess's greyhound had more body fat. 'Although some actors aren't as disciplined, and it gets to be a problem.'

'Really?'

'Let's just say that our Mann of Steel is at risk of becoming Man of Flab.' He flapped a candy wrapper at the two actors on the set, Selene and Johnny Tampa. Oh, how the mighty had fallen. He was a shadow of his former heartthrob self. Well, not a shadow. Something considerably more substantial than a shadow.

'He doesn't look so bad,' Tess said, out of loyalty to her teenage crush.

'He split two pairs of pants yesterday and we lost almost an hour finding a third. Okay, they're getting ready to film again, so you know to be—'

'Quiet on the set. Sound speed. Rolling. *Action.*'

Ben cocked an eyebrow at Tess and held a finger to his lips. He joined Flip and Lottie at the monitors, but she didn't feel entitled to jockey for the best view. Besides, she sensed that Greer might tackle her if she tried to get too close to Flip. She stayed in Ben's chair, catching only a glimpse of the actors through the equipment and personnel circling around the set, but able to hear every word they said over the headset. It was a short scene, nonsensical without the context of the larger story. Mann seemed to be trying to pass himself off as a sailor, but Betsy Patterson, who had dated a sailor or two in her time, kept catching him in lies and mis-statements. 'Are you wellborn?'

she asked at last, and the scene ended, apparently on a hilarious close-up of Johnny Tampa, considering the question. All in all, it was no more than two minutes, but they filmed it again and again from different angles, while the director, the stoop-shouldered man, kept pulling Tampa aside to chat. No one had anything to say to Selene, and Tess had to admit that she was convincing as Betsy Patterson, perhaps even more captivating than the real-life coquette, managing the trick of being innocent and knowing at the same time. But Johnny seemed tentative, off in a way that even a civilian could discern.

'Someone put Nair in Johnny's face cream yesterday,' Ben whispered to Tess during one of the breaks. 'He smelled it before he put it on, but it freaked him out. He could have ended up losing his eyebrows if he had used it.'

'Where was this?'

'In his banger. Trailer. We have a bank of trailers on the parking lot, which the actors and day players use as dressing rooms.'

Tess made a mental note that the trailers were something else she would have to be concerned about. Meanwhile, she was able to piece together much of what was happening on her own—two cameras, for example, took simultaneous 'A' and 'B' shots, which reduced the amount of time spent on coverage. The director never told either actor how to say a line but spoke more generally about the emotion he was looking for, the tone. They were on the ninth take, and even Tess could tell that they were finally getting what they wanted from Tampa when three bars of an Iguanas' song trumped the tender scene. *Para donde vas?* Her

107

cell phone. Oops.

'Whose fucking cell phone was that?' Lottie leapt from her chair—a not inconsiderable feat for her, given the distance to the ground. Her voice was soft but vicious. 'I was serious about the fine, I will fucking fine you, I will have your fucking head, what kind of idiot doesn't turn his phone off—' When she realized that the culprit was Tess, she softened her approach, but only slightly. 'Oh, you must be the . . . security detail. Monaghan. Well, I guess no one told you, but there are signs posted all over the fucking place. You can read, can't you? Greer—'

She motioned to the young woman and leaned toward her, giving her what Tess could only suspect was a whispery scolding.

'I'm sorry,' Tess said. 'It was all my fault. Greer *did* tell me.' She thought that might win her a look of gratitude from Greer, but the young woman had a panicky, stay-away-from-me expression. Flip looked sheepish, knowing he had arranged for Greer to bring her here, while Ben's usual smirk was in place. Tampa was clearly frustrated, having been interrupted just as he was beginning to calm down. Only Selene seemed oblivious to everything going on around her, playing with her hair even as a woman kept poking at the elaborate upsweep with a long comb.

'Thanks,' Tess said, waving as she stepped backward. 'I'm going to run over to my office, but I'll be back when Selene's finished for the day. Give me a thirty-minute heads-up, so I can be here when she's ready to go.'

Still moving backward, she gave what she hoped was a nonchalant wave, only to trip over a mass of cables. Righting herself, she fought the urge to run from the soundstage, settling for a brisk walk. It was only when she was in her car that she realized she had, in fact, fled with the headset that Greer had explicitly told her to leave behind. Poor Greer, she'd probably be blamed for that as well.

*　　　*　　　*

'Great hire,' Ben said to Flip a little later as they were preparing the setup for another scene, a dinner party. It was going to be an absolute ballbuster—three full pages of dialogue, half of it Tampa's. He was so good in his other scenes, but he seemed to fall apart whenever he had to act opposite Selene. A problem, given that the network kept pounding on them to write more for her. Their chemistry had been good initially but had deteriorated as Selene's part expanded.

Flip nodded absently, not catching the tone—a habit of Flip's, not catching the tone of things in real life. Then, on a double take: 'Hey, don't be an asshole. She's okay.'

'You really think this is going to solve anything, assigning her to Selene?'

Flip gave him a measuring kind of look. Ben wondered if his old friend guessed that Ben's real concern was how he could continue seeing Selene if she was watched every minute she was off set. But how could Flip know? How could anyone know? Selene was as intent on keeping their secret as he was. Or so she had said.

But all Flip said was: 'I think it's going to solve a lot of our problems. You'll see.'

'And if it doesn't?'

Flip shook his head, as if refusing to acknowledge this possibility. Greer—nearby, always nearby, always hovering, always spying, God, how Ben hated her—looked defensive, as if *her* work, her decision, had been challenged. Ever since she had started working for Flip, she seemed increasingly confused about her role in things, apparently believing that the orders she carried out were her orders. Ben wished that she would make a fatal mistake—insult Flip's wife, or confess to a profound admiration for Flip Senior. She was an operator, this one, although not as smooth as she thought she was, not nearly as smooth.

'She's kind of attractive,' Flip said. 'If I were single, I'd ask her out.'

Ah, good old Flip, always looking for a matrimonial noose to slip around Ben's neck, so they both could be monogamous and miserable.

'She has a boyfriend,' Greer said quickly. Flip, perhaps startled by the shrill tone in her voice, gave her a look, and she mumbled: 'I remember from when the newspaper wrote about her. They live together.'

Flip had a finite amount of attention for nonwork matters, and it was now exhausted. 'I'm going back to the writers' office, so you'll have to cover set for the rest of the day, Ben.' It was an order. To the world at large, Flip pretended they were two equals, two longtime friends who never quarreled. But someone had to be in charge, as Flip often said, and that person happened to be, well, Flip.

'You're the boss,' Ben told his oldest friend.

Chapter 11

Tess had a secret recipe for cooling the flush brought on by humiliation—she went to the nearest Baskin-Robbins and got a double scoop, chocolate chip and orange sherbet. It was a homeopathic cure of sorts, for it reminded her of a night when she was eight, when she had taken a lick of this admittedly odd pairing only to see both scoops fall and go rolling across the floor. But the clerk had been kind, giving her a new cone for free, and it was this kindness, the acknowledgment that everyone made mistakes, that the flavors brought back to her. She drove one-handed to her office, where she spent an hour on bills, paying and sending. In the end, she was dead even—assuming her clients weren't deadbeats.

Her nerves soothed, Tess raced home to walk the dogs. Her new assignment would be hardest on them, for they were used to tagging along to the office and even to some of her jobs. They were, in fact, great decoys on surveillance. A woman walking an unruly greyhound and a placid Doberman was so conspicuous as to be inconspicuous, Tess had discovered. If she struggled with her cell phone as leashes twisted around her like a maypole, no one would ever suspect she was actually snapping photographs. She should structure one of her classes around that concept, how to hide in plain sight.

Stony Run, the park that bordered her backyard, was empty at this time of day, and she enjoyed having it to herself. She scuffed her feet through the leaves, wistful for a time when people had made huge piles of them and started bonfires, environmentally unfriendly as she now knew that practice to be. Now, in upscale neighborhoods such as hers, leaves were piled along the curbs and sucked up by a huge city machine on an appointed date. She scuffed harder, enjoying the rustling sound. She stopped. The rustle didn't, not quite.

Glancing back over her shoulder, she saw what appeared to be an enormous mound of camouflage, tiptoeing from tree to tree. It was like something out of a cartoon, one where Wile E. Coyote dressed up as a cactus and attempted to blend into the landscape while stalking the Road Runner.

'Mrs. Blossom?'

The woman's considerable girth was visible from both sides of the tree she was using for cover, but she didn't acknowledge Tess, just stayed where she was.

'Mrs. Blossom, I *see* you.'

The woman peered around the tree. 'Does that mean I failed?'

Now that Tess had a chance to inspect the full, head-to-toe effect of Mrs. Blossom's surveillance costume—no other word would do—she was impressed almost in spite of herself. It was camouflage, yes, but not the usual browns, grays, and greens. This was purple camouflage, popularized a few years ago by fans of the Ravens, and Mrs. Blossom had found oversize men's cargo pants that actually bagged on her. To finish off her look, she had chosen low-heeled brown pumps and—this detail was utterly endearing to Tess—a moss green hat. She had thought about her costume, perhaps even opened up her pocketbook to complete it.

'We don't have grades. And you were on the honor system, right? You were to write up a report on how it went, good or bad. So how do you think you did?'

Mrs. Blossom stubbed her toe in the dirt. 'Not very well. You saw me.'

'Yes, but—not until we got to the park. Were you waiting here, or near my house? Did you follow me?'

'From your office,' Mrs. Blossom said. 'I parked there the whole day and—I was so worried, I had to go to the bathroom, which I know isn't allowed, but I went to this bar, which looked a little scary from the outside, although the bathrooms were really clean. Nice, even.'

Tess knew the bar, an unofficial lesbian hangout, and its bathrooms were, in fact, impeccable.

'I was getting ready to go home—Oprah is on at four, and I like to make a little snack first—but then you finally showed up. So I waited to see where you would go.'

And, still in a self-castigating snit over my loutish behavior on set, I didn't notice a car tailing me for seven or so miles. Tess couldn't decide whether to be proud of her student, or appalled at her own obliviousness.

'That's pretty good, actually. It's hard to follow someone in a car.'

The praise made Mrs. Blossom's cheeks flush pink.

'Do you want to walk with me?' Tess asked, holding out the Doberman's leash. 'Don't worry,

Miata just looks scary. She's a sweetheart.' Esskay, the greyhound, was the far more difficult dog to walk, lurching and bolting at every leaf, even the movement of the breeze through the grass, convinced that all motion was indicative of a smaller creature to be chased and eaten.

Mrs. Blossom looked worriedly at her watch. 'I don't know—there's the news, after Oprah. I like to watch that, be up on things. And then there's *Wheel of Fortune* and *Access Hollywood*.'

'*Access Hollywood*,' Tess said. 'That's what my life has become actually. I have all this access to Hollywood, and it doesn't interest me at all. I'm doing some work for that television show that's filming here.'

'Really?' Mrs. Blossom's voice rose to a fan-girl squeal. 'Have you met Johnny Tampa?'

Tess was surprised that Mrs. Blossom knew the details of the production.

'I saw him from across a room,' Tess said.

'What does he look like in person?'

She thought about this. 'Broader.'

Mrs. Blossom took Miata's leash, fell into step beside Tess. They were coming up on the synagogue, the busy street beyond it, and the dogs recognized this as the point where they usually turned around.

'But what's he *like*, Johnny Tampa? Nice. I bet he's nice.'

'I saw him for only ten minutes or so. You can't know anything about someone in such a short period of time.'

'I decided I wanted to marry Hamilton Blossom the moment I met him, and we got married four days later. The moment I saw him, I thought he

114

was the nicest, kindest man I could ever find. We celebrated our forty-third anniversary last year.'

'And forty-three years later, do you still think he is the nicest, kindest man you've ever met?'

'Oh, by then . . . well, by then, I realized that I didn't know the half of things. He was nicer than I ever suspected. He died this winter.'

Her matter-of-factness about her loss made it sadder somehow.

'I'm sorry,' Tess said.

'Me, too,' Mrs. Blossom said, sighing, not from self-pity but from the simple acknowledgment that she was sad, and likely to be so for some time.

The dogs, sensing the nearness of home—and the implicit promise of a treat upon their arrival—picked up the pace. Mrs. Blossom had to trot to keep up with Miata. 'What's Selene Waites like?'

Self-centered to the point of idiocy, the walking punch line to every dumb-blonde joke ever told, but a pretty good actress. 'About what you would expect, I think.'

'She looks so thin. She looks as if a good breeze would break her in two. Mr. Blossom always told me he liked a woman with some meat on her bones.'

A breeze eddied around them, fluttering the leaves, sending a few swirling to the ground. Both dogs perked their ears, as if they could pick up the scent of the changing season. The small shot of cool air reminded Tess that such golden autumn days were a short-term loan, and that winter would be here sooner rather than later, intent on being paid in full for all this loveliness. She would have liked to linger on the path, in the surprisingly not-bad company of Mrs. Blossom. But she needed a

115

nap so she would be fresh and alert for her first solo evening with Selene Waites.

Chapter 12

'Sorry about earlier today,' Tess said.

'About what?' Selene was standing in the living room of her rental condo, a place with the kind of sweeping harbor view that Tess had always coveted. Come to think of it, she *had* once enjoyed such a view, from the rooftop of her aunt's bookstore, when Tess had lived in the little apartment on the top floor. But with high-rise condos such as this one going up all over what was now billed as Harbor East, some longtime residents were living in shadowy canyons, barely capable of seeing the sun, much less the water.

'My cell phone going off in the middle of your scene.'

'Was that your cell phone?' Selene began pulling off the baggy sweater that she was wearing over tight, odd-looking jeans, along with a pair of freakishly furry boots. It was a fall night, barely in the fifties, and the actress was dressed for a hipster ski lodge. But then, given how thin she was, she was probably cold all the time.

If the outfit was strange, Selene's decision to remove it in the middle of her living room seemed downright bizarre. In seconds, she was down to nothing but a pair of panties and the ridiculous boots, and Tess couldn't begin to imagine how she had gotten the jeans off over the boots. Perhaps the denim had some stretch to it.

'Selene—'

'Hmmmm?' She headed toward the kitchen, separated from the living and dining rooms by a breakfast bar, and briefly disappeared behind the door of a vast refrigerator whose veneer matched the cherrywood cabinets. She emerged with a Red Bull and the largest bottle of vodka that Tess had ever seen in her life. And Tess had seen some pretty large vodka bottles in her day.

'You can't have that,' she said firmly, removing the vodka bottle from Selene's grasp while letting her keep the Red Bull. 'You're underage.'

The girl blinked once, twice, then burst into tears.

'It's in private, not in a bar,' she blubbered. 'Why can't I do what I like in the sanctuary of my home?'

Tess's lips twitched at the slight misstatement—Selene probably meant *sanctity,* although *sanctuary* wasn't necessarily incorrect—but she kept her tone stern.

'You're twenty. If this were wine with dinner, or even a beer, I might be a little more permissive. But coming home at eight o'clock and going straight for a vodka-caffeine cocktail, when you haven't had a bite to eat—that's not a good idea. Also, would you put a top on? I've spent a lot of time in locker rooms, but I'm not really comfortable with sustained nudity in people I hardly know.'

Selene looked down at her shallow, almost concave chest. Her tears had ended as suddenly as they started, and Tess wondered if the tantrum had been a bit of stagecraft, a test to see if she was susceptible to Selene's pouting. The men in

117

Selene's life probably fell apart at the first tiny blubber.

'Do you think I should get a boob job?'

'God, no.'

'Easy for you to say, walking around with what—' Selene curved her hand, as if she were going to feel Tess up, and Tess backed away so she was safely out of reach. 'A C cup?'

'D,' Tess admitted.

'Of course, they would be smaller if you took a little weight off, but still, a *D cup*. Would you trade that in for an A-minus? I'm built like a boy. My collarbone sticks out farther than my breasts.'

She smacked her clavicle, which was, in fact, more pronounced than the glands beneath it.

'If there was an operation to change your height, would you get it?' Tess asked.

'Is there?' Selene's eyes shone with excitement. The body may have verged on plucked chicken, but the face was almost inhuman in its beauty, a Botticelli come to life. Well, it was Botticellian in the coloring—the pink-and-gold glow in the cheeks, the masses of strawberry blond hair. The shape owed far more to the narrow visages of Modigliani, all cheekbones and almond eyes. 'Can you choose where you gain the length? Because I would love to have longer legs.'

'I was trying to make a point,' Tess said. 'We accept our height, and we don't think it signifies anything about our character or discipline. We should accept our body types, too, not fight to be what we're not. I could live off dandelion greens and never be a stick figure. You don't have big breasts. So what?'

'You don't understand,' Selene said. She walked

back to the pile of clothes she had left on the living room floor and fished out a tiny pink T-shirt. Tess couldn't help noticing it was printed with the slogan SPOILED BRAT. 'My body affects my career. I'm not going to get certain parts without tits. I got this stupid shit show because women back then, fashionable ones, wore those Empire gowns, so my body type works for this.'

Tess noticed she pronounced it the French way—*om-peer*.

'If your body is right for this, it will be right for other things.'

'I'll never be a Bond girl.'

'Why would you want to be a Bond girl? You should aspire to be James Bond.'

'Are they doing that?' Selene asked eagerly. 'A female James Bond? Because that would totally rock.'

She threw herself down on the sofa, sloshing some Red Bull but making no move to clean it up. Like almost all the other furnishings here, the sofa was huge and oversize, which gave Tess the sense that she had climbed Jack's beanstalk to arrive at the giant's aerie. But she couldn't help noticing that the apartment, for all its high-end details—the view, the top-notch appliances, the velvety upholstery—could not quite transcend the blandness that marked it as a rental unit, a temporary place for those with money, but no roots. It lacked the touches that quotidian life bestows—a teakettle, framed photographs, objects collected on travels. It was nothing more than an enormous hotel suite, and the size only emphasized its sterility.

'Do you like having a place this large, when

119

you're all alone?'

'I needed space in case my family visits,' Selene said. 'But they're schoolteachers, it's hard for them to get away.'

Tess had learned that much on her first Google pass. Selene was the youngest of five children from a relentlessly normal Utah family. When their youn-gest daughter decided she wanted to be in the movies, the Waites hadn't objected, but they also had refused to uproot the rest of the family. She had gone to live with her mother's sister in Orange County and sought emancipation as a minor at the first opportunity. It was curious to Tess that Selene's parents, who seemed sensible and solid, would essentially give their daughter license to be a wild child, but maybe people got tired by kid number five. 'Selene knows her own mind,' her mother had said in one of the few interviews to which she had ever consented. Asked if she was proud of Selene, she had said: 'I'm proud of all my children.' Selene might as well have been parentless Aphrodite, rising from the sea on a clamshell.

'Let's get dinner,' Tess suggested.

Selene made a face. 'I haven't found a single decent place to eat in this town.'

That stung a little. Tess thought that Baltimore, whatever its limitations, could put on a pretty good feed. 'There's Charleston, right here in the neighborhood.'

'Too much fish.'

'Do you like pizza—'

'I love it, but'—Selene patted her non-existent belly—'I can't risk it. I'll be all bloated tomorrow. It's got to be protein. Sushi is best, although I have to go easy on the soy sauce. Puffy eyes.'

'Well, I could do sushi,' said Tess, a little uncertainly. Hadn't Selene just vetoed fish? Besides, Tess wasn't big on raw things.

'Can I pick the restaurant?' Selene's manner was coy and wheedling, her default mode.

'Sure.'

'And wherever I pick, you'll go?'

'Yes.'

'*Wherever* I want to go?'

'Wherever you want to go,' Tess promised.

Which is how they ended up, not even thirty minutes later, in Selene's driver-equipped car, headed for New York.

*   *   *

They were just about to enter the Holland Tunnel when Selene pulled out her iPhone and, with a quick glance at Tess, began sending what appeared to be the *War and Peace* of text messages. Lloyd could do the same thing with his cell phone, whereas Tess was reduced to playing a virtual Gary Cooper when she texted, laboriously tapping out *yes* and *no*.

'Change of plans,' Selene announced. 'Nobu is mobbed. We're doing Mexican instead of sushi.'

But when the Town Car stopped in front of what appeared to be a very ordinary diner, Tess was dubious.

'This? We had to drive two hundred miles so you could eat here?'

Selene laughed at her. 'You'll see.'

Selene pulled on her hoodie and donned a pair of oversize sunglasses, despite the fact that it was now 11:30 P.M. They went inside, passing through the bright, quiet diner and into a concealed staircase that led to a very different establishment beneath, a truly subterranean lair of cavernlike rooms. The bar was jammed with people waiting for tables, but the bored-looking hostess raised one eyebrow at the sight of Selene and said: 'Of course.' The hostess, a ravishing creature in her own right, did not acknowledge Tess at all; she might have been a piece of toilet paper stuck to Selene's boots which, now that she noticed, weren't actual boots but spiked Mary Janes with knitted tops that reached just to her knees, worn with a skirt that barely covered her silky underwear. At least Selene was wearing underwear.

Come to think of it, Tess decided as she followed Selene's twitching bottom, *a piece of toilet paper might get more attention.* After all, someone might have felt obligated to point out that trailing tissue to Selene, however discreetly, while Tess was invisible to this young, chic crowd. How could they decide so quickly that she was a person of no consequence? There was nothing outrageously wrong with what she wore. In fact, her black trousers and sweater, paired with flat-heeled boots, weren't that different from what many of the diners here wore. Granted, most of the people dressed like her were men, but still, she was carrying the look. No, there must be something indefinably off about her, an unshakable whiff of hoi polloi.

Yet Tess recognized no one—except the young man who was waiting for Selene. But then, Buddhist monks, living in seclusion in the mountains of Tibet, probably knew of Derek Nichole, a pretty boy who had transformed himself into the actor of the moment by taking on a trio of foolproof roles—crippled man, developmentally disabled man, cancer-ridden gangster trying to make one last score so his small daughter would be financially secure. He hadn't been nominated for an Oscar, but the consensus was that it was a matter of when, not if.

'Hey, doll,' he said, not bothering to get up as Selene slid into the semiconcealed booth. No cheek kiss, no hug, just the smallest of waves, the fingers barely lifting from the table. Tess wondered if it was film or fame that taught one to modify gestures that way. 'I didn't know you were bringing your mom.'

'Joke,' Selene assured Tess. 'JOKE. I mean, Derek's met my mom, and she's a blonde like me.'

'I don't know,' Tess said. 'I could be your Baltimore mama. The city used to lead the nation in pregnancies to girls under fourteen.'

'Yes, but I'm twenty, so you would have had to have me when you were six.'

Tess waited a beat for Selene to declare again 'JOKE!' When she didn't, it seemed too late to correct her math skills. Yet Derek, his tone gentle, said: 'The numbers go the other way, baby. You add fourteen to your age to figure out how old— well, it's not important. Margaritas for everybody?'

'I'm working,' Tess said, 'and she's underage.'

Derek looked at Selene. 'I thought you were coming to New York to have fun. You told me you had a late call tomorrow.'

She shrugged prettily. 'I can have fun, within limits. I told you what the perimeters were.'

'Parameters,' Derek said. Again, he managed to correct her without being condescending or unkind.

'Isn't that what I said? I'm going to the loo.'

She didn't ask Tess to let her out from the banquette, just crawled over her as if she were a piece of furniture.

Tess started to stand: 'I should—'

'Don't be silly,' Selene said. 'It's a one-seater. Besides, you can see me from here. I don't need that much guarding, not here. It's *Baltimore* where all the strange shit is happening. Baltimore's the real problem.'

Tess settled for watching Selene thread her way through the crowd, then keeping an eye on the door marked CHICAS.

'She's a good kid,' Derek said.

'*Kid* being the operative word. How old are you?'

'Twenty-seven, so it wouldn't be exactly scandalous if we were dating.' He held her gaze. There were more handsome men in movies, with smoother, regular features, but Derek Nichole commanded one's attention. 'Look, it's not like that with us. We're pals. She wants to do what I did, careerwise, but it's harder for girls. All the media wants to write about is the bad-girl stuff. I ran with a tough crowd, back in Philly, wiseguys, but nobody cared where I went, or who I fucked, as long as I didn't break a bottle over somebody's head. Her, that's all they want to write about.'

'Poor thing,' Tess said, and it didn't come out as sarcastic as she had intended.

'I told her not to sign up for this stupid television show. I said go do theater in the West

124

End, make another independent film, but she began to worry that she didn't know where her next Chloe bag was coming from, and she jumped at the paycheck. Now she's got all this great attention from the film, and she can't leverage it. She's sewed.'

'Sewed?'

'Television shows require a minimum commitment of five years. And it's one way. You commit to them for five years, but they're not obligated to keep you. I made the same mistake, but I got lucky. The show I did ended up six and out. If it had been a success, I would have been stuck.'

'How did you do it?' Tess asked. 'I mean, you weren't much older than Selene when you. . . .'

He smiled at her inability to find a tactful way to finish her thought. 'When I went from a punch line to being touted for an Oscar? Let's just say I was smart enough to know I wasn't quite smart enough, and I found some people who understood what I wanted to do. Mentors. Or, Mentos as Selene calls them, and she's not far wrong. The fresh-maker, right? Well, they made me fresh again, made me someone who had to be considered in a different light. The only thing they couldn't change was my own stupid stage name. I meant to be Derek Nichols, but when I put my paperwork in, they misread my handwriting.'

Tess helped herself to the chips on the table, dragging one through a wonderfully subtle *salsa verde*. She was aware that people were glancing covertly toward their booth. *Who was that woman with Derek Nichole?* She also was aware that she was on the verge of enjoying herself, that Derek had shown more depth and subtlety in five minutes than Selene had over the course of an entire journey up the New Jersey Turnpike, where she had quizzed Tess on the origins of every rest stop name. Tess could forgive a twenty-year-old for not knowing who Joyce Kilmer was, but her ignorance of Walt Whitman and Woodrow Wilson had been a little staggering. Selene had asked if Whitman had invented the Whitman Sampler.

'What are you going to do next?'

'You know that best seller, the one about the two gay chaplains during World War I, one American, one British?'

Tess had managed to miss this novel.

'I'm producing that for my company, and I'm going to play the younger chaplain.' Her expression must have betrayed her, because he laughed. 'Don't worry, that's the American. I know I can't do accents.'

'And is there a part for Selene in it?'

'Afraid not. In fact, there are almost no women in it. You see, my character ends up shell-shocked—'

But here was Selene, back from the bathroom, holding a margarita the size of her head.

'Someone gave it to me,' she squealed in protest as Tess unwound her fingers from the stem. Tess took a sip—definitely tequila. Really good tequila.

'Don't waste it,' Derek said. 'That would be a crime.'

'You drink it, then,' Tess said, but he gestured toward the bottle of Negra Modelo in front of him.

'Okay,' she said. 'Just one, and only because I'm opposed to waste. I'm working after all.'

WEDNESDAY

Chapter 13

Tess awoke to a perfect sunrise, a piercing red-orange light that she normally would have admired. Today, it felt like dozens of needles stabbing her eyelids.

'Where am I?' she rasped, putting a hand to her head. Once she touched it, she realized it was throbbing. Strange, for Tess seldom had headaches and *never* had hangovers. And she felt as if she were moving. Could she have bed spins? No, she *was* moving, lying in the backseat of a car traveling swiftly.

'Delaware, for a few more minutes,' the driver replied. Selene's driver, in Selene's car, but—

'Where's . . . where's Selene?'

'Back in New York. Once you got ill, her only thought was to make sure you were taken care of.'

'I got . . . ill?'

'That's what she told me. She called and asked that I come get you, said you had reacted very strongly to something in your food or drink, that you seemed to be going into some kind of shock.'

'Not shock,' Tess said. 'And not food poisoning.' Her head felt as if it had been filled with wet cotton balls, but she could still find the thread of what happened. The drink that had materialized, Derek's insistence that she not waste it, a few sips, a few chips and salsa—and no memory beyond that. Fuck them. They hadn't even let her enjoy the *chorizo con queso* appetizer that she had ordered before the drink kicked in.

'They drugged me,' she said flatly. 'They
129

drugged me, and you obligingly whisked me away. How can you do that? You know I'm supposed to be with her at all times.'

'I work for Miss Selene,' the driver said. What had Selene called him? Moby? That seemed an unlikely name for a thin black man. 'I may have been hired by the production, but I quickly learned that it's better to do what *she* tells me to do. For one thing, she pays me extra. Besides, Mr. Nichole is a nice young man. A good influence.'

Tess had thought so, too. But now she was thinking that Derek Nichole was an even better actor than he was reputed to be. He had seemed so kind, so genuine. A genuine jerk.

'Where did Selene tell you to take me?'

'Initially, we took you to Mr. Nichole's suite at the SoHo Grand to assess your condition. When it became apparent that you didn't need a doctor, I started back to Baltimore at Miss Selene's insistence. And she said to tell you that she promises to make her call today. "Cross my heart and hope to die," if she doesn't. Those were her very words.' He sounded a little sheepish, repeating his employer's assurances.

'How's she going to get there if you're with me?'

'She'll hire another car, or even take the train. The Acela's only a little more than two hours, and her call's not until two P.M. She has plenty of time. Now where would you like to go?'

'Take me to the production offices. I might as well resign before they fire me. On the job for all of a day and I fuck it up.'

'You underestimated Miss Waites's ability to get what she wants,' the driver said. 'Don't feel bad—everybody does. You sure you wouldn't like to go home first? Take a shower? Maybe throw down a little mouthwash?'

Tess registered the metallic lime aftertaste in her mouth. 'That's not the worst idea I've ever heard.'

The driver laughed, a rumbling rolling bass that managed to charm Tess despite her foul mood and pounding head. 'And what would *that* be, exactly?' he asked. 'What is the worst idea you've ever heard?'

'Hard to say, but taking this job is in the top five.'

*　　　*　　　*

Once home, she released the driver, showered, then drove herself to the production office, feeling marginally better. It was embarrassing being undone by a roofie, the date rapist's drug of choice, but Tess was far more humiliated by being outwitted by two actors. They may, per Alfred Hitchcock's edict, be treated like cattle, but they had trumped her, so what did that make her in this barnyard analogy? A hen they had stomped on? A fly that they had swatted with their perfect little tails while never missing a beat in their cud chewing?

The production office parking lot was filled with patrol cars, and for one paranoid moment, Tess thought that someone had called the police to report Selene missing. *Shit, what if something had happened to her while I was out?* But then she registered the evidence unit and the yellow tape, and her self-centric fear was replaced by something more substantial.

131

She found Lottie in a cluster of people standing just outside the front door. Lloyd was in the group of production employees, and part of Tess's mind registered that fact, pleased he had shown up on time for his second day of work with no adult oversight whatsoever. She hoped he wouldn't be denied a third day on the job because of her ineptitude.

'What—' She stopped at the sight of Lottie's face, about as gray as any face Tess had ever seen.

'Greer. She was working late and—they don't know. They just don't know. A break-in—but I don't see how. Or why. There's nothing of real value here, nothing worth—and, Greer, who would—'

Lottie bit her lip fiercely, as if she'd rather inflict pain on herself than cry in front of employees.

Homicide detective Martin Tull, Tess's one true friend at the Baltimore Police Department, came out of the building just then, snapping off his rubber gloves.

'Hey, Tess,' he said, not the least surprised to see her there. Life in Baltimore was full of such coincidences. 'You working on this show?'

'I was,' she said. 'I'm not sure where I stand just now. What happened?'

He glanced at Lottie and the other *Mann of Steel* types, then motioned Tess to walk with him toward his car, out of earshot. 'She was beaten to death. The office is trashed, but all the major stuff, the computers and television, were left behind. That woman, Lottie, is going to look around once the evidence techs get through, see if anything was taken. But there's enough small valuable shit—

iPods, laptops—that it's hard to see it as a burglary.'

'When?'

'Last night, after ten. They say she worked late a lot, so it's either someone who knew that—or someone who didn't expect to find her here late.'

'Weapon?'

'We haven't found it yet. If the guy's smart, he tossed it in the harbor as he left.'

'They're not always smart, of course.'

'No, and this looks impromptu as hell. The little lady'—he jerked his head back toward Lottie— 'says there was a fiancé, though, and that there's been some trouble there, a bad breakup, maybe.'

'You have any information on him?'

'John "JJ" Meyerhoff—not one of *those* Meyerhoffs,' Tull added at Tess's sharp intake of breath. It was a surname that one found on big buildings all over Baltimore, most notably the symphony hall. 'I have a feeling I'm going to be making that point all day. This is a rough-and-tumble family out in the county. We've already sent a car there, but Mama Meyerhoff says her son took off for a fishing trip about two A.M.—she doesn't have any idea where he goes to fish, of course.'

Of course, Tess thought. An ex-fiancé. That made more sense than anything running through her head. It looked personal, it looked like an act of passion, and only a foolish detective would disdain such an obvious answer. So there was every reason to believe that this was a huge coincidence, someone at the production getting killed while Tess was in New York, sleeping off a roofie-induced coma. She wasn't on the hook for this.

133

Then why did she feel so guilty?

Someone grabbed her elbow. It was Flip, flipping out, and now her guilt was earned.

'Jesus, Tess. I just got off the phone with Selene's driver and he told me what happened, how you were in New York—'

She stopped him, unwilling to hear her incompetence rehashed. 'I'm sorry. It was a complete screwup on my part, and I know I have to resign and refund your retainer. There's no excuse for what I did. But if you could, consider keeping Lloyd on, okay? Don't hold him accountable for my mistake.'

'Resign? Because that little bitch drugged you and dumped you? This just convinces me more than ever that she's behind all the shit that's been happening.'

Chapter 14

Ben had taken to writing in a local Starbucks, much as he loathed the cliché of the whole enterprise, the screenwriter at Starbucks. But the room at the Tremont got old fast, and when he tried to write in his office in Locust Point, there were always interruptions. Flip could sequester himself in his office and no one would get past his little pit bull, Greer, but Ben's closed door didn't persuade anyone that he was working. Lottie, especially. Granted, Lottie had caught him napping once. It was after his first night with Selene, and he was exhausted because seducing her had required an actual courtship, the big

134

buildup of dinner and talking, not just the usual hump-and-dump, but he couldn't exactly explain to Lottie that he was worn out by the demands of getting a twenty-year-old girl in bed. *A twenty-year-old girl who knows far more than I do, not like I was her first,* he told himself now.

Even so, when he had come to work the day after he was discovered napping, the little sofa in his office was gone. Lottie had given him a supercilious smile, daring him to object. He hadn't said a damn word, just gone online and ordered another sofa from Pottery Barn, a much more expensive one that actually had a foldout bed, then put the bill on his expense account, with the scrawled notation: *writing supplies*.

The irony, of course—one of the ironies; there were ironies upon ironies in his relationship with Flip—was that Ben was the real writer of the two, the one who took the *final*-final pass on all the scripts. Everyone thought that Flip was carrying him, but Flip would be lost without Ben. Oh, Flip pretended to go over Ben's scripts, but it was acknowledged between them that this charade was for everyone else, because Lottie, the directors, and the various department heads were less likely to argue with Flip, whereas they would happily bust Ben's balls over any detail. When they had the tone meeting for one of the early eps, Lottie had tried a little divide-and-conquer. 'I'm not so sure about this beat,' she had said. 'It's a little glib, don't you think? The kind of conventional sitcom scene that you're trying to avoid.' The director, the has-been of the week, had nodded, although it wasn't clear that the guy could read, much less form an opinion about the words in front of him.

Flip said: 'Well, it was my idea, but if you think it could change. . . .' 'No, no, no.' Lottie had backtracked so fast that she almost ended up leaving the room. 'I guess I just didn't get it. Now that I see—sure, of course. And the next scene is even better, really pulls it all together, pays off the conceit.' 'Ben thought of that,' Flip said cheerfully. Yes, after that meeting, no one had tried to worm between them again. And when they were alone, Flip was generous in his praise for Ben. Plus, Ben finally had an executive producer's title and a 'story by' credit on every episode. What more could he want?

To do it by myself.

He glanced around the Starbucks, wondering if he had spoken this traitorous thought aloud. It had actually been hard finding a Starbucks in Baltimore. There was only one within walking distance of his hotel—well, two, if one took a more generous view of what was walking distance, but he was a California boy through and through—and almost nothing was near the production offices, stuck as they were on that godforsaken peninsula. Out there, they had to drink the coffee from a local purveyor, which tasted funny to Ben, although everyone swore it was better. Locally roasted, blah, blah, blah. As if local was necessarily a good thing here in Charm City, where the people, even the people in Starbucks, all looked weird to Ben. Pale, pasty. All right, downright doughy. Not to mention the teeth—God, the teeth. Living in California, where almost everyone had veneers and whiteners, one forgot what real teeth looked like. These relatively normal mouths were as shocking as a Shane McGowan convention.

136

Worst of all, Baltimoreans also had this—how to describe it—bovine happiness. No one seemed rushed or impatient here, a fact that drove Ben mildly insane when he was trying to order his morning mocha and get to work. The people around him were too dumb to know how miserable they should be.

Whereas, I'm smart enough to know exactly how unhappy I am.

His Treo, set to silent, vibrated on the table, and he glanced at the caller ID. Lottie. *No way, no how.* Flip was to have told her that Ben was off the reservation, trying to figure out how to beef up the Betsy part in episode 107, per the network's notes. He may have stayed up until three, waiting for Selene to visit as she had promised, but he had been awake by nine and out the door by ten, at his table in Starbucks by ten-fifteen, a very good boy, and he had actually . . . gotten nothing done. But he was trying. He had parked his ass in the chair and he had his computer open and he wasn't checking e-mail or voice mail or surfing the Internet. The phone chirped angrily, indicating he had a message, then began vibrating again. Lottie. And again. Lottie. About the fourth time, he decided to pick up, choosing to take the offensive before she could start haranguing him.

'I'm writing, Lottie. Don't you remember? Flip's orders. I'm trying to figure out how to add some scenes without losing some key beats, or else the final episode is going to be overstuffed with exposition. For every beat that goes in, one has to come out and—'

'Greer's dead,' she said. 'Killed at our offices, so we're canceling the shoot today and I'm reworking

137

the schedule accordingly. We'll probably have to shoot Saturday to make up for it. I assumed you'd want to know.'

He thought, but couldn't be sure, that he stammered out the appropriate questions—*what, how, when*? Lottie replied as if he had.

'She was beaten to death, last night or early this morning. The police want to interview anyone who had access to the office after hours, by the way, so they have your name.'

'I was in my room all night.'

'Jesus, Ben, no one's suggesting you're a suspect. Calm down. I just wanted to give you a heads-up that I gave this number to a Baltimore city homicide detective, Tull. If you see a three-nine-six prefix on your phone, take the call, okay?'

The last was laced with meaning, Lottie reminding Ben that she knew he didn't take most of his calls.

'Sure, of course, whatever they need. Do they . . . know anything?'

'Not really. I know they're going to be looking at her fiancé.'

'She was having problems with him.' *Shit, why had he said that? Why would Ben know the state of Greer's love life?* What did it matter what Lottie thought? What mattered was what the police knew, or might find out.

'Really? I mean, I knew they were on and off, but she still had the ring.' There was a silence, as if Lottie might be mulling her words, wondering if things might be different if Greer had felt free to confide her problems to someone. 'Well, that's the kind of thing the police will want to know, I guess.'

'It's so . . . awful.'

'You have no idea. I've been working in this business all my life, Ben, and I've probably seen every variety of murder there is in film.They all looked real to me, or real enough. But nothing I ever saw compares to . . .'

Her voice broke, and Ben was almost persuaded for a moment that Lottie was human, capable of normal emotion. But she quickly undercut that impression when she added: 'So it's a day off for crew but not for us. You, Flip, and I are having a working dinner tonight, and you should have the new beat sheet, so Flip can go over it.'

'So Flip can flip it, work his flippin' magic?'

'Right.' She hung up without wasting time on pleasantries she didn't mean. Lottie may have seen a dead body this morning, but the show must go on.

He stared at the computer screen in front of him, the few words that he had managed to peck out a jumble to him. Greer dead. Why? *Let it be the fiancé*, he found himself praying. Or a burglar, who didn't expect to find someone in the office that late. Let it be something that leads them away from the set and the production. Not that it mattered. He had an alibi.

Alone in his room.

Waiting for Selene.

Who had told him to wait for her there, who had promised that she would slip away from her babysitter, somehow, some way.

He got back in line for another mocha, this one with two extra shots. It took so long for the guy in front of him to order that Ben almost began to shake.

'You must *really* like coffee,' the barista

observed. She was young and well cushioned—fat by California's standards, but normal for Baltimore, and the extra weight gave her face a sweet roundness, true apple cheeks. She reminded him of someone.

She reminded him of Greer, the way she had been when she first started working in the office, so sweet and helpful, happy to do anything she was asked.

Chapter 15

'You can't possibly believe that Selene has anything to do with Greer's death,' Tess said.

'I agree,' Flip said in a loud clear voice, casting a nervous look at the waiter. 'That plot point wouldn't work at all in *Mann of Steel*. But I thought it might solve some things in the final episode, which is why I threw it out there. Could you bring us a bottle of the white Burgundy?'

'We have several. Did you want—'

'Just any decent white Burgundy. I leave it to you.'

The waiter gone, Flip dropped the plummy tone. 'Let's try to be a little discreet, okay?'

'It's Baltimore, Flip. It's not like the waiters have the *National Enquirer* on speed-dial. Read it, yes; tip it off, no. Waiters here are just . . . waiters. Not aspiring actors.'

Flip, unconvinced, studied their surroundings. The Wine Market on Fort Avenue was Baltimore hip, a mere five or six years behind the decorating curve—brick walls, exposed pipes threading the high ceilings, maple furniture. Tess forgave its derivative look because the food was good and the wine a bargain, sold at only 10 percent above retail.

'I was surprised that the police let me leave the scene without giving a statement,' he said. 'Your doing?'

'Luck of the draw,' Tess said. 'If anyone other than Tull had been the primary, we'd all be down on Fayette Street right now. Tull trusts me to bring you in later for a more detailed debriefing. Relatively sober,' she added, after watching Flip chug the Burgundy that the waiter had left in an ice bucket.

'Don't worry, this is just going to restore my equilibrium. Did you—'

'See her? No, fortunately. It sounds as if it was particularly . . . unsettling.'

'I've never seen Lottie that upset about *anything*,' Flip said. 'I didn't know she could get upset. The joke on *Mann of Steel* is that she's the Woman of Steel, an absolute ice queen. We're all a little terrified of her.'

Lottie was not the woman who interested Tess just now. She broke off a piece of bread and swished it through the little dish of olive oil and peppers. 'And Selene? What kind of emotions does she engender?'

Flip let loose a sigh so long that it was almost a whistle. 'Satanic spawn. A total nightmare. God, I wish the network would let us write her out of the show after the first season, have Mann continue on without Betsy Patterson.'

'And lose the whole blue-blood-meets-blue-collar thing? I thought that was the concept that

141

made this whole thing *go*.'

She didn't quite achieve the sincere tone she was trying for.

'Are you this obnoxious to all the people who hire you, or do you sometimes manage to fake enthusiasm for their enterprises?'

'It's the nature of my business to work for people with different tastes, values. Essential, even. I wouldn't work at all if I had to be gung ho about all my clients' professional lives.'

'Still, do you have to be such an asshole?'

A fair question, under the circumstances.

'I don't mean to be a jerk. The broad outlines of this show you're doing—I'll admit, I just don't get it. It's history, it's time travel, it's comedy, all set in the context of the never-never land of a thriving steel company in the twenty-first century.'

'Girl's house gets swept up by tornado and she's transported to a magical land where she expends all her power trying to get home again.'

'Okay, yeah, but *The Wizard of Oz* is a fantasy.'

'Billionaire media mogul whispers a mysterious name on his deathbed, launching a journalist's attempt to understand the private man behind the public figure. Yet the truth about Rosebud doesn't really solve any of those mysteries.'

'Although it was rumored to be William Randolph Hearst's pet name for Marion Davies's nether regions,' said Tess, grateful to have one of Crow's bits of trivia so readily at hand. 'Okay, when you reduce anything to a thumbnail description, it sounds a little silly, but—'

'Woman will do anything for the love of her ungrateful daughter—including confessing to the murder that the daughter committed.'

'*Mildred Pierce* and there's no murder in the book, which is a thousand times better.'

'Man builds a baseball diamond in a cornfield behind his house and Shoeless Joe Jackson appears—'

But now Flip had gone too far. A bridge too far, a baseball diamond too far.

'I HATE THAT MOVIE!' Tess said, and the bare brick walls sent her voice bouncing into every corner of the restaurant. She regained her composure. 'Sorry, but do not get me started on that cornball mush.'

'How can you hate *Field of Dreams*?'

'It's a male weepie, as I think Pauline Kael or some other critic said. And, you know, I'm okay with the male weepie. We all deserve our weepies. My issue is that what makes men cry is elevated to profundity, while what makes women cry is denigrated as sentimental. When you take my corn seriously, I'll grant yours equal respect.'

'What makes you cry? *Beaches*?'

'*Major League,* which is a better baseball movie than *Field of Dreams,* by the way.'

Even as Tess's mouth provided that glib reply, her brain was thinking about what really did make her cry. There was a certain expression on her greyhound's face, a wisp of a seeming smile. The Bromo-Seltzer Tower, glowing blue in the night. Old television footage of Brooks Robinson being inducted into the Hall of Fame. And there was the matter of a young woman, beaten to death just last night, but Tess wasn't hypocrite enough to admit that she felt anything but shock and dismay over that. The only thing that resonated was the violence of the death. A fatal beating took time—

and not a little passion.

Besides, Flip was talking about cinematic tears. Okay. Then—little Dominic dying in Noodles's arms in *Once Upon a Time in America,* but also Noodles coming back through the bus station door, thirty years of time summed up in a single shot. *The Wild Bunch.* The memory of a carrot-haired man who had loved *The Wild Bunch,* living—and dying—by the codes distilled from his beloved westerns. Had it really been just a little over a year ago? She reached for her knee. Maybe one day the scar wouldn't be there. Maybe one day, it would all be a dream. Just like in the movies.

'*Strictly Ballroom,*' Tess admitted. 'When the music goes out, and the father starts to clap, and they show they can do the *paso doble* without any music at all. . . .'

Her eyes started to mist, making her seem truthful, but she was still thinking of that carrot-haired man, dying on the cold cement of a parking lot, leaving her to fight for her own life—and avenge his.

'You haven't shot down my central point. *Anything* sounds ludicrous when boiled down to the pitch. But it's all in the execution. Why do you think Hollywood produces so much crap?'

'Because there's seldom any economic penalty?'

'No. Well, yes. I mean, *no.* People's careers do suffer from doing critically disdained work—'

'If it's also commercially inert.'

'The point,' Flip said irritably, as if unused to being interrupted, and he probably was. 'The *point* is that the writing, the performances, the visuals—those will combine to make this show something

144

really special. That's why we're starting small, on a C-list cable network with only eight episodes. People forget, but there was a time when getting a series on HBO was considered second-rate. *The Sopranos* was pitched to the networks first, and they all passed. By the way, has anyone ever proposed adapting your life story?'

Food arrived—a house salad for Flip, a much heartier steak salad for Tess—and she was spared answering right away. 'Last year—I was involved in a case of some notoriety, and some producers circled for a while.'

'You make them sound like vultures.'

Tess forked up a mouthful of steak and greens that required much judicious chewing.

'They were just doing their job,' he persisted. 'Look, you go to the movies. You read newspapers and magazines, right? Well, the material has to come from somewhere.'

'A friend of mine was killed in front of me. I killed a man. I never thought of it as *material*. A woman you know was killed in your office last night. Are you going to make a miniseries about that?'

Flip blushed, and she warmed to him. She knew he was pure Hollywood, bred and buttered, as the old Baltimore saying went. Flip's father was the one who had the claim to Charm City normalcy, a claim he had pretty much squandered years ago. But Flip did seem relatively down-to-earth.

'How—'

'Shot him.' *Over and over again, until the clip was empty. Shot him, but only after gaining advantage by almost gouging his eye out with scissors.* She withheld these details as a courtesy.

'That must have been awful.'

'It was. That's why I feel for Lottie, walking in on Greer.'

'I can't imagine—this is going to sound heartless—'

'Go ahead.'

'I can't imagine Greer engendering that kind of *passion* in anyone. She was a little machine. We used to joke about it, Ben and I, call her Small Wonder, after that sitcom.' He glanced at Tess to see if the cultural reference connected for her. 'The one about the robot? Voice Input Child Identicant, Vicki for short?' Tess couldn't even fake knowing what he was talking about now. 'Well, anyway, she was just extremely competent, her feathers never ruffled.'

'Still, they like the fiancé for it. Ex-fiancé, maybe. There seems to be some confusion about whether they were on or off.'

'Never met him. Frankly, I wasn't sure I would have believed he even existed if it weren't for the ring on her hand. Certainly, she wasn't spending any time with him, once we got into production.'

'How did you find Greer, anyway?'

'She found us, poor thing. Called my father's production company. My dad has a policy. If you have an area code beginning with four-one-zero, you get treated with respect and deference by his office. Maybe that was my problem. I had the wrong area code, so my dad never had time for me.'

Oh, poor little rich boy. 'So how does that connect you to Greer?'

'Her dad was a teamster, worked on one of my father's early films. She called my dad's assistant,

146

and I told Lottie to interview her with an open mind. She started off as an unpaid intern in the writers' office, basically an assistant to my assistant. Then my assistant left, and Ben came to me, said I should give the job to Greer, that she was actually fantastically competent. And, for once, Ben was right.'

'For once?'

'He's not the best judge of other people. Especially women. Although Greer isn't exactly Ben's, um, type.'

'You mean—he sleeps with women, then tries to find them jobs?'

'Sometimes. It's not as crass as you make it sound. Ben really is a fool for love. He falls for a girl—or thinks he does—courts her, builds her up big-time, then sleeps with her, and bam, all interest gone. It's like sex is the third act for him, and the only thing he knows to do afterward is to go to the credits. Over the years, he's doled out a few jobs to soothe their hurt feelings. Actors, usually.'

'Guys?' She hadn't figured Ben for being that inclusive in his sexual appetites.

Flip looked at her as if she were insane. 'Women. Oh—we call them actors, Tess, not actresses. *Actress* is considered derogatory.'

Whereas actor *is shot through with dignity.* 'Are you sure that Ben didn't sleep with Greer?'

'Let's just say I'd be shocked. So not his type. Why, you think the fiancé killed her in a jealous rage?'

Tess shook her head. 'I won't second-guess Tull, or get in his way. He's good police.'

'People really say that?'

'Say what?'

'"Good police." I've heard it on television, but I thought it was pure affectation.'

'It's what cops in Baltimore call themselves. Police, a police, a murder police. Where do you think the television shows got it?'

'Thought they made it up, like Ben and I do. You can be overreliant on reality, you know.'

Tess was unsure if Flip was explaining his rules for writing or his worldview.

'Let's leave the homicide investigation to Tull. I'm far more curious why you were so quick to blame Selene for what happened to me last night. You sold me on the idea that she was this poor little fragile actress—*actor*—at risk from her own bad behavior and, possibly, unwanted fan attention.'

Flip glanced around the restaurant, almost empty this late in the lunchtime hours. 'Okay, I wasn't entirely forthcoming when I hired you. But wouldn't it have been irresponsible of me to tell you that I suspected Selene of the various problems on set? I didn't want to prejudice you against her. In fact, I was hoping the two of you might bond, and she would end up confiding in you.'

'We were getting along famously until she drugged my drink. So why do you think Selene is the source of your problems?'

'Selene is signed to a five-year contract. That's standard. When she signed it, she probably thought the show had no shot of going five years, but then, when she signed it, she was thrilled to have any steady gig. Plus, she didn't know we planned to leave her in the nineteenth century.'

So Derek had been right: The producers demand commitment, but it's not mutual.

'Then *Baby Jane* was finally released, and Selene's success heightened the profile of our show. The network demanded we keep the Betsy character if we wanted any chance of getting a pickup for second season. They also ordered a lot of rewrites to beef up her part. I wouldn't be surprised if they don't change the name before it's over, which will freak Johnny Tampa out—and he's already plenty freaked. This was supposed to be his comeback. Instead, it's Selene's buildup.'

'So, you think Selene might be the source of the fires, the leaks to the newspaper, the community malcontents, even the Nair in Johnny Tampa's cold cream?'

'Maybe.'

'When you first hired me, you said all these things happened subsequent to the suicide of a man who might be Selene's stalker.'

Flip at least had the good manners to look embarrassed about lying. 'There were photos of Selene in his home, three or four. I was truthful about that. They appeared to be shot early on, when we were on location for the pilot last spring. There was some other stuff, too, the cops told us. Homemade movies of kids. Not porn, but kind of creepy. Selene looks fourteen, so maybe she was his type. The weird part was—he had a photocopy of the pilot script, the minipub.'

'The what?'

'The minipub is the first version of the script, which means it has the most limited distribution. In our office, each copy has a name and number. This was a photocopy, with the number blocked

149

out, so it couldn't be traced back to the source. The dead man also had the show bible, which outlines the first season. Lottie thought my previous assistant, Alicia, did it, and insisted she be fired. Alicia said she was innocent but agreed to be fired for the unemployment insurance, which makes me think she wasn't so innocent. After all, innocent people have nothing to fear.'

Tess didn't bother to contradict Flip on that score, although she knew from personal experience that innocent people are often the most vulnerable in a criminal investigation.

'And this is—?'

'Midsummer, right after we returned to shoot. Things escalated *after* that. And that's when I began to think Selene was involved.'

'Why would Selene give some stranger the script?'

'With a script, and the bible, he could get some sense of what we were doing, and wreak havoc. Of course, he'd need our shooting schedule to figure out where we were filming on any given day, but he could have figured that out via our permits, for example. Or, again, through Selene. The call sheet is faxed to her apartment every night, even if she's not needed on set the next day.'

'Do you think Selene was cultivating the dead man, using him to be her troublemaker, then moved on to someone else after the suicide?'

Flip looked at his wineglass with sudden distaste. He seized his water glass and gulped down its contents as if doing a keg-stand. 'Maybe he was just one of the people Selene was working with,' he said. 'I don't know. I was counting on you to keep tabs on Selene, making it harder for her to cause mischief. Look, I'm not saying she would have Greer killed. But she's stupid enough to hire someone stupid enough to screw up that way. Say she asked someone to break into the office last night, knowing she's going to have this elaborate alibi. Maybe the guy didn't expect to find Greer.'

'When the police came to talk to you about the suicide—did you tell them that you thought the script had been provided by someone in your office?'

'No. I suggested it could have been found in a Dumpster, which was a lie—we have a strict shredding policy in the office. But we had already started having problems with that crazy community activist, and I didn't want any more bad press.'

'Is that all? Is there anything else you haven't told me? Because, at this point, the lying has to stop. If I had known why you needed me in the first place, I would have been much more vigilant around Selene, approached the job differently.'

Flip took his time answering. 'I *think* so. Look, I never meant to deceive you. I needed someone to watch Selene. It didn't seem vital to me that you have all the background. As long as you were with her, I'd know what she was up to.'

'Only she dumped me, first chance she got, and went out on the town with Derek Nichole, someone who seems very sympathetic to Selene's desire to get out of her contract and establish herself as a legitimate movie star.'

'You're not suggesting—'

'No, just observing. How will Greer's death affect *Mann of Steel,* day to day?'

'We lost today,' Flip said. 'And the network types are blaming Baltimore, saying this would

151

never have happened if we filmed in L.A. Or Vancouver. Charm City's homicide rate is suddenly right at their fingertips, and it's being suggested that I pushed to film here because of some Oedipal issue, akin to George W. going after Saddam to placate Daddy.'

'Locust Point isn't exactly murder central. I won't speak to your Oedipal issues.'

'Thanks,' Flip said. 'That puts you in the minority, unfortunately. Everyone else feels very free to speculate on my "issues"—Ben, Lottie, columnists for *Variety*. Anyway, I talked the network down. For now. We've agreed we'll put up a reward for information leading to Greer's killer and we'll have a memorial service Sunday. By the way, when that rolls around, make sure Selene wears something appropriate.'

Tess hadn't expected this. 'I'm *still* on that detail? After what happened?'

'I've got no issue with your job performance, I just wish you could dial the sarcasm down a notch. The way I see it, I set you up by not telling you what a devious little bitch she is. I should have been straight with you, not try to play you. Besides, someone on the production was killed. Now we have even more reason to guard our precious little Selene, right?'

Tess grinned. She liked Flip's conniving streak when it wasn't directed toward her.

'I hate her, I wish I didn't have to work with her, but she may be my only hope for getting a pickup. From now on, don't eat or drink anything that she's had access to. In fact, if she offers you an aspirin from a sealed bottle, be skeptical. She's evil.'

'She's *twenty*. And not exactly a criminal mastermind.'

'She's precocious, and she's got great instincts. Probably what makes her such a good actress.'

'Actor, I thought. We're supposed to call them actors.'

'You're a quick study, Monaghan.' He raised his water glass in salute, and Tess was almost flattered—until she realized that was his intention. He was still playing her. Then again, she wasn't being completely honest when she told him she wasn't interested in Greer's death. Oh, she wouldn't interfere in the homicide investigation. But, as she interpreted her role, she now had free rein to figure out what was happening on set—and whether it was a coincidence that Selene was in New York the night that Greer was killed. She would need backup, of course. But at the prices she was charging Hollywood, she could more than afford it.

Chapter 16

That got out of hand fast.

What was that from? Something, something recent, seen on the cable with Marie, the two of them drowsing on the sofa together, too tired to stay awake, yet not wanting to retreat to the bedroom. It was like that game he and Bob had once played, dropping a line of dialogue into conversation—something deceptively ordinary, no smell-of-napalm-in-the-morning, no offers-you-can't-refuse, nothing instantly recognizable.

153

Anyone would know those lines. *That got out of hand fast. Did anything about that strike you as unusual? This shit just got serious.*

He thought he was doing pretty well, all things considered, until he reached for his coffee and the cup slipped from his hand and into the saucer—not enough of a fall to break the heavy cup, but coffee sloshed everywhere, irritating the waitress who had to mop up the spill.

'I shouldn't be drinking caffeine so late in the day,' he said, hoping to make a joke of it.

'You're having decaf,' she pointed out.

'So I am. May I have a refill?'

She stood over him, holding the orange handle that signified the decaf pot, looking as if she wasn't sure she was going to grant his wish, as if he had no standing to ask for anything, even something as small as a refill, and he was reminded of the very person, the very thing, he did not want to remember.

'Please,' he said at last. It was several minutes before he trusted himself to raise the cup to his lips.

She had been so young. It had been easy to lose sight of the fact when she was a disembodied voice—on an answering machine, picking up the phone in the production office. She was young, not that much older than the teenagers he used to teach. He should have been able to bully her, use his age and gravitas to his advantage. And for all her bluster, she was scared of him, at first. Then something had switched, and she had the upper hand. How had he betrayed his uncertainty, his desperation?

You have to pay attention to me, he had said. *You*

154

have to acknowledge me. A small word, a small thing. But she had shaken her head. 'You're wrong, it never happened. I'll swear you're lying. Besides, it doesn't work that way.' Kept repeating these things, in fact, over and over again. *It doesn't work that way.* In that moment, she reminded him of every customer service representative with whom he had ever quarreled, every bureaucrat on North Avenue, every medical professional and insurance company employee who had refused to authorize certain treatments for Marie. *It doesn't work that way.* As if they were talking about immutable laws of nature, instead of man-made rules and systems. Didn't this girl see that her very existence was proof that things *did* work that way? If there was room for her—young, barely out of school, with no discernible talent for anything— then there must be room for anyone. He said as much. She continued to shake her head, increasingly sure of herself, smug. The power had shifted. *It doesn't work that way.*

And she had pushed him. Don't forget that. She had pushed him, tried to rush past him, and he had grabbed her arm.

Later, standing at the water's edge, he regarded the bloody bat in his hand. It was no ordinary bat, but one inscribed to FLIP JR., A 'FLIP' OFF THE OLD BLOCK—BARRY. Oh dear, it must be from *The Natural,* a gift from Levinson to a little boy, probably no more than ten at the time. Had Redford held this bat? Or, at the very least, Joe Don Baker?

He had stood at the water's edge longer than he should, summoning the will to toss the storied bat, something he would have loved to own, once upon

155

a time, even twenty-four hours ago. He had to tell himself that no one of note had touched it, that it was probably just a leftover prop, something that otherwise would have been thrown away. Why, he wouldn't be surprised if the bat had never been in the movie at all. They had probably purchased them in bulk and given them away, telling the same lie over and over.

Still, he clutched it, realizing that his cynicism about the business had come too late to save him. Too late to turn back now. Was that a line of dialogue? It should be.

He threw the bat as far as he could, surrendering his piece of Hollywood history, with absolutely no regret.

PART TWO

BALTIMORE BABYLON

Would someone please tell Selene Waites that girls-gone-wild is so five minutes ago? The very wobbly demi-star was glimpsed leaving the SoHo Grand in what she obviously considered the middle of the night—that's 11 A.M. to you poor slobs with normal jobs. Clutching a Starbucks cup that was almost larger than she was, she jumped the cab line without an apology—or a tip for the doorman who hailed it for her, unless you consider a glimpse of lime green La Perla undies a tip. Hotel types insist that she wasn't registered, and we believe them. But we also know that Derek Nichole, who has taken a very proprietary interest in the rising star—all professional, of course—is staying at the SoHo Grand and was seen with Selene just last night in the hotel's bar. Of course, the semilegal blonde was drinking Shirley Temples. (Ginger ale, cherry grenadine, and a shot of vodka chased by Red Bull—that is the traditional recipe for a Shirley Temple, right?)
—*From an Internet gossip column*

'Gawker Stalker'
Selene Waites, lurching around Penn Station, trying to find the first-class waiting room. Very pretty in person, but scary thin, and her clothes looked as if she had slept in them, assuming she had slept at all. Shot video of her on my cell and posted it to YouTube.

THURSDAY

Chapter 17

Although twenty-four hours had passed since the Internet had provided helpful video of Selene wandering dazedly through Penn Station, Tess expected to find a young woman still suffering the effects of her long night's journey into day. Yet the actress—*actor*—made her 11 A.M. call time without any sign of wear or tear. Her skin was glowing, her eyes fresh and bright. Oh, to be twenty again.

'I'm so sorry you got sick up in New York,' Selene said, sitting in the makeup chair. It took more than an hour to arrange her hair in the elaborate style that had been copied from one of the portraits of Betsy Patterson, a so-called triple portrait by Gilbert Stuart, which was pinned to the mirror, a reference point for the stylist. 'But that's the risk with Mexican food—what do they call it, Petaluma's revenge? I wanted to take you to a hospital, but Derek said you'd be okay if we just let Moby drive you home, and I could follow on the train. Did you know the train is actually faster than a car?'

So that's how you want to play it, Tess thought. She and Flip had discussed at length how she should behave with Selene, and he had urged her to pretend to accept Selene's version of events— even as she allowed Selene to suspect that Tess was running her own game. As someone who could flub a role as a spear carrier—this was not hyperbole, Tess had been fired from her bit as a supernumerary in *Aida* a few years ago—Tess wasn't sure she had the acting chops to achieve the

163

desired effect. But then, the whole point of the exercise was to act badly.

'Oh, it was fine,' she said. 'When nausea comes on that way, the only place you want to be is your own bed. I *so* appreciate you getting me home. I'm not quite recovered—that's why Flip hired a rent-a-cop to guard your condo last night. But I'm getting better.'

'And you're not mad at me?' Selene put on a little-girl voice, her eyes sliding away from Tess's reflected gaze.

'No, it's not *your* fault I had a bum quesadilla.'

'I don't remember you eating a quesadilla. . . .'

'Didn't I? The chips, then. Although we all ate the chips, didn't we?' Selene had licked the salt off one chip, exactly one chip, as Tess recalled, while still maintaining that she could eat whatever she wanted, thanks to her *fantastic* metabolism. 'Oh well, what does it matter what caused it? The thing is, I'm still a little shaky, and I can't let that get in the way of Job One, which is looking after you, especially now that we're going twenty-four-seven. Which means, of course, I'm going to require backup. I'm only one woman, I can't be with you constantly.'

'Back'—Selene paused almost five seconds before squeaking out—'up?'

By then she had registered the tall blonde entering the makeup trailer. It was Tess's oldest friend, Whitney Talbot, whose very posture seemed to scream 'boarding school headmistress on crack.' This was Jean Harris before she shot Dr. Herman Tarnower. Mere moments before. Whitney was wearing riding pants and boots, although Tess knew that her friend hadn't ridden

164

for years, and the kind of gone-to-seed Burberry blazer whose elbow patches weren't for show. In fact, Tess was certain that she recognized the blazer from their freshman year in college, and she had thought it looked like a dog's blanket then.

'Around the clock?' Selene said sharply, dropping her usual little-girl lilt. 'Isn't that excessive?'

'Not at all. What if something had happened to you in New York when I got sick? And, truthfully, this isn't just about you, Selene.' The girl gave the tiniest bit of a pout, as if she found it sacrilegious to suggest that anything was not all about her. 'This is a twenty-five-million-dollar production. If anything happens to you, all that money will be lost.'

'But they have insurance for that,' she said, her antennae up.

'Some. But they wouldn't recoup all their losses, and they wouldn't be compensated for the money that they expect to make when *Mann of Steel* takes off. Anyway, this is Whitney Talbot.'

Whitney shook Selene's hand so hard that what little flesh the girl had on her arms wobbled up to the shoulder and back again. Skinny as she was, Selene didn't have a lot of muscle tone.

'Delighted,' Whitney said. 'What was your name again? I'm afraid that I don't get to the movies much.'

'Selene Waites.'

'Right. You were in the movie about the prodigy.'

'P-p-prostitute.'

'Well, that's a kind of prodigy, isn't it? And I'm sure you were utterly convincing in the part.'

165

'Th-thanks.'

Whitney was acting, too, of course, but only a little. Tess knew that her friend really did go to the symphony more often than the cinema, and she wasn't inclined to be impressed by any actress, even one who insisted on being called an actor. The movies that Whitney knew tended to feature Katharine Hepburn, Myrna Loy, or Jean Arthur. Or, as she liked to say: 'They were called the *talkies* for a reason, once upon a time.'

Tess patted Selene's bony little shoulder, and the girl shot her a look, as if it were a breach of etiquette to touch her without permission. 'Anyway, Whitney's going to hang here on set today, then I'll meet you back at the apartment, where we'll both be sleeping for the duration of the shoot.'

'You and me?' Selene's voice squeaked.

'You, me, and Whitney. Quite a threesome, don't you think, but you've got all those empty rooms, right? Oh, I might sneak home to check up on my house-guest, Lloyd, but Whitney will be there *every* night.'

'With my rifle,' Whitney added.

Selene bit her lip, studying the two women. Tess was determined not to underestimate her again, and she doubted that the girl would give in easily. But, for now, she seemed cowed, and Tess felt more than comfortable leaving her in Whitney's care.

'My family was distantly related to the Pattersons,' Whitney said, peering over Selene's shoulder to study the facsimile of the Gilbert Stuart triptych. 'Of course, we *kept* our money.'

*   *   *

The production office was still cordoned off, an official crime scene for at least one more day, and the writing staff had set up a makeshift workstation in another suite of offices one floor down. Tess was impressed to see Lloyd at the photocopier, running off pages with the rapt attention of a young novice.

'He doing okay?' Tess asked Ben, who was working nearby. Well, lolling, but he could have been thinking deep thoughts about the script in front of him.

'He's great, actually. Seems thrilled to do anything we ask, and never complains, even about the most trivial assignments. I think he would draw my bathwater if I asked him—and drink from it afterward.'

'We are talking about Lloyd, right?'

Ben nodded. 'But you didn't come up here just to check on Lloyd, I'm guessing.'

'Take a walk with me,' she said. 'It's gorgeous outside.'

They wandered through the Tide Point complex. Built on the old Procter & Gamble site, it had taken the names of P&G products for the various buildings—Cascade, Joy, Dawn, Ivory. Perhaps the developers thought it a whimsical tribute. Tess remembered the hundreds of jobs lost when the plant was closed and found the theme in dubious taste.

'Want coffee?' Ben asked, gesturing to the outpost of Daily Grind just outside the fenced parking area.

'A little late in the day. I try not to drink coffee after ten or so.'

'Vodka, then?'

She laughed. 'Maybe a little early.'

'Ah, it was ever thus for me. Too late or too early, never right on time.'

They settled on a bench overlooking the harbor. He extended his long legs and stared straight ahead, which suited Tess fine. There were advantages to talking to a profile. The eye was freer to roam, notice body language.

'About Greer—'

'Fucking tragedy, that.'

'The cops like the ex-fiancé for it.'

'Well, that makes sense, doesn't it? Isn't that how most women become homicide victims, at the hands of a husband or boyfriend?'

Normally, Tess would like a man who had that information at his fingertips. But Ben's use of the statistic struck her as glib and incurious, a way of trying to shut down the topic.

'Actually, about one-third of the homicide cases in which women are victims are classified as "intimate" homicides. So the majority *aren't*.'

'Still—the broken engagement, the threats . . .'

'Was there a broken engagement, much less a threat? Lottie told police that you mentioned something to her yesterday, but no one else seems to know exactly where they stood.'

He crossed one leg over the other, resting his foot on his knee. He wore jeans and sneakers, with an Oxford shirt that he hadn't bothered to tuck in, or maybe he just couldn't keep his shirt tucked in for long.

'I was just inferring. Greer had been pretty

jumpy the past couple of weeks. And there were other signs that seemed to indicate a breakup.'

'She was still wearing an engagement ring when I met her.'

'Yeah, well, Greer wasn't one inclined to let go of anything once she got it in her grasp. I guess she persuaded herself that she was within her rights to keep the ring. Look, why do you care? This is what homicide detectives do, right?'

'I was hired because of problems on the set. This could be connected.'

'Then the problems will stop, won't they, once they have the guy locked up.'

'Maybe. Maybe not.'

Ben was getting irritated. 'Fuckin' Flip. Look, I know what he thinks. It's *not* Selene.'

'How can you be so adamant?'

'Because, well . . .' He scratched his cheek. At least he shaved every day, didn't cultivate the stubble look. 'Because that girl doesn't have the necessary IQ to organize a trip to the 7-Eleven, much less play these kind of pranks. As for murder—'

'Selene went to a lot of trouble last night to get out of town, establish an alibi.'

'She went to a lot of trouble to dump your ass the way I hear it, Sam Spade.'

'I fancy myself more as the Continental Op. After all, he has his roots in Baltimore.'

'Bullshit. Hammett wrote about San Francisco.'

'He was born in St. Mary's County and grew up in Southwest Baltimore, and started work as a Pinkerton here. In the Continental Building at Baltimore and Calvert streets. Which, by the way, has two birds above the front door, birds that were

169

once painted black.'

Now he was interested. 'No shit?'

'Why would I make up something like that?'

'I live in a place where people tell a dozen lies before breakfast, just to stay in practice. Myself included.' He almost seemed to be boasting.

'Don't lie to the cops when you talk to them,' Tess said. 'Although, admittedly, almost everybody does.'

'Why would I lie to them?'

'Where were you last night?'

'In my hotel room. Alone. Oh, by the way, *fuck* you. I didn't kill Greer. Why would I?'

He was staring straight out at the water. Tess was watching the suede Nike balanced on his left knee. He had been jiggling his foot from the first mention of Selene, although he had been the one who brought her name into the conversation. Or had the jiggling begun with Greer? It was tricky sometimes, not taking notes, but it made people so nervous that it wasn't worth it.

'I don't know. Why does anyone kill anyone? And yet they do, almost every day in this city.'

'I hate this place.'

Normally, Tess took such statements about her hometown about the same way she responded to imprecations against her mother. But she decided to play along.

'It's not an easy town to be an outsider. A lot of Baltimoreans—they've never been anywhere, so they don't know what it's like to be new to a place, and they don't reach out to newcomers. But won't you have to live here if *Mann of Steel* gets picked up?'

'Probably. Makes it hard to know whether to

root for a success.' He must have caught something in Tess's face because he quickly added: 'Kidding. I'm *kidding*. I don't want to shut the production down. Frankly, Flip and I need a hit. We've been critical darlings and wunderkinds long enough. We're older now, the rules have changed. We need to be straight-up *wunders,* and being beloved by the critics isn't enough anymore. It's time to make serious money for somebody.'

'But it does appear that someone wants to hamper the production. And now Greer is dead.'

'That stuff that's been happening . . . it could just be bad luck. And if Greer's fiancé killed her, that has bupkes to do with the production. I'm not big on conspiracy theories. Real life is simple.'

'Yes,' Tess said agreeably. 'In real life, for example, sometimes people are just hanging out in their hotel rooms, alone, on nights when it would be nice to have an alibi.'

'You know, you're the first woman I've ever wanted to call an asshole.'

It was the second time in two days a man had used this word to describe her. Tess decided it was a compliment of sorts. She'd rather be an asshole than a bitch.

'What about Lottie?'

'What about her?'

'My sense is that you're not too fond of each other.'

'Look, Miss Marple—'

'She was an amateur. I'm paid to do what I do.'

'Did you know there has never been a successful television show about a female private investigator?' Ben asked abruptly. 'Spies, yes. Amateurs, yes. Straight-up cops, sure. But no

171

female private investigators. I know, it's what killed *Ottoman's Empire*. What does that tell you about your chosen profession?'

'It tells me,' Tess said, 'that you'll go a long way out of your way to change the subject, rather than talk about last night, or Greer. Or Selene.'

'I don't care what time it is,' he said, rising to his feet. 'I need coffee. *And* vodka. Right now, what I really want is coffee with vodka in it. You think I can find that in this godforsaken peninsula?'

He walked away but didn't stop at the Daily Grind, just kept going toward Fort Avenue. It was almost as if he planned to turn right and start walking westward, all the way home to California. And that was fine with Tess.

Chapter 18

Lottie MacKenzie held up one finger—one tiny, rigid index finger—and Tess froze on the threshold of her office like a well-trained dog at the edge of an invisible fence. *I could learn things from this woman,* she thought. Tess had yet to hear Lottie raise her voice or threaten anyone, yet she somehow managed the trick of being formidable. The fact that she didn't try to fight her size only served to make her more intimidating, even in her overalls and voguish Skechers. No heels for Lottie, which was shrewd. If she had attempted a more grown-up outfit, a suit and heels, she would have looked like a doll, or a child playing dress up. Instead, she appeared to be a precocious sixth-grader who happened to be in charge of a $25 million production.

Her office furnishings did make one concession to her height—a footstool next to her Herman Miller chair, but she wasn't using that just now. She sat with her legs crossed, in the style that the un-PC still called 'Indian fashion,' and her body sang with such palpable energy that Tess wouldn't be surprised if she could levitate from that position. She reminded Tess of a hummingbird, a very industrious one, hovering in the air with so much to do, so much to accomplish.

A hummingbird—and Tess was scared to death of her.

'I thought,' Lottie said, when she hung up the phone, 'that your job was to watch Selene, not hang around here. Although, if I had my way, you wouldn't have that job anymore.'

'I've added personnel. At no extra cost,' Tess added swiftly when Lottie's eyes narrowed. 'Someone will be with her at all times now, even during filming. But Flip also has given me latitude to look into the other problems you've had on set.'

'You think Greer's murder . . .'

'I don't *think* anything. My job is to have an open mind. However, if I find a connection, I'm obligated to go to the police.'

'But you'll talk to us first.' Lottie tried to make it sound like an order, but there was the tiniest hesitation in her voice, the hint of a question mark. 'I mean, we pay you, so whatever you learn is proprietary to us, I assume.'

'Maybe,' Tess said, determined not to have that fight until it was necessary. 'Right now, I'm more interested in how proprietary *materials*—the pilot script, the show's bible—ended up in the home of that man who committed suicide. A man who might have been stalking Selene.'

Lottie had a pencil holder filled with actual pencils, old-fashioned yellow no. 2s, uniformly, lethally sharp. When did she find the time to sharpen them all, how did she maintain them at the same length? She pulled one out of the lumpy ceramic mug that held them and pressed the point into her palm. Tess was reminded of the old story about G. Gordon Liddy, the Watergate burglar, passing his hand through a flame to show how tough he was, and she relaxed a little. If Lottie needed to make a show of strength for Tess's sake, then she wasn't that strong.

'That's a personnel matter, and I can't discuss it with you. Liability issues.'

Tess took a moment. She didn't count to ten—experience had taught her there was no number, whether it was ten, a hundred, or a billion—that could reverse her temper's trajectory. Instead, she studied her surroundings, thought about what she wanted, and how saying something rude or snappish, while providing a fleeting satisfaction, would not get her any closer to that goal.

'Lottie, I work for you. For the production. We're on the same team.'

'You were hired by Flip, who didn't even consult me beforehand. I was against this from the start, and given what's happened, I wasn't wrong.'

Tess remained calm, but she didn't bother to hide her exasperation at Lottie's logic. 'Greer isn't dead because I came to work here.'

Lottie didn't blush when embarrassed, not exactly, but color rose slightly in her face, two freakishly perfect round dots of red. Tess would bet anything that older people had grabbed those cheeks once upon a time, pinched them, and told Lottie how cute she was. How she must have loathed it.

'I wouldn't go that far,' she conceded. 'But it's hard not to consider the . . . juxtaposition. The other things, before, were relatively minor. Trash can fires when we filmed outside. The sudden flak from the community people and the steelworkers. Nair in cold cream. This—murder, ransacking the office—is something different.'

'And, as far as the police can tell, probably unrelated. They're looking for Greer's ex-fiancé.'

Lottie resumed testing the pencil points against her palm.

'Did you ever meet him?' It was a hunch, but Tess was no enemy of hunches.

'Once. Greer tried to get him a job here. He has some carpentry skills, he thought he could work with the art department, but we have a full complement. The guy who's doing our set is a local, a veteran who came up with John Waters, and he has all the people he needs. I wasn't going to force some nepotism hire on him to make an intern happy.'

'So Greer put her fiancé up to it?'

Lottie suddenly seemed to become aware of her own strange behavior and put the pencils back in the holder, brushing her palms together. 'That's what I thought at the time. But, later, I wondered if it was his idea, if he wanted a job here so he could keep an eye on Greer.'

'Was Greer involved with someone on the production?'

Lottie didn't speak right away, and Tess willed

175

herself to wait it out, let the silence work on Lottie. *The person who speaks next is a loser,* she chanted in her thoughts. *The person who speaks next is a loser.*

'No, but—'

Loser! I win, I win. High-five me. It's my birthday, it's my birthday. Yes, it was ridiculous, but Tess wasn't above a little end-zone celebrating in her head.

'I think she aspired to be.'

'With whom?'

'Anyone. Anyone, that is, who could help her. Greer would have initiated a relationship with me, if she thought that would be beneficial to her career goals.'

Lottie's gaze dared Tess to ask the question. But she had a different tack in mind.

'Interesting, that she would think that a married woman with kids might be open to that. She must have been casting a wide net.'

Lottie, surprised, held out her hands, as if to check that her ring finger was, in fact, quite bare.

'I noticed you don't wear any jewelry,' Tess said. 'No earrings, no necklaces, not even a watch. Perhaps your skin doesn't do well with any metal, even gold? Or maybe it's just part of the androgynous look you cultivate. And while there may not be photos of your family here in the office, your leather satchel is a mom's bag, and that ceramic mug you use as a pencil holder—a child made that.'

Lottie eyed her skeptically. 'Flip told you.'

Having won the point, Tess didn't mind revealing her source. 'Yeah, he did. But I like to think that I'm not the sort of person who assumes

176

a woman is gay just because she wears overalls and paint-er's pants. Okay, so Greer was putting out the vibe that she was open to—we'll call it off-the-books overtime. Did anyone take her up on it?'

'Not to my knowledge. The crew is too tired at this point to get anything going. Flip's almost as happily married as he says he is, and Ben always says he doesn't shit where he eats. Still—have you ever seen *All About Eve*?'

Tess nodded, fighting the urge to sigh. After just two days among the Hollywood crowd, she longed for a good nature analogy, a food metaphor, or even a reference to one of Aesop's fables.

'Greer was shaping up to be quite the little manipulator. I gave her the original internship. I was impressed that a teamster's daughter had made it to L.A., gotten a toehold in the business. It wasn't her fault she had to come home when her father got sick. In the beginning, she sucked up to me big-time, and I thought I might train her to be an A.D., but she didn't have the patience to work her way up that way. She decided the writers' office was a faster fast track, so she put in for the assistant's job after the pilot was picked up. Then, when Alicia was fired, the job as Flip's assistant fell into her lap. Greer was very good at being in the right place at the right time.' Lottie's face crumpled a little. 'Until the other night.'

They had circled back to what Tess wanted to discuss all along.

'Alicia was the one who gave the materials to the man who killed himself?'

'Wilbur Grace,' Lottie said, and Tess realized she was the first person in the production to concede the man had a name, that he was

177

something more than just a link in their chain of bad luck. 'She swore she didn't, that she had never heard of the guy, but when the phone logs showed he had called her repeatedly, she offered to resign. I told her that she could at least collect unemployment if she was fired, and she agreed. And who would admit to doing something they hadn't done, just to get benefits?'

Flip had all but said the same thing. Hollywood must be a charmed place, where no one was ever wrongly accused of anything, never forced to choose between principles and pocketbooks.

'Why would the guy have wanted those things in the first place?'

'Fans are obsessive. There's nothing they don't want, and there's no show or actor that doesn't have its own set of fan-boys and fan-girls. Johnny and Selene have lots of fans, and there's even a cultish sect for Flip and Ben. Plus, with the advent of eBay, a lot of stuff is making its way to the Internet. There's always been a small tradition of graft on sets, as there is in any office, and I'll turn a blind eye to some props walking off. But scripts—look, it's not as if *Mann of Steel* is the final episode of *The Sopranos*. Still, we can't have our scripts floating around out there. That was a serious transgression, and Alicia had to go.'

'But, to be precise—she never admitted to being the person who gave the documents away? She tried to resign when it became clear no one believed her and agreed to be fired so she could collect unemployment.'

'Who else could have done it?'

'Lottie, you're the one who said Greer was a schemer. And she's the one who benefited when

178

Alicia was fired, getting her job.'

Lottie eyed Tess thoughtfully.

'I'm still not sure I like you,' she said in her blunt way, 'but I like the way you think. Only here's something else for you to consider—we only found out about the scripts after the guy killed himself and the police notified us. So was that part of Greer's plan, too? Goad the guy into killing himself, in order to get Alicia fired? Or maybe you think Greer hunted this guy down, hung him from his own ceiling fan?'

The two women shared a look, the kind of grudgingly respectful gaze more often seen between two adversaries in a western—oh, crap. Now Tess was falling into the habit.

'I'm guessing someone has Alicia's particulars? Home address, phones?'

Lottie detached a Post-it from a hot pink pad and handed it to Tess.

'You had this ready, all along?'

She nodded.

'I'm always three steps ahead. I have to be. I know tomorrow's weather forecast and every actor's call time and what kind of sandwiches they're going to hand out at break tomorrow. I know Saturday's schedule and how the set designers are going to create a faux chapel on the soundstage, for Sunday's memorial service, and how much the catering is going to run us, and if I have to put that against our budget or can get accounting to keep it outside the line costs. I know *everything*.'

Tess believed her. That is, she believed that Lottie *thought* she knew everything. There was a difference.

179

Chapter 19

No one said outright that it was Johnny Tampa's fault that they had to have second meal that night, but he knew they were blaming him. The crew seemed to have fallen into the habit of believing everything that went wrong was Johnny's fault, which was so unfair. He was in almost every scene of this goddamn thing, and he was always meticulously prepared—had his lines cold and was even making a good run at a Baltimore accent before Flip and Ben decreed that he shouldn't. But he *needed* to understand the mechanics of this time-travel gig, why his character seemed to move between present and past in ways he couldn't control or predict. Until that was made clear, he was going to have trouble in certain scenes.

'It doesn't matter,' Ben had said tonight, clearly exasperated that Johnny wouldn't let the subject drop. 'Mann doesn't know how it works, so why should you know?'

'Mann also doesn't know that he's going to end up living in the present, with Betsy as his wife, and I do, so it's clearly okay for me to be privy to information that Mann doesn't have,' Johnny countered. 'This is about the implicit integrity of the show, whether viewers will feel cheated. If the time travel doesn't have a logical explanation, even if it's never spelled out for the viewer, then the character, the world, won't feel real. People will reject it instinctively, sensing you're not playing fair.'

Ben had sighed, and gone to summon Flip, the

great soother and smoother. But Johnny wasn't looking for an ego stroke, or even assurance that it was his part that really mattered, that the show was called *Mann of Steel,* and it wasn't likely to change. Likely—wait, had Flip said *likely* the last time they spoke? Likely meant it *could* change. Was the network going to build up Selene's part even more? There had been a lot of changes in the last script; they had gone all the way to buff pages. Johnny couldn't remember a single episode in his career that had gone even as far as cherry.

Second meal was pizza from a local place called Matthew's, and it was pretty much the best pizza in Baltimore. Johnny circled the table sadly, knowing he should skip it. A year ago, he had hired a life coach who had put him on an intuitive eating program, dictating that Johnny should eat what he wanted when he wanted it. The result was that Johnny had intuitively eaten his way up to almost two hundred and thirty pounds. He watched Selene take a single slice of the crab pizza, which was kind of like a soufflé on a crust, rich and creamy and cheesy. . . . She took exactly one bite, then left the slice on her plate, which only affirmed his belief that she wasn't human. A succubus, maybe, or were women incubuses? Incubi? Borg?

Ben and Flip could tell themselves all they wanted that they weren't trying to make a time-travel show, but they would need that sci-fi core audience to get a second season. Johnny Tampa knew this because he *was* the core audience, a diehard science fiction fan. Over the last five years, when he had been on what he now called his hiatus, he had spent most of his time in his Santa Monica condo, reading fantasy and science fiction.

181

It was the time-travel angle that had interested him most in *Mann of Steel,* not that beggars could be choosers. Truthfully, his dream gig was that vampire show that HBO was doing, but they hadn't even given him a courtesy audition. 'Not ethereal enough,' they had said, and everyone knew what that was code for: too fat.

He decided to retreat to his banger, away from the temptations of second meal. He realized Selene had nibbled just enough pizza so that her breath would be all crab-and-cheese stink in their next scene, when they were supposed to kiss. Very clever, Selene, but had anyone else noticed? Flip and Ben melted in her presence. Lottie didn't seem quite as impressed, but then Lottie didn't like anyone. The fact was, it probably didn't matter if everyone saw through Selene, if everyone realized what a phony and a bitch she was. It was understood that *Mann of Steel* had a shot only because Ben and Flip had been lucky enough to sign Selene before *Baby Jane* earned her that Golden Globe nomination.

Johnny wondered if they still considered themselves lucky, or if they had stopped to consider why Selene had been so convincing as an amoral, scheming teen whore. Johnny, who read the trades and the tabloids as obsessively as he read science fiction, knew all the rumors about *Baby Jane.* Moreover, he believed them, too. It was said that Selene had an affair with the director, which had been dicey, given that Selene was barely legal at the time. The bigger sticking point, however, Hollywood being Hollywood, was that the director was married to the screenwriter, and she tried to block the release. At least, they were married when the project started. Part of the reason the film had languished for two years was that its distribution rights had to be divvied up in the divorce. The screenwriter couldn't decide, for a while, what she wanted more—to destroy Selene's career or make a bundle off a low-budget movie with a star-making performance. Ultimately, she had chosen the bundle. Didn't everyone?

Johnny had left *The Boom Boom Room* at the height of his popularity to pursue the movie offers that were pouring in. Of course, he hadn't known it was the height, far from it. He thought there was still plenty of sky over his head. Separated from the part that had made him a house-hold name, he seemed to lose whatever charisma he had. On television, he was handsome, in an interesting way. On a movie screen—he just disappeared, couldn't hold the frame. 'It's kind of like Samson,' his agent had said. 'When he cut his hair.' Which was confusing, because Johnny hadn't cut his hair. He hadn't changed at all, and that seemed to be the problem. It was as if the rules of the universe had been subverted, as if all the physical laws, such as gravity, had reversed when he wasn't looking. Hot was cold. Up was down—and out. That's when he started reading science fiction.

There was an envelope propped up in front of his mirror, addressed to him in care of the set's street address, which few people knew. Inside was a recent tabloid, with a paper clip attached helpfully, pointing him to an article headlined: who says men age well? There were photographs of Mel Gibson, Alec Baldwin, and, shit, *him,* circled with a big red pen mark, just in case he couldn't find his own fat mug on the page. The photograph was at least six months old, when he was thirty pounds heavier. So unfair. He was—he looked in the mirror, lifted his chin, lifted it higher. There was the old jawline. Sort of.

Suddenly, it seemed as if the mirror was the only place to look, there was no angle in the trailer where he couldn't see himself. He charged back to where the crew was eating, eager to show Ben the magazine. Selene gave him a triumphant little look, her eyes flicking to the rolled-up tabloid in his fist. He ignored her and, when he couldn't find Ben, turned his attention on the icy blonde who had been lingering around set all day, Selene's babysitter or bodyguard, take your pick. She looked to be in her early thirties, which was his demographic. She would have been in high school about the time he was playing high school senior Trip Winters on *Boom Boom*.

'Johnny Tampa,' he said.

'Really?'

'Really,' he said, with an aw-shucks grin, waiting to hear how much she had loved him when she was in high school, how his posters had covered her room.

'I mean, that's your real name? Or did you change it from something?'

That question was so tired that he had long ago developed a standard answer. 'I was born Johnny St. Petersburg, had to shorten it when I went into show business.'

After a small delay, as if she needed time to process the fact that he had actually said something clever, she laughed. It was a rather metallic, *rat-a-tat* sound, but it seemed genuine enough. She had a hard, almost scary edge to her. He liked it.

'Whitney Talbot,' she said. 'I'm here to—'

'I know. You follow her everywhere? To the bathroom and stuff?'

'I let her have her bathroom breaks in privacy.'

'Maybe you shouldn't.'

'What?'

'I mean, this soundstage, it's a big space. And it might seem secure, but who knows? I mean, you're here to protect her, right?'

'Right,' she said, after a beat.

'If I were you, I'd never let her out of my sight. You never know what she's going to be up to.' He turned his head to the side, in case his profile jogged her memory. Pride vanquished, he said: *The Boom Boom Room?*'

She looked puzzled. 'Is that one of the strip clubs still operating on the Block?'

'No, it was a television show, about kids put in a school-within-a-school on special detention, kind of like *The Breakfast Club*—oh never mind. A lot of people watched it, back in the day.'

'I didn't watch a lot of television, growing up. I was kind of outdoorsy.' She said it nicely, apologetically, not in the snobby way some people had. He almost believed her, except he didn't believe anyone who claimed not to watch television. Who didn't watch television? It was like . . . not brushing your teeth, or refusing to shower, odd to the point of being uncivilized. Everybody watched television. There had been a time, around season four of *Boom Boom,* when he couldn't go anywhere or do anything without being recognized. He hadn't always enjoyed the attention, but he hadn't been stupid enough to wish it away, and he had been genuinely surprised when it stopped. Since then, it was as if he couldn't get quite enough oxygen in his blood, as if he were living at 75 percent. He had plenty of money, he had been smart that way, but his financial stability was scant comfort. He wanted another success in this business, and to get that, he had to pretend to be in love with some twenty-year-old twat. He hated her. He needed her. Well, that's why they called it acting.

Dinner was wrapping up. He couldn't help noticing there was a lot of leftover pizza. He wondered if he should take it home. No, it wouldn't be any less fattening at breakfast tomorrow, only colder. He wondered if he should try to take the blonde home, but he supposed she had to stick close to Selene. Besides, she hadn't seemed terribly interested. No, he would just go home and get into bed, read a few pages of the latest Robert Harris. He had tried to get Flip and Ben to read Harris, engage them in the rules of alterna-history, but to no avail. They seemed to think that because Napoleon had, in the end, forced the divorce between his brother and Betsy Patterson, they could remove her from history with no real effect. But what about Betsy's son? You couldn't just eliminate people from history. That was a kind of murder.

The PAs were calling them back to work, but Johnny spotted Lottie huddled with the director and showed her the magazine.

'Look what was in my trailer.'

Lottie glanced at the photos. 'It's not so bad, Johnny. Besides, it can't hurt to be considered in

186

the same class as Mel Gibson and Alec Baldwin.'

'That's not the point. Someone sent it to me, to unnerve me.'

'You've got to start locking your door,' Lottie said. 'I thought, after the Nair—'

'It came in the mail. And it proves the Nair wasn't an isolated incident. You know who's behind this. Why don't you do something about it?'

'Selene's got a bodyguard now,' Lottie said. 'She can't go anywhere without being seen.'

'Well, maybe the bodyguard is in on it, then. Someone's doing her dirty work. We can't go on like this. She doesn't want to be here. I hate working with her. How are we going to get through this season, much less another one if we're lucky enough to get picked up?'

'Johnny.' She sighed, weary as his mother, although she was several years younger and barely came to his collarbone. 'Let's just get this scene and let everyone go home, okay?'

The stand-ins had cleared the set, and he and Selene took their places. In this scene, Mann had brought Betsy to his home in twenty-first-century Baltimore—although, damn Flip and Ben, he still didn't know *how*—to persuade her that he really was from the future, that it was possible for him to know her fate. Tomorrow, they would go on location in Green Mount Cemetery, and he would show Betsy her own tombstone. He wasn't crazy about that scene, which seemed unduly influenced by the graveside scene in *A Christmas Carol*—and the Mr. Magoo version at that. But that was Ben and Flip for you. They hadn't read Dickens, but they knew their Mr. Magoo. Today, however, they were in the Mann family rowhouse, and Betsy was supposed to be overwhelmed by the modern ingenuity of the La-Z-Boy recliner. Was this stuff really as sly and ironic as everyone else seemed to think? Or was it stupid and vapid? You couldn't tell everything from the words on the page. So much depended on the editing, the look. And the performances, although Ben and Flip seemed to have lost sight of that as well.

'Quiet on the set. Sound speed. Rolling . . . *action.*'

Selene, in character, gave him a flirtatious look. Sure enough, garlic fumes were everywhere. He gave her one back, topping it with a wink, and they ran their lines, building up to their big kiss in the La-Z-Boy. Johnny Tampa could kiss, he knew that much about himself. There was no one he couldn't kiss, under any circumstances. He could tongue a dog, a real one, or even French a potato if that was what he had to do. He was a great kisser, on camera. Off camera, it didn't interest him that much. He preferred it *impersonal* because he had grown tired of girls staring at his face, as if they couldn't believe they were with Johnny Tampa. And then there were those who hadn't known they were with Johnny Tampa, and that had been even worse.

'Cut,' yelled the director, who then walked over to Johnny. He lowered his voice, his style when giving notes. 'Lose the wink, okay, Johnny? It's way too lecherous for Mann.' As usual, Wes had no notes for Selene.

The crew was too professional to sigh, but Johnny could feel everyone slumping. After all, they were now three hours over the day.

Meanwhile, Selene, who had set him up to flub the scene, could barely suppress her smile as she threw herself back into the La-Z-Boy.

Chapter 20

It was Tess's nature to be suspicious of anything that came too easily, and finding Alicia Farmer fell into that category. With Lottie's piece of paper in hand, all Tess had to do was drive to the address listed and wait for someone to show up. Was Lottie trying to manipulate her? 'Trust no one' was beginning to seem a very apt motto for this job.

At least the address itself was surprising, a working-class neighborhood in Northeast Baltimore. Tess had assumed that someone in the television business would have settled into one of the hip, emerging areas favored by the postcollege crowd. Alicia Farmer lived in a small brick bungalow on a large, irregular plot, a diamond shape that looked as if it had been created by accident when the street was widened a few years back. The result was that the house sat slightly apart from the others, lonely and isolated, like the first kid to go in the stew pot in a game of Duck, Duck, Goose.

No one answered her knock, so Tess took a quick walk around the house, which looked well tended, although a new deck seemed to have been abandoned in midconstruction. She then took up residence on the bench at the bus stop across the street. Sitting in a car for long periods of time caught the attention of nosy neighbors, but one could sit at a bus stop all afternoon and no one would notice.

It was after eight when a woman not much younger than Tess parked a Chevrolet Caprice at the curb and trudged toward the door, head down, a single plastic sack of groceries dangling from her right hand. Tess let her get inside, then waited another ten minutes before knocking, allowing the woman to decompress a little—put her groceries away, make the transition from work to home. She wouldn't have thought of such a tactic when she started this kind of work, but she knew how she felt at the end of a long day, and she saw no harm in letting this woman decompress before Tess peppered her with questions about a workplace she had left involuntarily.

*   *   *

'I'm from the state unemployment office,' she said exactly twelve minutes later, 'and we're doing spot checks of departmental efficiency. Do you know where we might find Alicia Farmer?'

'I'm Alicia Farmer,' the woman said, as if confessing to something unpleasant. 'But I never put in for unemployment. I got another gig.' She indicated the insignia on her blouse. CHARM CITY VIDEO.

'So you're still in the film business?'

'Yeah.' Alicia laughed, a little unwillingly. 'For now, until Netflix or the idiot management puts us out of business. Now if you don't mind—'

'I wasn't exactly truthful,' Tess said, smiling in a way that she hoped would take the sting out of her confession, all the while positioning her body

190

slightly forward, so the door couldn't be closed without real force. Alicia seemed too downtrodden, too defeated, to slam a door on someone's foot. Speaking swiftly now: 'I'm an investigator working for *Mann of Steel,* and I'm looking into some of the security issues on set.'

'Security issues? Like the death of Greer Sadowski? Yeah, I guess that was a real security *issue.*'

Alicia had reddish brown hair, pulled back in a ponytail, and such dark shadows beneath her light eyes that they might have been bruises. She reminded Tess of someone she knew, although it took her a second to pin it down. She reminded Tess of *herself,* the woman she was on the verge of becoming after she lost her job at the *Star.* God, she had been lost for a while. *If* she hadn't allowed Tyner to talk her into becoming a private investigator, *if* she hadn't taken the risk of opening her own business, *if* she hadn't met Crow and, yes, allowed him to woo and pursue her, this could be her, in a red CHARM CITY VIDEO smock, living in a safe, but not particularly desirable, Baltimore neighborhood, sarcasm her only defining trait.

'The police are looking into Greer's death, not me.' Then, on a hunch. 'Should I give them your name?'

'I didn't hate her *that* much.' Tess liked the precision of Alicia's candor. Not wanting the girl dead, but not pretending to care more than she did. 'Look, I'm exhausted and all I want is to drink a beer, watch some stupid television. Can we sit down? I'll even give you a beer.'

Tess took the offer, sitting with Alicia in a small den off the kitchen, an addition that appeared to have been made circa 1982, judging by the butternut squash-colored appliances, with a Formica breakfast bar separating the kitchen from the pine-paneled alcove. With only a few small tweaks, it could have passed for cheerfully funky, a retro gem. Instead, it seemed resigned to dowdiness.

'My folks' place,' Alicia said. 'My father died ten years ago, my mother just two years ago. When I have the time to renovate, I don't have the funds. When I have the funds, I don't have the time. I don't know. I watch all those home improvement shows, but I think it's decadent, the way we fetishize our homes. Or maybe that's a convenient rationalization for my crap house.'

'It's cozy,' Tess said, sucking up, but not completely insincere. 'I'm guessing your parents died kind of young?'

'Dad had that cancer no one can pronounce, the one that steelworkers get from asbestos. Mom went out the old-fashioned way, good old lung cancer.' Alicia Farmer fired up a Lucky with a great deal of style and ceremony. 'Me, I'm invincible. Or I don't give a shit. I haven't figured out which one it is yet.'

'Wasn't it weird working on *Mann of Steel* when your dad had worked at Beth Steel?' Tess may have been trying to ingratiate herself, but she also was genuinely interested. 'I mean, you had to realize how bogus it was, a thriving steel plant in modern-day Baltimore. Plus, you probably know some of the steelworkers who have raised a stink about it.'

The question seemed to catch Alicia by surprise. She blew smoke at the ceiling while she thought about it. 'It's a television show. A guy time-travels after he gets hit on the head. It wasn't exactly a *documentary*. I have to say, though, you're the first person who ever asked me that particular question about my job at *Mann of Steel*.'

'What do people usually ask?'

'What's Johnny Tampa really like, do I ever get to ride in a limo. Shit like that.'

Tess smiled. 'I've worked there less than a week, and I've been asked the Johnny Tampa question.'

'What do you say? I told people he had all the personality of particle board, and everyone thought I was kidding. Me, I thought it was kind of unfair to particle board.'

'How did you end up working for them?'

'The usual Baltimore thing—I know a girl who knows a girl who does the hair of an old friend of John Waters. John's been working with the same people forever and didn't have anything for me. But when his casting director, Pat Moran, heard that *Mann of Steel* was coming to town, she made inquiries on my behalf. I got hired as Flip's assistant before the pilot was shot, and it was great . . . for a while.'

'What happened?'

Alicia looked to the ceiling again, blew more smoke. 'Oh, the usual girl-on-girl action. Greer got hired, she wanted my job. Somehow she made it happen.'

Time to go straight at it, Tess decided.

'Lottie MacKenzie says you photocopied a script and gave it to someone outside the production, that you resigned when asked about it.'

'I resigned because I was so damn sick of

193

Greer's manipulations by then. Who do you think ran to Lottie, blaming me? She was going to get me one way or another. If I had been smarter, I would have gotten out of her way the first time we clashed, asked Lottie for another job in a different department. But by this time, Greer had trashed me so thoroughly that I didn't have a chance. Besides, she had a protector. I never had a chance, once she got him on her side.'

'A protector? Flip?'

'Ben Marcus.'

Strange. Tess had the impression that Ben didn't particularly like Greer. And then she wondered why she thought that. Perhaps it was just that Ben didn't seem to like anyone, starting with himself. Or perhaps it was because Ben wanted her to think he wasn't particularly fond of Greer, that he had taken every opportunity to run her down. Lottie had said that Greer seemed to be open to any kind of liaison that would give her career a boost.

'Are you saying . . . ?'

'I can't say anything for sure. Still, she wheedled her way into the writers' office as an intern, when we really didn't need anyone. Then, all of a sudden—bam, she's got a paying gig, as the second assistant. She was very efficient, however. Meanwhile, phone messages were disappearing from my desk, I didn't get e-mails that I was supposed to get. Penny-ante shit like that.'

'And the script? The one that was found in the dead man's house?'

Alicia stubbed her cigarette out in a bright yellow ashtray that could probably fetch an outrageous price in some hip little secondhand store. 'Truthfully? I don't know shit about it. The guy's name was in the phone log, but I don't remember him, and I never said anything to him beyond "I'll pass that on to Flip."'

'Pass what on?'

'Who knows? He was one of a dozen people who called or e-mailed every day, claiming an urgent need to talk to the executive producer. My job was to be politely *unhelpful*—take the message, send a "Thank you for your inquiry" e-mail, whatever. He was one name among many, Wilbur Grace. Hard to forget a name like that. But I sure as shit didn't give him anything. All he ever got from me was "Hello," "I'll tell him," "Yes, he's got your number."'

'Someone gave him the script and the bible. The man killed himself. And now Greer is dead.'

Alicia studied Tess. 'But you just said they're looking for her boyfriend, right?'

Actually, Tess hadn't said that. 'He's officially a person of interest at this point.'

'But it makes sense, especially if she was sleeping with Ben Marcus.'

'Are you saying that you know this for a fact?'

'I'm saying that I know Ben Marcus has sex so often, and with so little thought, that I wouldn't be surprised if he started humping a doughnut off the craft services cart one day.'

Flip had alluded to the same behavior on Ben's part but said an affair between Ben and Greer was unthinkable. And it was, Tess decided—not because of Ben but because Greer wouldn't settle for anyone less than the boss.

Her beer finished, Tess decided to let her doppelgänger have the oblivious eve-ning she so

195

clearly desired. She stood. 'One last thing—'

'Home alone, sleeping. That's one thing I don't miss about the old job, those crazy hours.' Alicia smiled. 'That is what you were going to ask me, right? Where I was the night Greer died?'

'Actually, I just wanted to use your bathroom.'

The powder room proved to be one of the few projects that Alicia had found the time and money to complete. It had a pretty pedestal sink, a striking light fixture, and one of those state-of-the-art toilets that used a minimum of water. Tess flushed it twice, giddy as a child.

* * *

A few blocks away, Tess pulled over and found a little free wireless bleeding into the air, possibly from the McDonald's. She used it to look up Wilbur Grace on her laptop, see if he was still listed in Baltimore. There he was, Wilbur R. Grace on Elsrode Road, mere blocks from where she sat. How could she not at least drive by, given that it was all but on her way back to Selene's condo?

And once she found the house, on a dead end that ran into Herring Run Park, how could she not get out, walk around. It was never her intention to break in, of course—or so she told herself as she fiddled with the kitchen window, which slid up so effortlessly that it seemed rude to resist its invitation.

She flicked the kitchen light switch. No power— it must have been turned off by now—and it only would have drawn the neighbors' attention. But there was a streetlight outside, and once her eyes adjusted, she began to look around, feeling silly.

196

What did she expect to find? A man had killed himself here, hung himself from the ceiling fan above the charming, old-fashioned table, a white metal top with an elaborate black design. It was sad, but it probably didn't have anything to do with *Mann of Steel,* despite what had been found among his effects.

'Don't disdain the obvious, Monaghan,' she said out loud, keen for company in the dark, achingly quiet house. She wandered into the living room. Like the kitchen in Alicia Farmer's house, it was a Baltimore time capsule, only this one was stuck in the early 1960s. Why was the furniture still here? Maybe Wilbur Grace had died without a will and everything was being held up by probate. That was a mess, Tess knew from experience, but it would be sorted out eventually. Until then, the house would sit, and—she heard a creak back in the kitchen. Someone else was opening the kitchen window, which Tess had been careful to close behind her.

Flight or fight? She chose neither, crouching behind the sofa instead. Her eyes had adjusted to the light; that was her one advantage. If someone else was entering through the kitchen window, he—or she—had no more right to be there than she did, so that was a push. She had left her gun in the car—distinct disadvantage. Burglars tended to be averse to violence, hence their choice of profession. But when confronted, they could be unpredictable.

Voices. There were two of them, male and female, trying to whisper but not having much success. *'Are you sure—?' 'Yes, I've done it before.' 'But what if—?' 'He's dead, no one's here, no one's ever here.' 'It's creepy, though, him dying here.'*

By then, the duo was in the living room, heading toward the stairs, two teenagers, a six-pack of beer dangling from the boy's hand. Tess should have let them go. It was no business of hers if two kids wanted to take a shot at adding another stat to the city's out-of-wedlock pregnancy rate. She could have let them pass, then retreated silently out the window. She was trespassing, too.

'You come here often?' Tess called out when they were about halfway up the stairs.

The girl screamed, and the boy dropped the six-pack, which bounced down the steps and broke free of the plastic rings, rolling across the wooden floor. Surprised and overwhelmed, they couldn't begin to figure out what to do. The girl tried to run down the stairs as the boy ran up, only to block each other.

'Don't choose a career in any kind of crisis or emergency work,' Tess said, picking up a beer. She was tempted to open it for the sheer insouciance of it, but it would only spray everywhere, making a mess. Besides, she wasn't in the mood for a Natural Light. She was never in the mood for a Natural Light.

'Who are you?' the boy asked. 'What are you doing here?'

'Let's just say I have a right to be here,' she bluffed, 'which is probably not your situation. Breaking and entering, drinking alcohol when you're under twenty-one, getting ready to have sex with a minor—'

'*I'm* a minor,' the boy protested, even as the girl said: 'We were not!'

'The law doesn't care about the boy's age,' Tess

198

said, having no idea if this were true. 'But I'll tell you what. I'll forget about everything I saw and everything you've done, if you'll just tell me some things I need to know about the man who lived here. You did know him, right?'

'Mr. Grace?' the boy said. 'Yeah.'

'What was he like?'

'Weird.'

That was more than she had hoped for, actually. She was counting on getting the usual 'Nice man, quiet man' rap, the default of incurious neighbors everywhere. Translated: *I never paid attention to him.*

'How so?'

'He'd invite the neighborhood kids over to watch movies.'

Well, Crow did that with Lloyd.

'And that was okay, he would give us sodas and stuff, screen us these old movies, then ask us what we thought.'

Again, not so different from what happened in her home.

'And he even wanted to make movies with some of us.'

Shit.

'Not like that,' the young man added hastily. Perhaps he had told the story before and always gotten the same reaction. 'Movies with stories, that he had written out. Short. They weren't exactly the *Matrix,* but they were kind of good. Only he stopped doing that, like, a year ago or so.'

'Did he keep the movies?'

'Shit, I don't know. His equipment was old school, some big clunky camcorder, VHS tapes. Who still has that shit?'

Tess glanced around the room. There was a large armoire in one corner of the living room. Using a pinpoint flashlight on her key ring, she opened it and found a television and a cable box, but no DVD player, and no VCR. Below the television was a shelf with films in both formats, mostly classics, but there were no homemade movies among them.

'You steal this stuff?' she said.

'What stuff?'

'You said he watched movies, he had to have something to watch them on.'

'No,' the boy said, adamant, even a little offended. 'I wouldn't do nothing like that. I come over here to—you know, have fun. I'm not a thief.'

The girl spoke up, outraged. 'This is the first time I've ever been here.'

The boy smiled sheepishly at Tess, as if expecting her to take his side, to understand that a super-suave Herring Run stud such as himself— hadn't he sprung for an entire six-pack of Natural Light—couldn't be expected to be tied down to just one girl.

'But there was equipment,' Tess insisted, examining the armoire. In the back, several small holes had been bored into the wood so cords could be passed through.

'Like I said, I hadn't come over to see Mr. Grace for a couple of years. He liked the younger kids, mainly.' Again, he seemed to know what Tess was thinking. 'Not like that. When you're little, it's not embarrassing, doing that shit, running around and pretending to be other people. But you outgrow it, you know?'

Tess studied the living room, best as she could

200

see it in the dim light. Nothing else seemed missing, or off. The television was light enough and, although not a flat-screen, new enough to fetch a decent sum at a pawnshop. If there had been a burglary, why not take that as well?

'What's upstairs?'

'Bedrooms,' said the playboy of Northeast Baltimore, leering, and Tess froze him with a look. 'Not trashed or anything,' he added. 'I been coming and going from here since he died, and I ain't noticed anything missing. He didn't really have any friends. Just the little kids.'

'You left the window unlatched?'

He shrugged, almost proudly. He wasn't altogether dim-witted. Tess stared him down.

'The first time, I came through the cellar,' he admitted. 'He has them *Wizard of Oz* doors.'

It took her a second to get that reference, but it made her smile. Some old Baltimore houses did have storm cellar doors, although tornadoes were rare.

'Once I pried them open, I bolted 'em shut from the inside. I just leave the one window unlocked, on the back porch.'

'Very considerate,' Tess conceded. 'How about I give you guys a ride home? It's getting late, and it's a school night.'

'Well, we don't live far . . .' he began, then realized it hadn't really been a question.

'And I'll take the beer,' Tess said. 'For your own good.'

'Like you never drank when you was my age.'

'I'm not saying that. I'm just saying I didn't get caught.' She regarded the beer with little affection. Crow could always use it for crab boil, she guessed.

'By the way, drink what you want, but when it comes to birth control, don't do that on the cheap, okay? That'll cost you.'

Chapter 21

Martin Tull was, as Tess had assured Flip, good police. Smart, methodical, with a kind of confidence that can't be faked and a work ethic that few could equal. While some detectives welcomed homicides because they started the overtime clock, Tull was inclined to work eighteen-hour days no matter the circumstances. Going on nine-thirty, it was a toss-up whether he would be free, but Tess decided to try to lure him out anyway.

'A man has to eat,' she said persuasively. 'And drink.'

He agreed to meet her at Burke's, a reliable all-night refuge, the kind of place that made its living off cops, emergency room personnel, reporters, and insomniacs. Tess decided to have mozzarella sticks and a beer. Tull, as was his habit, ordered coffee, black. Tess wasn't sure she had ever seen him drink anything else. Come to think of it, in all the years she had known Tull, she wasn't sure she had ever seen him *eat*.

'A shot of whiskey would be healthier,' she said. 'It reduces stress. And who knows how long that coffeepot has been sitting on the burner?'

'I love the coffee here,' he said. 'It's boiled down to the essence. It's like . . . caffeine syrup.'

'Are you trying to get a second wind, or just

maintaining for the drive home?'

'Home, I guess. We can't find the boyfriend. Which, of course, makes me happy in the long run—just convinces me that he's the one we want—but I wouldn't have minded finding him today.'

'So, a dunker?'

'I think so, yeah. Based on how his family's acting. Alternating between *"Oh, JJ just disappears sometimes, goes fishing up at Deep Creek Lake when the weather is like this,"* then, in the next breath, mentioning what a bitch the dead girl is, how badly she behaved, and then "Not that we'd wish any harm on her."'

'Behaved badly how?'

'JJ was convinced there was another guy—his mother let that slip, and tried to backpedal. From what I gather, the two were high school sweethearts, years ago, got back together in the past year, but the mother never thought the girl's heart was in it.'

'What did they say at his job?' Tess asked, knowing that Tull would have checked with the suspect's co-workers as well.

'All they know is that his mom called in early Wednesday, said he was sick, too sick to even talk on the phone, expected to be out all week. Look, I've got a patrol on his house. He's going to try and come back, maybe as early as tonight. He's not bright. Even his own mother isn't putting him forward for genius status. He's probably scared and freaked out, trying to figure out if there's anywhere he can go on the lam. But he doesn't have the resources.'

Tess whisked a mozzarella stick through the

marinara sauce. She had always liked this particular brand of bar food, but her fondness for it had soared when it was demonized by the Center for Nutrition and Public Policy as one of the worst possible foods to eat. She kept a mental list of such foods—pad thai, kung pao chicken, fettuccine Alfredo—and tried to eat them as frequently as possible.

'I know the rule of thumb is that the obvious suspect is the obvious suspect,' Tess said. 'My only concern is if there's any connection between him and the problems that have been dogging this production. Could this guy be our arsonist, for example?'

'If the problems stop now, you'll know.'

'Yes, or maybe someone else will have figured that out as well, and will use this as an opportunity.' She was thinking of Selene. If she had been creating the problems on set, what would she do now? What if she had hired Greer's ex-boyfriend to be her private little troublemaker, and he had been sidetracked by whatever had happened between him and Greer? Selene's trip to New York could have been an elaborate alibi. Only—did it even count as an alibi? She could have left the restaurant anytime after Tess passed out. She was spotted at Penn Station at noon, but it had been a very conspicuous sighting, the kind of thing tailor-made for cell phone video cameras and TMZ.com. The gossip item put her at the SoHo Grand about 11 A.M. That was at least eleven hours—more than enough time to return to Baltimore, and go back to New York, with six hours in between. Do it in a private car without an E-ZPass, pay cash for whatever gas you need, avoid red-light cameras at intersections, and it was possible to make the trip without leaving a single electronic footprint.

It was all very interesting, but Tess was working for Flip, and the last thing Flip wanted was for his star to be connected to Greer's death. Tess was supposed to be using her relationship with Tull to ensure that the production was shielded, as much as possible, from scandal. And based on what Tull was saying, she should be happy on that score. Yet she felt a mild, nagging discontent. Maybe it was nothing more than the cheese inside its deep-fried coat, growing rubbery and cold.

*   *   *

Back in Selene's condo, Whitney poured Tess a glass of port.

'Roomies again,' she said, toasting her. 'After all these years. But is this the future we envisioned for ourselves, babysitting a spoiled twenty-year-old?'

'I can hear you.' Selene's voice came from the living room, where she was watching a huge plasma television with the sound turned off. Selene used the television the way a baby interacted with the mobiles hung over a crib, lying back and letting the images wash over her, although without any evidence of intellectual stimulation.

'I wanted you to,' Whitney assured her. 'I want you to hear every syllable that emanates from my mouth. I'm going to school you, girl.'

Tess snorted port. Whitney attempting the outmoded slang of *school* was too funny. She suspected Whitney knew as much.

'So, who did we expect to be, all those years ago? How are we different?' Whitney asked. Tess didn't jump in. She knew Whitney had her own set of answers and would want to go first. 'We've traded Coors for Taylor Fladgate. And instead of Kent House, our dorm, we're in a Baltimore high-rise that neither of us can afford.'

Tess was sure that her friend *could* afford such an apartment, but she had the WASP habit of cheapness when it came to big-ticket items. Whitney would probably live and die in the guest-house at her parents' mildly run-down valley home because it was free.

'We were both going to be journalists,' Whitney continued. 'You, a crusading investigator, part Nellie Bly, part Woodstein. Me, a globe-trotting foreign correspondent. Now you're the owner of your own business, and I run the family foundation. Upgrade?'

'Downgrade, I would think,' Selene snarked.

'My uncle Toddy married an actress,' Whitney said, addressing Tess in a stage whisper. 'He was disinherited.'

Selene got up and flounced into her room, slamming the door behind her.

'She hates me,' Whitney said cheerfully.

'Good, then you're doing your job. How was the day on set?'

'*Tedious*. Why do people think it's glamorous, spending hours in a big drafty barn of a place, watching people say and do the same things over and over again?'

'Did they give you one of those little headset thingies that allows you to listen to the scene?'

'Yes, but I turned the sound off after the third

take. I couldn't take listening to that dialogue. I felt like my IQ was dropping by the minute.'

'And the day was problem free?'

'For our purposes. The tiny woman, Lottie, said the energy was a little off, because people are upset, but it seemed to be going well. Johnny Tampa was pissed because someone left an unflattering photo of him in his trailer. What a fat load he is. Remember how—'

'No,' Tess said quickly, knowing where her friend was heading and prepared to disavow it, three times if necessary, like Peter denying Jesus before the cock crowed. She was never going to admit to her youthful yearnings toward Johnny Tampa.

'Oh you did too have a crush on him when you first got to school.' Whitney spoke with the smugness of a true friend. 'What were you thinking? Even thin, he wasn't that attractive.'

Tess looked out at the harbor, so beautiful at night. Her thoughts followed her eyes eastward, to the mouth of the bay and then across it, time-traveling to the pretty little college campus where two girls had met, two girls who were at once so much younger and older than the girl who had just closeted herself behind her bedroom door. '*We* thought that we would never get old, much less fat. Well, fatter, in my case. We thought our metabolisms would never change. We thought we would get everything we wanted. We were, in short, twenty.'

Whitney laughed in rueful agreement. 'What if someone had made you a bargain, all those years ago, offered you all this? Not just the apartment, but the life, too? The money, the beauty, the

207

attention. Would you have wanted it under these conditions—life in a fishbowl, a job at which you have very little control?'

'Honestly? At twenty? I think I would have said yes. I think almost anyone would. At twenty. Not now.'

'Poor baby,' Whitney said, looking at the closed bedroom door, sotto voce for once. 'She's already beaten the million-to-one odds by becoming a successful actress. Now she has to face the ten million-to-one odds of becoming an actress who finds work past the age of thirty-five. Remember the silent stars whose careers ended when the talkies came along? For women, it hasn't really changed.'

'Marie . . . Dressler, the one whose dog ate her,' Tess recalled.

'Wrong Marie,' Whitney said. 'Marie Dressler was in *Dinner at Eight*. You're thinking of Marie Prevost. Remember, Nick Lowe had a song about her. He rhymed *winner* with *doggie's dinner*. And then there was Lupe Velez—'

'She was in talkies,' Tess said.

'Right. But she went bankrupt and ended up drowning in her toilet when she vomited up all the Seconals she had taken in hopes of a slightly more, uh, picturesque suicide. Don't you know your *Hollywood Babylon*? Hollywood kills its own.'

'Well, there was Thelma Todd, whose murder was never solved,' Tess said. 'But I'm not sure that was actually Hollywood's fault.'

'You've forgotten the starlet who jumped from the thirteenth letter of the Hollywoodland sign— back when it had thirteen letters. Oh, and another one who immolated herself on a pyre of her own clippings. What a way to go.'

The two old friends fell silent, and Tess assumed that Whitney must be thinking, as she was, of the fates available to actresses of a certain age. To women of a certain age. The distinctive ring of Selene's cell phone broke the silence, followed by her side of the conversation—not the words, only the tone, which was suffused with a husky, flirtatious giggle.

'I wonder who she's talking to,' Tess said. 'Then again, knowing Selene, she'd talk to the dry cleaners in that breathy little voice.'

'Easy enough to find out.'

'How?'

'She has an eleven o'clock call tomorrow. Grab her cell while she's still asleep, check the received call log, make a note of it.'

As it happened, Tess didn't have to wait until morning. A few minutes later, the water started running in Selene's bathroom. Tess knocked softly on the bedroom door in a pretense of courtesy, then pushed inside, Whitney trailing her. While Whitney kept an eye on the closed bathroom door, Tess grabbed the iPhone. It took a second for her to figure out its protocols, and when she did find the received call log, the latest call wasn't particularly surprising: DEREK. He and Selene had probably shared one more laugh over drugging Tess; that gag never got old. The other calls were from her driver, Lottie, and Selene's mother. In fact, it looked as if Selene's mother called every day about the same time, which surprised Tess. She hadn't thought the Waites family was particularly supportive of their daughter.

The received call log exhausted, Tess was about to put the phone back on the nightstand when she remembered Selene's furiously tapping thumb, texting in the car on the way to New York. She found the text function and clicked back two days in time. Derek again, checking Selene's ETA. And, in between Derek's calls, one from a different number, a text that read simply: aching for you. where are you? The absence of text shorthand—no *4* for *for,* no *u* for *you,* no *r* for *are*—might have been enough to tip Tess off to the sender—someone who had enough pride, or time, to use the language in full. But she didn't have to guess. The text was from someone named 'Benny,' who happened to have a number in Selene's phone book.

She pressed the call button, hanging up when Ben Marcus picked up breathlessly on the second ring: 'Have you figured out a way to get rid of them?'

Chapter 22

He waited until Marie was asleep to put in one of Bob's movies. Marie knew about the stash of VHS tapes, of course, and the old VCR that had suddenly materialized. He could never hide anything in this house. Marie knew their home the way some people knew their bodies—she could detect any change in it, no matter how small. The house *was* her body, in a sense; she inhabited it the way a hermit crab lived in its shell, only she never outgrew it. She could be resting on the sofa in the evening, yet tell by sound alone if he put something away in the wrong place in the kitchen. Where would he hide her Christmas gifts this year, now that he didn't have an office? But everything should be solved by Christmas, one way or another. It had to be. Bob's estate would be settled, the other matter resolved as well, and he could tell Marie everything. Well, not *everything,* but he could tell her that he had decided to take early retirement, thanks to this windfall that Bob had engineered for them before he died. Even then, Marie probably wouldn't want to watch the films. They always made her cry, even the silly ones.

When he brought the VHS tapes home, he had told a semitruth, as he liked to think of it. It was hard for him to think of anything he said as a lie, because then he would be a liar, and that didn't fit with his sense of himself. He told Marie that while Bob's estate was held up in probate, the Orphans' Court had determined that certain items of no financial value could be removed from the premises. And a judge might have ruled that way, if a judge had been asked. In reality, *he* had made the ruling, after a fashion, entering and leaving with the set of keys that Bob had given him years ago—the same keys he had used to unlock the back door that day, after a week of Bob not answering his phone.

In his mind, he framed the memory as Bob might have framed the scene in his viewfinder. He did not see the kitchen through his own eyes but saw it as if the camera was watching him from the other side of the room—the door opening, his eyes moving slowly upward, only Bob's feet and ankles

211

on view. It was a clichéd way of seeing, a scene stolen from someone else—but then, he didn't have Bob's eye.

He had wanted to believe it was despair, nothing more, Bob finally laid low by some variant of the same odd brain chemistry that affected his only sister, Marie. But then he discovered what a mess Bob had left behind—the debts, the second mortgage, the refinance on the first mortgage, a balloon that was going to come due in a year, kicking up to a disastrously high rate. Then there was the lawyer, saying he was still owed money, even though it was his bills that had driven Bob to near bankruptcy in the first place, and that he planned to attach the house. Who cared if some VHS tapes disappeared? Even a grasping lawyer wouldn't assign them any value.

Still, they might try to take the movies from him, if they knew. He wouldn't put anything past these people. Thinking about them, thinking about all the people who were allied against him, made his face grow hot, then anger and humiliation overtook him again, just as it had the other night. Quickly, he pushed the play button, desperate to lose himself in Bob's meticulous fantasy world.

The film opened on a shot of a castle—this would be the decrepit old mansion on St. Lo Drive, but it looked so elegant on film, so much better than it did in life. Most things did. A knight and his squire entered the frame. *Don Quixote*? *Ivanhoe*? While some of Bob's movies had dialogue, this one had only a musical score, and it quickly burst into a choreographed battle, with other knights emerging from the forest to challenge the hero. *Ivanhoe*. He and Bob were

212

infants when that film was first released, the version with the two Taylors, Elizabeth and Robert, but they had probably caught it in reruns, on the old *Picture for a Sunday Afternoon*. Had that been Channel 2 or Channel 11? He could no longer remember, but he did recall that there were two movies, at most, on Sunday afternoons, and people waited years for a big movie to make its way from the cinema to the television. Now movies were everywhere, all the time, available with one click of a computer mouse, on sale at the grocery store, in rental bins at McDonald's. This easy accessibility should cheapen the experience, but it somehow never did. Nothing could break the spell of a good movie.

On his screen, the eleven-year-old versions of Ivanhoe and his squire broke free and ran across the undulating hills of Clifton Park. Okay, he wasn't objective, but it seemed to him that Bob's camerawork was outstanding.

In the bedroom, Marie was snoring. He picked up the phone, called his contact.

'Have you seen the call sheet for tomorrow?'

'Yes, only—look, I'm not sure I should be doing this anymore. Someone was killed. There's a lot more attention.'

'I know,' he said. 'But that has nothing to do with us, does it?'

A short silence, as if the question was being considered. 'You had the code, to get into the building. I gave that to you weeks ago.'

'I never used it,' he said swiftly. 'As you pointed out to me, access to the building wasn't worth anything, if I couldn't get into the offices, and you said they were always locked tighter than a drum.'

'Of course, yeah, but—you can see why I'm creeped out. What if they find out I'm the one who gives you the information about the call sheet?'

'You told me the list is set up on a bcc, so they don't even see the addresses. Even if someone goes looking for it, they'll just think it was a mistake, an oversight.'

'I suppose. . . .'

He turned off the video player, and watched the CNN crawl on mute, relying on silence to get him what he wanted, an old teacher's trick. He could bring his classes to order simply by staring at the students, back in the day, although that had gotten more difficult toward the end of his time in the classroom. The children became so hard, so mean.

A resigned sigh. 'They're going to be at Green Mount Cemetery most of the day. With both Mann and Betsy.'

'Thank you—'

'Also, there's something else, something extra.'

'You already told me they'll be shooting Saturday to make up for the missed day. But I don't think I'm going to worry about that.' It was hard for him to get away on weekends. Besides, the person he needed was dead now.

'No, not shooting. Something else.'

'Yes?'

'You see, it's extra. Outside our agreement, which covers only the information on the call sheets and other production-related e-mails. So . . .'

A childhood taunt came back to him—*greedy guts*. 'How much do you want?'

'Fifty?'

The matter was open to negotiation, but he was

214

too tired to barter. The fact was, when you were going broke, small sums became less urgent, paradoxical as that might seem. With only a few months between him and an abyss of debt, he couldn't worry about the stray fifty here or there, especially if it led to his windfall. 'Fifty it is.'

'There's a memorial service Sunday, on the soundstage. For Greer. Everyone will be there. There's going to be security—they don't want any press—but I don't think they'll question anyone who claims to be family, and she's got some uncles and cousins. You could blend right in.'

This was good information, although not in the way she thought. He could definitely use this. 'Okay, look for an extra fifty in your pay envelope Monday.'

'I've been thinking—what will you do now? Without Greer, I mean. Didn't everything depend on her?'

'You let me worry about that.'

'I might figure out a solution to your problem. I might be able to help.'

The impudence! So now it was to be a partnership—and he didn't need or want a partner. He might not resent an extra fifty dollars here or there, but he wasn't sharing the jackpot with anyone.

'I really don't want you to worry. Good night, and look for your *bonus,* come Monday.'

FRIDAY

Chapter 23

The Starbucks barista seemed to know Ben Marcus, at least by sight and coffee preference, calling out his order before he reached the cash register. Hidden in a corner, Tess watched him, happy for the chance to observe an unwary Ben. He was always so *on* during their encounters—picking even his most sarcastic words with care. But maybe that was Ben's way of speaking to everyone. Although she couldn't hear what he was saying to the peppy young barista, Tess could tell from his expression that he was his usual arch self. If he was nervous about this meeting, it wasn't apparent. Last night, when Tess had called him on her own phone for a more substantive conversation, he had been caught off guard and had even stammered in a place or two. But in the intervening nine hours since he agreed to this meeting, he would have had time to think about what he wanted to say, to shape his story. He was, after all, a professional storyteller.

He doctored his mocha with extra sugar, then plopped down in the upholstered chair opposite Tess.

'Thanks,' he said, although neither his tone nor his expression indicated gratitude. 'For meeting me here, instead of the office. There's not much privacy there.'

'Is that how Greer found out you were sleeping with Selene?'

He seemed surprised that she was so direct—and a little relieved. Ben was probably used to

219

meetings that began with more smoke blowing and ass kissing.

'I suppose so,' he said, after a beat. 'I never really knew how Greer found out. She was sneaky that way.'

'And she used the information to force you to get her—well, which job? She was promoted twice, first to the production assistant's job in the writers' office, then to Flip's assistant. At what point did she play the Selene card?'

'Greer wasn't that direct.' Ben's characterization surprised Tess; she thought the girl had bordered on tactlessly blunt at times. Perhaps she was different with her bosses. 'She asked for my help, yes, but it was never a strict quid pro quo. Look, no one cares who Selene sleeps with.'

'If that's so, then who's keeping the tabloids in business?'

That earned a wan smile from Ben. 'I mean, no one on the production cares about Selene's love life, as long as she shows up for work on time. Underage drinking, breaking the drug laws of this country? That makes us nervous, because if she gets busted, we're not insured for that. But she can fuck anyone she wants to.' His own words seemed to give him pause. 'As long as it's someone or something that can give informed consent.'

Tess allowed herself the luxury of thought, of not coming back at Ben too quickly with another question. She had the same sensation that she had when speaking with Flip. She was being tricked, diverted—but from what? Alicia had suggested that Ben was Greer's protector, and Tess was curious about that dynamic. But the fact that Ben was sleeping with Selene was of interest to her because it meant he might have information that would confirm whether Selene was the source of the problems on the set. Why hadn't Flip asked his old friend what he knew about Selene, tried to use him as a double agent? Certainly, Ben's loyalties to Flip and the production had to trump this—Tess groped for a noun but found none. Relationship? Fling? Soulless carnal encounter? She settled, in her head, for *thing*.

'No one cares who Selene sleeps with,' she repeated. 'Does anyone care who Ben sleeps with?'

Bingo. He flushed, dropped his eyes to his coffee, began jiggling his foot as he had the other day.

'I would be really grateful,' he said, 'if you didn't mention this to Flip. Or Lottie, but only because she would tattle to Flip. I could give a fuck what Lottie thinks about my extracurricular activities.'

'But you don't want Flip to know? I thought guys talked freely about such things.'

'We've been friends a long time, since grade school. It gets complicated. Do you have friends like that?'

Tess shrugged. Of course she did, everyone did. But she wanted Ben to keep talking, building up enough momentum to run into some inadvertent truths.

'I love the guy. *Love*. We've been there for each other all our lives. Look, he has the name, the connections, and no one can match him when it comes to the big picture for a show. But he can't match me on the line-by-line writing. That's just the way it is. Flip has never envied my ability to write, and I've never wanted to be the son of Phil Tumulty—God knows, I saw how that fucker neglected Flip through much of his childhood. I mean, yeah, I took a summer job from him when I was twenty-one—I wasn't going to turn down my best connection in the business—but I was never blind to his flaws. Even so, it bugged Flip, that summer I worked on his dad's last movie here in Baltimore. He considered it a betrayal. That was the last serious fight we ever had. The only one.'

'Would he really care about you and Selene? He keeps telling me how happily married he is.'

Ben's jiggling foot, the tapping toe of denial, began working the floor beneath the table. 'Flip got married at twenty-three, to his college girlfriend. And he's determined to stay married to her, no matter what. It's like a religion with him, not repeating his father's mistakes. But that's not to say it's easy, saying no, especially when he has a partner, me, who's free and unfettered. Usually, he eggs me on, encourages me to be a wild man, then asks for all the details. But every now and then, he makes an arbitrary ruling that someone is off-limits. And the minute he does that . . .'

Tess faked sympathy. 'That's the one person you have to sleep with. So Flip told you to stay away from Selene?'

'Yeah.'

'Is that why you've been so quick to defend her whenever someone suggests she might be the cause of problems on the production?'

'Yes. I mean—no, I'm not so blinded by sex that I can't think rationally. But some of the stuff that happened—well, let's just say I know she wasn't involved. One time, when we had to evacuate set,

222

because someone set a fire in a city garbage can? We were in my trailer. That was tricky, getting out and not being seen.'

'Maybe that's not a coincidence. You being her alibi.'

Quick as Ben was, he needed a second to get Tess's meaning. 'Hey, I decided to pursue her, not the other way around.'

'That's what men always believe.'

'Are you trying to say that Selene set her sights on me, and let me think it was all my doing? That's pretty subtle for a twenty-year-old who can barely read a newspaper.'

Tess didn't have a particularly high opinion of Selene's book smarts, but she had a hunch that her boy-Q was in the genius stratosphere.

'Men always believe they're in charge, the author of their own lives. But, in my experience, women make a lot of things that happen, and let men think it was their idea.'

'Now *you're* being ridiculous.'

'The night that Greer was killed, Selene told you that she would find a way to dump me and meet you at your hotel room, right? Then she went to New York. She never had any intention of seeing you, but she made sure she knew where you were—alone, in your room, waiting. But what if the plan was to send someone to the offices that night to make some more mischief with the production? The file drawers were open, papers were strewn about. Police think that Greer's missing boyfriend did that to make it look like a burglary, but what if Greer interrupted the set gremlin and the person panicked?'

'File drawers were open?' Beneath the table,

Ben's feet were tapping so hard that he was practically doing a Mr. Bojangles buck-and-wing. 'But this was in Flip's office, right?'

It seemed an odd detail to fixate on. 'In Flip's office and the anteroom where Greer worked. As I said, the theory is that someone tried to make it look like a burglary after the fact.'

'What kind of burglar goes through files in the writers' office?'

'I didn't say it was a *good* plan. The point is, if this was part of the ongoing campaign against the production, then Selene's New York trip becomes a very visible alibi. Derek Nichole made a point of telling me he grew up in a tough part of Philadelphia, all but suggested that he was connected. And he did say that he wanted to help Selene.'

'Is she sleeping with him?'

'What?' Tess asked, even as she realized that Ben Marcus, for all his flippancy, was far more interested in Selene Waites than he wanted to admit, perhaps even to himself. 'Look, Ben—as I keep telling you, it's not my job to look into Greer's murder. But if there is an organized campaign of vandalism against the production, and Selene is involved—I think it would be a good idea for you to come clean with Flip about the relationship.'

He shook his head. 'I can't, I just can't.'

Tess remembered the online sexual harassment course she had been required to take as a condition of her contractual employment at Johns Hopkins night school. She had gotten a 93 percent and blamed her less-than-perfect score on a poorly worded question. 'Is it a firing offense? Sleeping with an actor?'

'Is—God, no, I'm not sure it's even possible to sexually harass an actor. Especially one who wants to get written out of the show. That's the one thing I *can't* do for Selene, and I made that clear early on. Although, I have to say, the networks are fucking the show over by switching the emphasis to her and making us keep Betsy as a character. Screwed up a lot of stuff we had planned for season two, if we get a pickup. Then again—without Selene, we won't have a season two or three. It's a real Hobson's choice.'

'Were your plans for the show in the'—she needed a second to pull up the jargon—'the bible?'

He seemed to find her use of the lingo amusing. 'Certainly, it was spelled out that Betsy would be left behind in the nineteenth century, where she belongs. Now she's going to follow Mann wherever time travel takes him. Sort of like Mary Steenburgen's character jumping into the time machine with H. G. Wells in *Time after Time*.'

'And there's only one bible?'

'One copy? God no.'

'One version, I mean. It's not a document that gets revised?'

'No, not really. It's a planning document, a blueprint for the pitch. Next season—if there is a next season—we'll take on some new writers, spread the work around, and we'll have to work up some pretty detailed beat sheets for them. But the bible's mainly for the network, when you're trying to sell the show. There's no reason to go back and change it. Why the interest in this kind of insider knowledge? You want to write for television?'

'God no,' she said reflexively.

'Then you're the only one.' He flapped a hand at the people sitting around them, as if they were so many flies he'd like to swat. 'I bet at least half the people here think they have a television show or a movie inside them. Of course, they don't want to do the grubby work of actually *writing* it. They just want to tell someone their idea and share the money, fifty-fifty. Which, by the way, they believe is incredibly generous on their part, because their idea, as they'll be the first to tell you, is a million-dollar idea. But here's the thing that civilians don't get—ideas are worthless.'

'I don't know,' Tess said. 'Some ideas have value. *E* equals *mc* squared, gravity. Those were kind of important.'

'It's the application of ideas that have value, even in the sciences. They don't give you a patent for the idea, they give you a patent for the execution of the invention. Television is the same way. It's not the idea behind *Mann of Steel* that got us a deal—'

That was easy enough for Tess to believe.

'—but our ability to execute it. Flip is an experienced show runner. I'm a writer with producing experience. We know how to make a television show. The idea is the easiest thing to have.'

Tess could see his point, although she was startled by Ben's fervency on the topic. He smacked his hands against the table as he spoke, creating a counterpoint to his still-dancing feet.

'At any rate, I've seen enough of television production to know it's not for me,' Tess said. 'You guys work longer days than anyone I know, and the

226

tedium—I wouldn't have the patience for it. It's worse than surveillance.'

Ben seemed mollified, or at least calmed by Tess's token respect. 'Sorry, I just thought—I mean, given the questions you were asking, about the bible and everything, I thought you were another screenwriting wannabe.'

'To throw some movie dialogue back at you— who would admit to being that?'

He continued to drum the table, but with less hostility. 'Don't tell me, don't tell me, don't tell me—*The Untouchables*. Sean Connery to Kevin Costner, when he says he's an ATF guy. You didn't get it word for word, though.'

Tess nodded. 'We watched it recently. Part of Lloyd's continuing education, although I'm not sure De Palma is the best influence on a kid we're trying to keep on the straight and narrow.'

'I like Lloyd,' Ben said. He seemed vaguely surprised by the concept. 'I'll help him, anyway I can. He really should be working with Lottie—he's clearly got more aptitude for the visuals than the words—but if *I* make that suggestion, she'll shoot it down as if it were skeet. So I'm going to plant that idea in Flip's head. Lloyd should be a P.A., work his way up on the production side of things, where his lack of a formal education won't matter as much. Television and film are still democratic that way. If you can do the job, no one cares about your degree or pedigree. I knew a kid, started as a P.A. in high school, and he's directing episodes of network television now. Ditto, if you *can't* do the job—a big-deal degree is worthless.'

For a moment, Tess almost liked Ben Marcus. But then she registered that was exactly what he

227

wanted. That he had, in fact, fastened on the topic of Lloyd's future to divert her from something he didn't want to discuss. Selene, Greer, Flip? It was like the childhood game of hot and cold, and Tess had been very hot there for a second, or at least warm. Now under the table Ben's feet were still, his hands calm.

'Ben?'

'Yes?'

'Last night, after we spoke, Selene and I had a little chat. She told me her relationship with you began three weeks ago.'

'Give or take. I didn't write it down in my diary, draw a big heart around the day, but, yeah, give or take, that's when it started.'

'Greer was already working as Flip's assistant by then.'

He was a bright guy. He didn't need for Tess to connect the dots for him, to point out that this meant much of what he said was bogus. He was so bright that, when caught in a lie, he didn't rush in with more words, or try to explain himself.

'That sounds right,' he said. 'You know what, you're good at continuity issues. You'd be a good script supervisor, if you put your mind to it. See, that's what I do—I help people. I'm lovable that way, but I wouldn't want it getting around.'

He grabbed his cup, rising to his feet so quickly that the small table rocked and Tess had to rescue her own cup of coffee before it toppled. 'See you around, Sam Spade. Don't take any wooden nickels.'

Chapter 24

As she left Starbucks, Tess once again had the sensation that an overstuffed sofa was following her down the sidewalk. Yes, there was Mrs. Blossom, trying to be inconspicuous on the south side of Baltimore Street. Tess couldn't fault her clothing—a large, flowery dress was not particularly out of place in downtown Baltimore—but there was something about Mrs. Blossom that drew the eye, a delicacy of movement, not unlike the tutu'ed hippos in *Fantasia*. Caught, she gave a cheerful wave, and dashed across the street to join Tess. For a large woman, she moved pretty fast.

'You only had to do the surveillance exercise *once*, Mrs. Blossom,' Tess said.

'But I keep getting caught,' she panted out, a little breathless from her sprint through traffic. 'Except the other night, but I lost you for part of the evening, so I didn't think I should count that.'

'The other night?'

'Yes, when you were with Selene Waites. And then you came out of the bar with Derek Nichole. I like him.' She frowned. 'Well, I liked him better, before he started doing movies with so much cursing. I don't like cursing.'

'You—you followed me to New York?' Tess had been trying to do a walk-and-talk, hurrying toward her car—and a meter that was due to expire any moment—but this conversation was worth slowing down for, even if it meant a twenty-seven-dollar parking fine. 'All the way in?'

'Yes, although it seemed kind of cheating

because you weren't driving, so you wouldn't have been as alert. I didn't go into the restaurant—'

Tess made a conscious effort not to smile at the thought of Mrs. Blossom trying to make her way into that achingly hip eatery. That would have been something to see. Then again, they might have mistaken her for the latest drag queen to play Edna Turnblad in Broadway's version of *Hairspray* and welcomed her as a star.

'And, you know, it's so hard to park in New York, I just kept circling. I know that's not a good technique—and if you had been in there a long time, I could have run out of gas—but I decided to *commit,* like you told me. I got lucky, too. I had just turned on the block when I saw you come out.'

'Did you pay attention to the time? Did you see him pick me up?'

Mrs. Blossom fished through her purse, a bright purple bag the size of a small suitcase, and pulled out a memo pad. 'It was about eleven-thirty when you went in, ten to midnight when you came out.' She looked up from the pad, her eyes sorrowful. 'Miss Monaghan, you looked like you'd been *drinking*. That doesn't seem very professional.' Mrs. Blossom consulted her memo pad again, all Joe Friday just-the-facts seriousness. 'At twelve-ten A.M.—should I use military time?'

'No, you can use A.M. and P.M.' Tess didn't want to bother with the math.

'At twelve-ten A.M., the Town Car arrived at a hotel.'

'Name of the hotel?'

'The SoHo Grand.'

That was the hotel where Selene had been seen drinking later, where Derek Nichole was staying.

'I found a parking place around the corner and went into the bar, off the hotel lobby. It was tricky, because the lobby is on the second floor, and I couldn't be sure I would see you coming and going, but I figured if I sat next to the window, I'd be able to see you leave. I went up there and had a nonalcoholic beer. It cost ten dollars! And they were so rude, made me wait forever, and it was *loud*. I don't know why people go to places like that. But I could see the lobby from where I sat, and pretty soon, Derek Nichole and Selene Waites showed up, and they were given one of the sofas, although the table said it was "reserved." She's so pretty in person. And little. Is she as sweet as she looks?'

'Hmmmmm,' Tess said, trying to be diplomatic. 'What did they do?'

'They came in and ordered drinks—a beer for him, a cocktail for her, although she kept drinking cranberry juice—and they were talking very low to each other, kind of serious. I tried to hear what they were saying, but I wasn't close enough. And then the bar closed, so I went outside and got in my car, and waited until I saw the Town Car come back. That was about four A.M., and this time, it was Mr. Nichole who brought you out.'

It was oddly embarrassing to think about Mrs. Blossom watching her drugged body being hauled around New York like a sack of potatoes. True, it wasn't her fault that she had been dosed with roofies—or ketamine or GHB—but it was still humiliating. Where had she been during the interval, in Derek Nichole's hotel room? If the two had wanted privacy, hadn't that put a crimp in their plans? Was Selene that desperate to drink

231

that she had to knock Tess out in order to party hearty? Nothing really added up. She thought about the multiple gossip items, her text messages to Ben—what was Selene doing?

'Wait a minute, Mrs. Blossom—are you sure Selene was drinking cranberry juice? The gossip columns said she was drinking it with vodka and Red Bull.'

'Oh, she ordered a drink, but she had a bottle of Nantucket Nectar with her, and she drank from that. The waitperson tried to give her a hard time about bringing in an outside beverage, so she tucked her bottle under the table and ordered a drink, but she kept sneaking sips from the bottle under the table and barely touched her drink.' She snorted. 'I don't blame her. They probably charge fifteen dollars for a glass of cranberry juice!'

They had arrived at Tess's parking spot, but she was too fascinated by Mrs. Blossom's story to worry about the meter. The woman may have signed up for the class to give herself something to do on Monday nights, but she seemed to be a bit of a prodigy. A woman such as Mrs. Blossom, properly trained, could learn to be so visible as to be invisible.

'Look,' Mrs. Blossom said, pointing skyward.

They were at the corner of Charles and Baltimore streets, where the downtown outpost of Johns Hopkins ran an old-fashioned electronic news ribbon around the top of the building. The headlines were written by the staff of the *Beacon-Light,* and they were well known throughout Baltimore for their wordy obtuseness and not infrequent grammatical errors. But the message that had caught Mrs. Blossom's eye was crystal clear to Tess: MAN WANTED IN TV SET MURDER KILLED BY POLICE IN STANDOFF.

Part of Tess's mind couldn't help deconstructing the headline. 'TV set murder'—that made it sound as if a large Magnavox had been the weapon. Besides, Greer hadn't been killed on set; she had died in the production office, which was across town from the soundstage. But even as she picked those nits, Tess had no problem discerning the larger meaning—Greer's boyfriend had been killed when police officers caught up with him. If running was a good marker of guilt, in Tull's worldview, then resisting arrest was an unsigned confession. So, a dunker for Tull. The obvious answer was the obvious answer.

She was happy for her friend but disappointed that she would never have a chance to talk to JJ Meyerhoff about his ex-fiancée, Greer, and whether she had any connection to *Mann of Steel*'s problems.

Chapter 25

Ben should be happy. Well, not happy—Greer was dead, and now her fiancé, poor fucker, God bless him, had gone down in a hail of bullets. But it tied everything up, neat as a bow, and Ben was in the clear. Which was only fair, because he hadn't actually *done* anything.

But what if someone else materialized? What if Greer had confided in someone? What if he was, in fact, in some sort of fiendishly creative hell where he had to live forever with the idea of

233

someone else popping up, full of . . . *insights*. That had been Greer's airy-fairy term. 'I had the most interesting insight.' Even Greer had seen his side of things, though. Then again, it was in Greer's interest to be persuaded, because it meant she could collect endless bennies from him with a relatively free conscience. It was a relief that she was gone. Like all blackmailers, she had already started angling for what she wanted *next*. The last few weeks, Greer had reminded Ben of *The Leech Woman,* a B horror film in which a woman found the elixir to eternal youth. The trick was that it required killing a man and harvesting some gland, and each hit of the youth juice provided a shorter lease on wrinkle-free immortality, so the woman had to kill more and more frequently, until she finally killed a woman in desperation, which turned out to *accelerate* the aging process. Greer had been getting greedy that way, insatiable.

But that wasn't what killed her, Ben reminded himself. She had been killed, fittingly enough, by one of the people she had stepped on as she climbed her little ladder.

'If *Mann of Steel* gets a pickup for season two,' she had said in the car just the other day, on the way to set, 'do you think an associate producer credit would be appropriate?' Then quickly, before he could answer, she conceded the impossibility of her own ambition. 'Oh, never mind, I guess I'm being silly.' Ben would have been charmed if he hadn't remembered, in vivid, glaring detail, how she had played the same trick with her current position. 'I know I just got promoted to the writers' office, but I wonder—could I be considered to fill Alicia's job, now that she's been let go? I guess not, that's silly, although I am the only one who's been on board since preproduction, and I'm the one who knows all of Lottie's systems—no, it's ludicrous, forget I ever said anything.'

Ben hadn't forgotten exactly, but he had thought that Greer had talked herself into seeing that she was pushing too hard, too fast. He had been shocked when Greer became more pointed a few days later: 'Look, you'll see that I get an interview, right? With Flip? And you'll put in a good word for me? I mean, that's not too much to ask, is it? After—well, I just thought I had demonstrated to you what a conscientious employee I am, that I am absolutely loyal to the pro-duction.'

God, it had probably been only a matter of time before he was one of the bodies who fell under those sensibly shod size seven feet.

He should be happy. Or something. Whatever he felt, he had to start revising Flip's version of 107, the penultimate ep. Flip had brought it in at sixty pages, twelve too long, knowing that Ben would fix it. *Yassuh, yes, Master Flip, I'll tighten up your flabby-ass script.* He sighed, glancing at the bedside clock radio, thinking about the all-nighter ahead. Now that Monaghan knew about his affair with Selene, what did he have to lose? Why couldn't Selene just come over here, while Monaghan or her cohort waited in the lobby? Isn't that what a real bodyguard would do? Sure, he had implied that he would stop if Monaghan wouldn't rat him out to Flip, but he hadn't *promised.* Okay, the idea was crazy, but he could call Selene, flirt with her. Maybe phone sex? He selected her name from his address book but ended up going straight to voice mail. When had they spoken last, outside work? He couldn't remember. When had she last called or texted him? It was the night Greer was killed, the night she went to New York. Since then—nothing.

Suddenly, it seemed essential to walk to Little Italy, the littlest Little Italy he had ever seen, and grab a cup of real espresso to power him through the night of writing ahead. Vaccaro's was only a mile or so, and it was a nice night for a walk—crisp, autumnal. The fact that Vaccaro's was blocks away from Selene's apartment—well, that was mere coincidence, didn't enter into his decision at all.

Within an hour, he found himself standing on the sidewalk across the street from her building, feeling like the most pathetic sap that ever lived. He wanted to scream her name, hold a boom box above his head in the pouring rain, all the clichés. Instead, he stood there, blowing on his espresso, wordless. And what could be more impotent than a writer without words?

*　　　*　　　*

Johnny Tampa's bedtime ritual took almost an hour, but he was proud of the fact that he used inexpensive products—cold cream on his face, generic shampoo, the drugstore knockoff of Oil of Olay. His mother had raised him to believe in thrift, and he had never broken faith with her ways. Some of his peers had, and where were they now? Johnny may have endured a long dry spell, work-wise, but he would never have to worry about money. The hardest part had always been reconciling his private habits with his public image, which demanded a certain amount of extravagance. It killed him, buying a first-class ticket with his own money, but he had to do it from time to time, lest he be seen flying coach. He couldn't afford being marked as a loser. He had to keep up the pretense that he had been waiting for the right job all these years.

The television droned in the background, keeping him company. One of the cable channels was doing an all-weekend marathon of *The Boom Boom Room* with 'extras'—shopworn trivia that would be old news to diehard fans, and who but diehard fans would watch a marathon of *The Boom Boom Room*? Besides, some of the so-called trivia was just plain lies. He and his mom had not lived in their car when they first went out to Los Angeles. They had a perfectly nice apartment, in a building favored by lots of young actors. And, yes, he had been in the Mickey Mouse Club, but not the cool one, which spawned Britney, Justin, Christina, et al. He had been in the lame 1970s version. But no reason to sweat that inaccuracy, given that it made people think he was a lot younger than he was. Then again, if people thought he was doing the Mickey Mouse Club back in the early 1990s, they might conclude he had aged horribly.

It was so odd, watching his young self. He was a better actor now, no doubt, and his face was more interesting. But who knew that age was so *thickening*? Not just the waistline, but everything— face, features, even his feet. Then again, some of his peers seemed to get thinner, and that wasn't attractive either. They looked gaunt, dried up. Maybe it was just his imagination, but it seemed the previous generation of actors—Nicholson, Connery, Hackman—had aged much better.

Depressed, he grabbed the remote by the sink and clicked away, running through the channels rapid-fire. He rested for a moment on the news story about Greer's boyfriend, getting killed when he wouldn't surrender. Man, that was weird. But then, other people's passions always struck Johnny as mildly ludicrous. In a movie or a television show, when both people were hot, you could get it. Besides, it was in the script. But just two ordinary people, getting all crazy over each other? Johnny had been married briefly in his twenties and taken a big financial hit in the divorce, and that had been enough to decide for him that he didn't want anything long-term, ever again. In California, he used an escort service—very discreet, with nice girls, ones who weren't too hard or used up, and he was careful to keep things relatively kink-free, lest he ever show up on a client list; you'd never catch him having to explain some girl dressed up like a Brownie. God, he would kill for a brownie. Maybe he should find someone, sublimate the hunger with sex. Here in Baltimore, he had assumed he would hook up with someone in the production, but it hadn't happened. Yet. He still thought the scary blonde, the one who had pretended not to know who he was, had potential. Yes, she was kind of terrifying, but he found that attractive in a woman.

But she was assigned to watch Selene, and he would be crazy to try and get close to anyone who was part of Selene's camp.

Fully oiled and moisturized, he slid into bed, switching the television back to his own marathon. The trivia box popped up beneath his chin, his beautifully sharp chin: *Where is he now*? The answer was provided after a string of commercials for erectile dysfunction cream and some magic stain remover. 'Johnny Tampa has retired from Hollywood, but a comeback is rumored for 2008.'

You betcha, he thought.

*   *   *

'That was fast,' Marie said sleepily, watching the ten o'clock news. 'People will get mad, wait and see.'

'People will get mad because they solved a murder?'

'They'll say that it was because it was a white girl, and she worked on that television show, that they never put that much effort into the drug murders. But it's so obvious that the boyfriend must have done it.'

He shouldn't ask any questions, shouldn't draw the conversation out. Change the topic, change the channel. But he couldn't help himself. 'Obvious because he ran away and didn't surrender?'

'Exactly. It would make a good *Law and Order* episode, only it would need more twists. On television, the boyfriend wouldn't be guilty. It would be someone else.'

Change the topic, change the topic, change the topic. 'Who?'

'Why, someone with the production. Like, she'd be having an affair with her boss, and maybe his wife found out. Or that skinny little actress girl

239

killed her because . . . she wouldn't sell her urine so she could pass the contractual drug test.'

'The actress in the movie has a contractual drug test?' News to him, but Marie often knew such things, thanks to her steady diet of magazines.

'Not in real life. I'm making stuff up. Like you and Bob did, when we were younger. Remember? I never said anything out loud because you thought I was just the stupid little sister, but I would be doing my homework at the dining room table while you talked in the kitchen. You had the best ideas.'

'Bob did. I could barely keep up with him.'

'Bob added the flourishes, fleshed them out. But all the ideas started with you. Bob always gave you credit.'

'Talking about Bob makes me sad.' *And anxious, so very anxious.*

'I'm sorry.'

Only he was not thinking of Bob just now but of Marie, the Marie he re-met the summer he and Bob graduated from college, the Marie who had somehow outgrown her scabby knees and pigtails and turned into a really striking girl. Not exactly beautiful, but sexy. The early 1970s had suited her. He supposed he should have realized then that one dramatic transformation indicated there could always be another. If it had been hard to find little Marie in that long-haired girl, then it was impossible to see the traces of twenty-one-year-old Marie in the puffy features and swollen ankles of the woman lying next to him on the sofa. And yet, he didn't love her any less. The case could be made that he loved her more than ever, especially since they had lost Bob. *Oh, Bob—why didn't you*

240

come to me earlier, tell me the truth sooner? Why did you let it get so out of hand, why did you lie to me?

'*Law and Order* always has a second twist, in the second part,' he said to Marie. 'A legal maneuver, a conflict of interest. So there would have to be a third thing, something really mysterious.'

'Like what?'

'I haven't a clue. As you said, Bob was the one who made my ideas work.'

'But you had good ideas, too,' she said, her voice soft with sleep. She would be asleep before the weather forecast. He couldn't carry her to bed anymore, but he would shake her gently, guide her there, as if she were a sleepwalker. 'You always had the best ideas.'

Oh, yes, he was just teeming with good ideas. They were in this fix because of his good ideas, because he thought he knew better than Bob how to go about things.

Stop, his mind advised him, in the cadence of a telegram. Had he ever received a telegram, or did he know of them only via the movies and cartoons? Had he ever lived a life, or was he still waiting for life to start? Fate had given him a chance to make things all right. Stop. Stop. Stop.

Why was it taking so long for Marie to fall asleep tonight?

*   *   *

Lottie sat in her office, free at last to still her mind and try to absorb the news. Alone, she allowed her legs to swing free, kicking against her chair, a little-kid habit she was careful to police around others, because she knew it made her look cute, precious. But it was going on eleven-thirty, the end of a long and turbulent day. She should feel relieved, not anxious. Not only was Greer's murder essentially solved, but there hadn't been an incident on set for almost a week—unless you counted Johnny Tampa's complaint that someone had mailed him an unflattering tabloid article, and no one was taking that seriously—except Johnny. No fires, literal or figurative, to put out, no locals trying to State-and-Main them, no snafus with permits. Even the weather had been kind, beautiful October day after beautiful October day. The production had been blissfully uneventful—except, of course, for Greer's death, and the police had removed that from the movie's moral balance sheet as well.

Lottie wished she could be as quick to absolve the production. If she had hired JJ, would that have made a difference? She told herself that a man who would kill his ex-fiancée—or girlfriend, or wife—wasn't susceptible to cause and effect. A violent man would always find a reason to act violently. Still, Lottie couldn't help thinking that the production had changed Greer. The young woman who had volunteered to work for free on the pilot had been so eager, so sweet. Had she been changed by her proximity to Flip, by her glimpses into the money and perks provided by such a lifestyle?

They hadn't found the murder weapon, but that didn't seem to bother the police. It bothered Lottie, though, as did the memory of Flip's trashed office. Why hadn't JJ taken anything if he wanted to make the incident look like a burglary? Flip's Emmy, for example. It wasn't hockable, but you

242

could imagine someone trying to sell it on eBay. Flip's iPod, in the dock next to his computer. Okay, so the killer wasn't really a burglar, and he hadn't thought like a burglar. He was an unstable young man, hopped up on adrenaline, desperate to cover his tracks.

Still, something tugged at Lottie's logical, meticulous mind. Part of the reason that Lottie hadn't hired JJ was because he was so obviously pussy-whipped. He hadn't wanted the job, he all but admitted, but Greer had pushed him into applying for it. He had smiled goofily at the mere mention of Greer's name, and it was clear that he thought her a tremendous prize, that he was the luckiest man in the world to have her as his future wife. It had been cute, if unfathomable. Really, if you had asked Lottie then where she thought the relationship was headed, she would have predicted that Greer was more likely to kill *him* one day. Or, more correctly, shed him for his lack of ambition, his limited potential—which was exactly what happened, she reminded herself now. Greer, dazzled by Hollywood, broke up with her loser boyfriend, and he lost it. End of story.

Well, the good news was that their troubles were over. They could probably fire the Monaghan woman, save that expense. It had been ridiculous, hiring a watcher for Selene, given how much they already paid for security on set.

Checking her computer clock, she used her office phone to call home, where it was only eight-thirty. She couldn't bear to talk to her children over the unreliable cutting-in, cutting-out buzz of a cell phone. It was hard enough to have a conversation with four-year-old Angela, the

243

younger one. She could never decide which was worse—Angela's distant, distracted mode, when she prattled about the day's events and seemed slightly vague about who Lottie was, or the dramatic, melancholic wail: *When are you coming home, Mommy? I miss you.* To-night, Angela told her a long, hard-to-follow story about preschool and a goldfish, but Lottie had hung on to every word. Her seven-year-old, Topper, was stoic, inured to her absences—and that was more painful still.

'They're fine,' Jason assured her, taking the phone. Perfect Jason, as he was known among her friends and family, P.J. for short—good-looking and strong and capable. One of Lottie's more tactless friends had even wondered if it was fair of Lottie to take a six-footer out of the dating pool. 'That's a foot more than you need.' Of course, Lottie saw it differently—she had to marry up, literally, so her children would have a fighting chance to escape the curse of her genes. How she had worried, every year, over the height percentiles. So far, both children were reliably above the eightieth percentile, but she had been fairly normal, too, until puberty. Jason said she worried too much, but show her a unit production manager who didn't. It was practically the job description.

'If we get a pickup,' Lottie said to him now, after checking in with both children, 'we could live here. We could live like kings, in fact. You can buy a Victorian mansion for the price of a two-bedroom bungalow in Glendale.'

'It will all work out, even if the show doesn't go,' Jason said. 'You always find a gig. You're in demand.'

'I want a gig that allows me to live with my family full-time,' she said. 'I want to look after my own children, not tend to those who simply behave childishly. But—*shit*.'

'What, babe?'

'Fire.'

'You had to fire someone *again*?'

'No, there—I think—look, I have to go.'

Smoke was creeping under the door, lazily, almost prettily. Her mind detached briefly, as if she were watching an effect created for the screen. *Nicely done. Sinister, yet not over the top.* She willed herself to be calm and approached the door with a tentative hand. It wasn't warm to the touch. Cautiously, she opened it, peering out. The hallway was filled with smoke, although she couldn't pinpoint the origin. She groped her way toward the elevator, pushed the buttons, then remembered that she should take the stairs. Where was the stairwell? At the other end of the hallway. She crouched low, practically crawling. The smoke seemed to be thinning, but that could be wishful thinking on her part.

Once outside, she gulped for air, and it was almost as if she could taste it, drink it down. She walked to the edge of the parking lot before she called 911 from the cell phone in her pocket. The fire station was mere blocks away, and it was a great comfort to be able to hear the sirens start seconds after she called, although it was also unnerving, standing alone in the parking lot. She couldn't see any flames, but where there was smoke. . . . What could be burning? Electrical malfunction? *If the fire had been set*—her mind

245

didn't want to follow that train of thought, but she couldn't stop it—*if the fire had been set, someone else was here, or had been here.* Yet her car was the only one on the lot. She locked herself in it, but that didn't make her feel safe enough. She drove a few blocks away and parked in a busier, better-lit area, listening to the sirens drawing closer.

PART THREE

DESPERATE LIVING

SUNDAY

Special to the Beacon-Light

Firefighters and police were summoned yet again to the production offices of Mann of Steel *late Friday—for what turned out to be a homemade smoke bomb.*

Only one person was on the premises, unit production manager Lottie MacKenzie, and no one was injured in the incident, which appears to be another in a series of pranks that have plagued the production.

Asked if she thought the smoke bomb had been planted by someone unhappy about Mann of Steel—*the troubled production's detractors include some community activists, local historians, and disgruntled steelworkers—MacKenzie said she was sure it was an isolated incident, 'Probably a prank by kids, nothing more.'*

Firefighters have been called three times before to the Mann of Steel *set, although always when the production was filming in Mount Vernon and Fells Point.*

More seriously, the production office was the site of a murder earlier this week, but police are adamant that there is no connection, given that the suspect, John 'JJ' Meyerhoff, was killed early Friday in a standoff with police.

'Still, every incident like this is just another example of Mann of Steel's *drain on our resources,' said Mandy Stewart, a community activist who has complained about the inconveniences caused by the production when it's on location in Fells Point. 'They take and they take and they take, but they're not putting anything back.'*

251

Chapter 26

'And Greer said, in that terribly earnest way she had, "But it's *chartreuse,* Mr. Tumulty."'

The mourners laughed in that delayed rueful way common to memorial services, as if they needed a second to grant themselves permission. Tess had to admit—Flip was a good public speaker, and he had found the perfect tone for his eulogy. Thanks to him, the service was doing what a memorial or funeral *should* do, but so often didn't: respecting the memory of the deceased while cheering people slightly, but not too much. In Flip's experienced hands, Greer's story became one of a hardworking local girl who hadn't been afraid to reveal her ignorance if it meant doing her job better. It was a nice story. Tess wondered if any of it was true. She wondered if it mattered if it was true. Probably not. God forbid that anyone tell the truth at her funeral. Maybe she should write that down somewhere, leave it behind in a safe-deposit box with the will she had yet to write: *No truth telling at my funeral!*

Flip's achievement was all the more remarkable when one considered how few genuine friends Greer had among the cast and crew of *Mann of Steel.* As for her family—there wasn't much, not here, just her mother, two stocky men who appeared to be her brothers, and a few older women, aunts or cousins. And no high school friends, Tess decided, studying the crowd. No friends of any stripe? She glimpsed Alicia Farmer in the back, which seemed curious. She had been so candid about disliking Greer. Was she here to *network*? With Greer dead, would she try to persuade Lottie that it was Greer who had released the proprietary materials? A few months at Charm City Video could make a woman pretty desperate.

Flip paused, taking a sip of water, and Selene's voice jumped into the silence—that is, the ring tone on Selene's cell phone, blaring her pallid cover of 'Call Me,' made its presence known, buried deep as it was in her huge leather bag, a designer brand Tess couldn't identify, although she was fairly sure it cost as much as her first car, even after adjusting for inflation. Before Selene could grab the phone, Whitney literally slapped the girl's hand, reached into the bag, turned it off, and then put it in her own purse. Tess had other reasons for wanting Whitney with her today, but chaperoning Selene through a memorial service had turned out to be a job that required both of them. Just getting her properly dressed had taken hours, as Selene's idea of suitable garb ranged from a thigh-high skirt to an overly theatrical black Dior suit. The suit would have been appropriate under some circumstances, but it made Selene look like a little girl playing dress-up—a Eurotrash princess or the grieving widow of a president cut down in his prime. 'No one has ever confused Tess or me with Diana Vreeland,' Whitney had hissed at one point, 'but I think even *Vogue* agrees that funerals require *panties*.' In the end, they had managed to assemble a safe-for-Baltimore outfit of navy dress and cashmere cardigan.

'I can't be photographed in this!' Selene had protested. 'I'll be on the "What was she thinking?"

253

list in the *Star*.' Tess pointed out that because the memorial was on private property, the landlord was within his rights to restrict press access, just as he had forced the steelworkers to hold their informational picket on the narrow strip of grass alongside the parking lot. As it turned out, press in this case was a lone *Beacon-Light* reporter, juggling a notebook and a video camera, and two of the local television crews, no reporters in tow. Would the memorial have attracted more attention if Greer's homicide was still considered an open case? Or was Baltimore simply getting blasé about Hollywood? Tess wanted to believe it was the latter.

Flip finished with John Donne, his only misstep to Tess's mind. It seemed a bit clichéd, and not at all central to Greer's life. Whitney, on the other side of Selene, must have had the same thought, for she passed Tess a note: *With Greer dead and no replacement, he probably doesn't have anyone to look up appropriate poetry for memorial services.* On Tess's right, Lloyd frowned, embarrassed for them. Lloyd took funerals seriously.

Flip asked Greer's mother if she wanted to say anything, but she shook her head. She looked so *old*. Based on Greer's age, Tess calculated that Mrs. Sadowski could have been as young as forty-five, as old as sixty-five if Greer had been what was once called a change-of-life baby, but she definitely *looked* as if she fell into the high end of that range. Her hair was gray, the kind of faded, washed-out gray that appeared to have given up on color out of sheer exhaustion, her face weathered and haggard. She had an understandably shell-shocked expression, and although a handkerchief

254

was balled up in her fist, she had yet to cry that Tess could see. She just kept squeezing the handkerchief tighter and tighter.

'Well,' Flip said, caught off guard by the mother's refusal to speak, which he clearly had been counting on for his big finale. 'I guess we should, um, eat.'

*   *   *

Next to the 'chapel,' which had been created in one of the unused corners of the cavernous soundstage, a local caterer had set up an elaborate spread. Given the circumstances, someone—the set designer or art director—had made the impromptu catering hall pretty, draping dark cloths and hanging a large blowup of a photograph of Greer, bent over her clipboard. The photo had clearly been taken on set, as Selene was in the foreground, yet the eye was drawn to Greer, who was in sharper detail. The photo was, in fact, extraordinarily good, very well framed, arresting in a way that Tess couldn't define for herself.

'Selene, who took that photo?' she asked.

'That guy. What's-his-name. Somebody. I'm dying for a cigarette. Can I go outside?'

'In a few minutes,' Tess said, conscious of her other agenda. She, Whitney, and Selene needed to be conspicuously in the thick of things, at least for a while.

She continued to study Greer, mostly forehead and hair in the shot. Tess remembered the young woman who had fished her out of the water, a mere week ago. Like Alicia Farmer—who had slipped out as soon as the service was over, clearly

255

anxious not to mingle—Tess couldn't pretend that she cared for Greer. In fact, she had found her rather obnoxious. But, no, you wouldn't wish someone dead for that, or even for the annoyance of being overly ambitious. *The obvious answer is the obvious answer,* she reminded herself. Greer broke up with her fiancé, and he killed her. Happened all the time.

Flip was steering Greer's mother through the buffet line, helping her fill her plate. Whitney followed with Selene, picking the most fattening foods in the spread, which included miniature crab cakes, deviled eggs, and a ten-layer cake in the Smith Island style. Lottie, alone in a corner, looked miserable. Grieving Greer or the cost of this shindig? Tess immediately felt bad about her own snarky thoughts, remembering the scare that Lottie had experienced Friday night. It had turned out to be a smoke bomb, like two of the other incidents on location. But, innocuous as the homemade smoke bomb may have been, its presence meant someone had broken into the offices after hours. That was genuinely troubling. Tess thought they should change the code, but the management company didn't want to inconvenience its long-term tenants for the sake of the short-term *Mann of Steel.* Lottie had admitted to Tess that she had been a hard-ass in negotiating the lease, and the management company couldn't wait for them to vacate. If they did get a pickup, they wouldn't be coming back to Tide Point.

Tess saw Lloyd across the warehouse, giving one of Greer's relatives a tour of the set itself, explaining various technical details—the drops used to create views through 'windows,' the lights

256

that could mimic day or night. Tess was amazed at how much Lloyd had absorbed in his first week at work, but she was even more stunned at his unflagging enthusiasm. True, it had only been a week, but she had never seen Lloyd excited about anything, except certain action films and, on occasion, a chicken box from one of his old haunts.

The reception was breaking down now into its natural subsets—cast and crew in one cluster, Greer's family in another, Ben off by himself, a can of soda clutched in his hand. Tess saw another gray, haggard-looking woman moving toward Greer's mother and assumed it was one of the relatives, although she didn't remember seeing this woman during the service. But when the woman spoke to Mrs. Sadowski, whatever she said caused Greer's mother to reel back so quickly that Flip just missed having a plate of food smashed into his shirtfront.

'You have some nerve,' Mrs. Sadowski rasped at the woman. 'Coming here, to ask me that.'

'You won't talk to me on the phone, so what am I supposed to do? It was his property, plain and simple, should have been given back weeks ago. He owes on it. You want me to make payments on an engagement ring that your daughter wouldn't give back, when everyone knows she should've? My son is dead, too.'

'He broke up with her,' Mrs. Sadowski shrilled. 'You don't have to give it back under those circumstances. Especially when he killed her.'

'He broke up with her because she was cheating on him. That's different. And we'll never know what really happened, will we?'

Even as Tess moved forward, anxious to help

257

Flip keep order, her mind was stumbling over that fact. *He broke up with her* . . . but Greer had told everyone at work that it was the other way around. Saving face? Or had she lied to her mother? And, wait—cheating? Greer was cheating on her fiancé? With whom?

But she didn't have the luxury of sorting out her thoughts just now, not with Mrs. Sadowski flinging a plate of food into the face of JJ Meyerhoff's mother, who let out a banshee wail and pushed back, so that Mrs. Sadowski was propelled into Flip, who landed backward on the buffet table, which went down in a heap under his weight, the ten-layer cake landing on his chest.

*   *   *

Ben had been looking for an opportunity to sneak out, and he couldn't have asked for a sweeter moment than the mother melee. Man, it felt as if he had been waiting for this moment for weeks, although Greer had been dead barely four days. Well, he supposed he should be grateful it was a service, not an actual funeral or, worse, a viewing. He found those barbaric. But an open casket probably hadn't been an option after what Greer's ex had done to her.

And it was JJ, right? It had to be JJ. Because if it was someone else, then someone else knew.

Before the service began, Ben had made a point of introducing himself to Greer's mother, clasping her shoulder. Put a house-dress on Mrs. Sadowski, and she wouldn't have been out of place in a Dorothea Lange portrait. Someone should show Selene this face, let her see what a lifetime of

258

smoking could do to one's complexion.

'Mrs. Sadowski,' he said, extending his hand. 'Ben Marcus. I worked with Greer. We're so sorry this happened.'

She gave him a look, but it was dull and glazed over. His name didn't seem to mean anything to her. Greer hadn't spoken of him to her mother. *Good.* For once, he had never been happier to be lost in Flip's shadow, just the sidekick.

And now here he was, literally lost. He could never find his way in Baltimore, especially outside the Beltway. It took him almost an hour to locate the apartment that Greer had shared with her boyfriend up until a month ago. Luck was with him, for once—it was a so-called garden apartment on a split-level, the windows on the front barely above the ground, but with a small patio on the rear. Once, while researching a cop show, he had read that sliding doors could be rocked open. The information had seemed dubious, but he tried, and the door gave way with surprising ease.

Only maybe it wasn't so surprising. Someone had already been here. The place was a wreck. Had the boyfriend stopped here on his way out of town? Drawers and cabinets had been pulled open, sofa cushions tossed. In the narrow galley kitchen, all the items from beneath the sink had been left on the floor.

Flip's office had been ransacked, too—stop, don't think about that, it's crazy.

He found his way to the bedroom, which was even worse—the mattress flipped, clothing scattered everywhere. Whoever had been here seemed to have begun in a fairly systematic way, then become increasingly antic. The mother had

259

said something about a ring, but Greer had worn the ring even after the breakup. Besides, JJ almost certainly hadn't returned here after Greer was dead. Police would have been watching the place. Someone else had been here, looking for something. The same something that Ben wanted? How could that be? There was no one alive who knew of its existence—right? Greer had sworn to him that it was their secret, that no one else knew, not even her fiancé.

There was no percentage in staying here. He went out the way he had come in, realizing that the patio door had opened for him so magically because someone else had jimmied it before. When? Days ago, hours ago, minutes ago? He tried to walk nonchalantly to his car, just a guy in a suit, passing through a suburban parking lot. *Jesus, that woman was morbidly obese.* How do people get like that? And if you had the misfortune to weigh three hundred pounds, why would you wear a huge flowery dress with a purple belt emphasizing your non-existent waist? He waved at her, figuring that the more attention you drew to yourself, the less likely people were to remember you.

*   *   *

Tess had set her cell on silent for the service and then forgotten about it, what with helping to clean ten-layer cake off Flip and trying to get the dueling mothers to a point where the police wouldn't have to be called. The plan had been to let the reception take the place of a late lunch, but with most of the food on the floor, they ended up at Chili's, Lloyd's favorite restaurant. Crow had made a lot of headway with Lloyd's taste in films but virtually none with his taste in food. Tess didn't mind. She shared Lloyd's love of Chili's nachos. She was helping herself to the wonderfully cheesy, gooey concoction when she felt something vibrating close to her thigh.

'Yes, Mrs. Blossom?'

'You were right!' The woman screamed with such glee that Tess had to hold the phone away from her ear. 'He left the soundstage and went to the girl's apartment. But he didn't stay long, not even five minutes. And I peeked in the windows after he left, and the place is trashed. *Trashed*. He couldn't have possibly done it, not so quick. So someone else was there, too.'

'Did he see you?'

'Yes, but not in a way that counts. He waved at me, going to his car, but he clearly thought I was just some dumb lady who lived there. Then he drove back to the Tremont.' She laughed, and Mrs. Blossom's laugh, even on her cumbersome, clunky cell phone, was a thing of wonder, a sweet, high bubble of sound that had been held captive far too long. 'This was *fun*. I hope you have more things like this for me to do. I don't even care about the extra credit.'

'Remember, Mrs. Blossom, you're the only student who has qualified for extra assignments, so keep this to yourself when we meet tomorrow. I wouldn't want the other students to get jealous.' Actually, Tess was trying to work out the ethics of using Mrs. Blossom this way. The woman was a surveillance prodigy. Maybe Tess should put her on the payroll when the semester was over.

Lloyd, who had been apprised of the setup,

261

looked up expectantly. 'So he left the viewing and went to Greer's apartment, just as you thought he would.'

'The weird thing is—someone else had already been there.' Tess was thinking of her own trip to Wilbur Grace's home, how she had found the window open. Yes, the neighborhood kids had been using it as a makeout pad, but there was still that rectangle of dust in the armoire, the VCR or DVD player that had gone missing, and maybe not because it was so easy to pawn. Then there was the office, ransacked the night of Greer's death, and the smoke bomb Friday. 'What is everyone looking for?'

'The black bird,' Lloyd said, in a remarkably good imitation of Kasper Gutman, as he had been embodied—so fully, magnificently embodied—by Sydney Greenstreet. 'Or maybe it's one of them Hitchcock MacMuffins.'

Tess took a sip of beer. Lloyd had failed the GED on his first attempt, but Crow had insisted at the time that it wasn't lack of ability but a lack of interest that had undermined him.

'Are you saying a *MacGuffin* is irrelevant?' she asked, supplying the correct word without calling too much attention to it. That was how Crow corrected Lloyd.

'Of course, that's what it always is,' Lloyd said, rolling his eyes at her ignorance. One week as an unpaid intern and he was Cecil B. De Mille. 'Besides, Greer was killed by her boyfriend and he's dead. So who cares what's in her apartment?'

Out of the mouth of—well, not babes, but a pretty savvy seventeen-year-old. Lloyd had a point: If Greer was killed by her boyfriend, who was now dead, what possible treasure or item could have at least two people looking for it so frenziedly?

Two people. Tess shuddered, realizing after the fact how heedlessly she had exposed Mrs. Blossom. Granted, she didn't think Ben was a threat to anyone—except, perhaps, the television viewers of America. But she couldn't be sure to what lengths a second person might go to find this thing, this object, this *MacMuffin*.

Chapter 27

Marie was snoring—full-out, raucous snores, nothing delicate or ladylike. She would be horrified if she knew what she sounded like, but he found it endearing. Snoring was the kind of normal problem that other married couples had. Snoring, stealing the covers, leaving the seat up, nagging. These were the sorts of things a person could confide to a friend, over a beer at the local tavern. If a person actually had any friends. His only friend was dead. Besides, he never had been able to talk to Bob about Marie, the one drawback of marrying his best friend's sister. He never even discussed her illness with Bob, which was strange, as Bob might have been one of the few sympathetic ears he could find in a world where almost everyone else thought Marie was simply a lazy good-for-nothing.

It was fifteen years since Marie was diagnosed, and he realized in hindsight that her problems went much further back. Probably all the way back to her childhood, he knew now, but he hadn't been paying close attention to Bob's kid sister back in the day. *High-strung,* they said then, *delicate,* and he found both terms more on point than the rather bland 'panic attack' that the first doctor had scrawled on her chart. Now the official papers that flew back and forth read 'APD'—avoidant personality disorder. He preferred the old-fashioned term *agoraphobia,* which translated literally as fear of the marketplace, because it seemed to be the best definition of what ailed Marie. She didn't want to engage with the world of the market, i.e., *work.*

Maybe it was only fair. Marie, born in the early 1950s, had already formed her ideas of what a woman's life should be when the concept of women's liberation put everything up for grabs. She wanted none of it, and had explained as much to him, in their early days of going together. 'Any woman who has ever snapped a garter is never going to burn her bra,' she said, utterly earnest. It had made him laugh. They had been sitting across from each other at the old Pimlico Hotel, having cocktails and feeling very grown up—he at twenty-four, she just twenty-two. He had liked the fact that she was old-fashioned, that she wanted to be a homemaker. Since graduating from UB, he and Bob had been sleeping with the early hippie girls around Mount Vernon, but he had known that was only temporary. Easy sex, no strings, empty as hell. When Marie graduated from Towson, teaching degree in hand, he realized she was a girl he would have to take seriously, and not just because she was Bob's little sister. She was the Real Thing.

Marie didn't actually like teaching, as it turned

out. She didn't like kids. She took a job at Social Security, and people assumed they were trying for a family that simply never arrived. People were kinder then, it seemed to him, with only parents and relatives daring to ask nosy questions about when they would hear the patter of little feet. With everyone but Bob, they had floated the impression that they were waiting patiently for fate to smile on them. And when Marie started visiting doctors about her growing little assembly of symptoms— dizziness, heart palpitations, shortness of breath, a reluctance to ride elevators, her fear of malls, her gnawing worry that she was going to black out while driving—people had assumed that the various specialists she consulted over at Johns Hopkins were going to help her conceive. They didn't know that Marie was visiting the old wing, the home of the Phipps Clinic, where she was told for years that it was all in her head and all she needed was traditional psychotherapy and that would be seventy-five dollars, please.

And then, finally, her condition had a name, and an array of drugs that could treat it. Yet once she was told it *wasn't* all in her head, that she had a legitimate disorder, Marie abandoned herself to the condition, growing ever anxious, ever more frightened. She quit her job, and it had hurt, losing that paycheck, especially when their disability claim was disallowed. That was a nice irony, Social Security denying one of its benefit programs to a longtime employee, but Marie didn't have the stomach to go through the multiple appeals that everyone said were part of the game. That's why *he* had left the classroom and moved into administration, trying to make up for the loss of

265

Marie's income. He wasn't unhappy, as he told himself frequently. But he also knew that the double negative, *not unhappy,* didn't equal happy.

Then he lost the very job he hated, axed unfairly in a housecleaning staged by the new superintendent, one of those show-offy flourishes meant to establish what a tough, hands-on manager the guy was. Hadn't anyone noticed that the new guy had eventually hired a fresh team of bureaucrats, cronies from his old system, and paid them even more? He had talked to a lawyer about a reverse discrimination suit, but the guy said it was a lost cause, and he was forced to take the severance package offered, or risk losing the health insurance.

That's when he had gone to Bob for money, and Bob had told him there would be plenty of money soon, more than enough for both of them, but he needed legal assistance—a retainer for a lawyer, then more money for the so-called expert who was supposed to be their ace in the hole. But the lawyer and the expert disappeared when things went south, leaving nothing but their bills behind, and Bob had killed himself. Not so much because of the thousands he owed, but because of the dream that had been choked in its crib. That girl had killed Bob. She deserved to be dead.

Where had she put it? He had spent an hour in that tiny apartment, and he was pretty sure it wasn't there. The office was still a possibility, but security there would be impossibly tight, thanks to the stupid smoke bomb incident. Had she confided in anyone what she knew? God—what if, after all this, it didn't exist? But, no, she had seen it, and she was the one who had called Bob, after all those weeks of him getting dicked around by Alicia Farmer.

He left Marie and her buzz saw snoring and went back into the living room, putting another one of Bob's videos in the VCR. He kept hoping that he might find what he needed among them, but that was silly, of course. If Bob had what he needed, he wouldn't have killed himself. The title came up: THE TAMING OF THE SHREW, DIRECTED BY WILBUR R. GRACE, WITH ADDITIONAL DIALOGUE BY GEORGE SYBERT. That was an inside joke, Bob's tip to the apocryphal story about Sam Taylor and the Pickford-Fairbanks talkie. But it had been George's idea to update the story to modern-day Baltimore. As Marie had said, George often tossed out an idea, half-formed at best, and Bob then ran with it. But he always gave George credit.

It was only this year, after seeing Bob's strange passive reaction to defeat, that George had come to realize that Bob had some of the same problems as Marie. The difference was that Bob had coped by inserting a camera between himself and the world. He could function as long as he had a lens, as long as he was on the sidelines, framing the story. This year, for a few heady months, Bob had seen himself as the hero, in center frame, the little guy who was going to take on the Goliaths and win. But he was one of the ordinary folks that Goliath trampled, one of the people you never heard about. In the end, it was Bob's dream that killed him. A case could be made that all George was doing now was trying to avenge his best friend's death, by any means necessary, and in a movie, that would make him the hero.

In the bedroom, Marie's snores roared on, a

strange sound track to the dreamy, beautiful creations her brother had left behind.

MONDAY

Chapter 28

Tess's reporting career may have been short-lived, but she still had met her share of famous people. Presidential candidates, Nobel Prize winners, a couple of minor movie stars, and, in a rather startling turn of events, Boris Yeltsin, who had mistaken her for a member of his welcoming party and swept her up in a vodka-infused bear hug. Tess had actually been on deathwatch, a morbid little reporting detail in which a ju-nior staffer ensures that luminaries arrive and depart a city safely, but it had seemed more tactful to let Yeltsin have his version of the event.

Tess had enjoyed those encounters for the anecdotes they provided, but she had never gone civilian on a source, or felt the smallest whiff of fan-girl excitement. Until now, going for coffee with Johnny Tampa, something she had actually imagined when she was in middle school. Well, not coffee. She had probably envisioned an ice cream date or a romantic dinner in some candlelit venue. But she would settle for Bonaparte Bread, the high-end pastry shop only a few blocks from the high-rise where Selene lived. The request had seemed to unnerve Johnny, yet it apparently didn't occur to him that he could say no. Tess knew from the call sheet that he wasn't scheduled for pickup until noon.

He was waiting for her when she arrived, a true non-diva move. The lean, sharp features that she had idolized as a teenager were somewhat obscured by middle-age fleshiness, but when he smiled, he was the heartthrob that she recalled. Tess noticed that other women in the pastry shop also responded to Tampa's smile and manner.

'You're the one in charge of guarding Selene, right?'

'I'm handling that detail with my friend, Whitney, yes.'

'Right, the scary blonde. So how come one of you didn't catch her sending me that stupid magazine?' He brushed off Tess's reply before she had a chance to formulate it. 'Oh, she's too smart to do it herself, but I know she put someone else up to it. Someone on the crew, or maybe even Ben Marcus.'

'Why do you think that one of the producers on the show would be willing to do that for Selene?' she countered, fishing. Maybe Ben's relationship with Selene wasn't the well-kept secret he believed it to be.

'Because he's *mean*. He's always teasing me about my weight. A young skinny guy like him, he probably thinks it's funny that I have a . . . glandular problem.'

A glandular problem. Tess couldn't remember the last time she had heard that euphemism. Then again, current science was on Tampa's side, making the case that willpower wasn't enough for some people to lose weight.

'But Ben wants you to be happy, right? Ben and Flip. They see you as the linchpin of the show.'

'So they say.' He chewed thoughtfully on his chocolate croissant. 'They say they wrote the show for me, and they can't help that the network is hot for Selene. They talked pretty big, when they were trying to get me for this. Now I'm wondering if I

272

shouldn't have entertained some of the other offers I had. At least I wouldn't have to live *here*. Sorry. No offense.'

It happened to be one of Tess's least favorite phrases, a have-your-cake-and-eat-it-too bit of rhetoric that demanded the listener forgive the speaker for saying something impossibly rude.

'If the show goes,' Tess said, 'you'll be here quite a bit.'

'Yeah,' he said. 'And in winter yet. I don't do winter.'

'It's relatively mild.'

'No such thing to someone like me, who grew up in Florida and has lived in California since age sixteen.'

'How did you get into acting?' She knew, of course. She could recite much of Johnny Tampa's biography from memory. But she was trying to get into a groove with him, find an innocuous topic that they both could enjoy, and she figured that Johnny Tampa was one of Johnny Tampa's favorite subjects.

'Mickey Mouse Club,' he said.

'So you were in the Mickey Mouse Club and then you went out to California to do'—she pretended to grope for the name of his first show—'*High School Confidential*.'

'I went out to California with nothing promised to me. But my mom believed in me, and she agreed to go out for a year, see what I could get started. The year was almost up when I landed the featured part on *High School Confidential*, then got the lead in *The Boom Boom Room*. And the rest is history.'

Of a sort, Tess thought. If one had very low

273

standards for what constituted history. 'But you've been taking some . . . time off, as of late?'

He had moved on from the chocolate croissant to a Napoleon. It was hard for Tess not to wonder if he was a bulimic, albeit one who had mastered the binge without learning how to purge. Tess hadn't eaten this much even in her competitive rowing days. Or, come to think of it, her own bulimic teens.

'You're very polite,' he said. 'Everybody knows what happened to me. I left television to make movies, and not a single one of them hit. It wasn't my fault—in every case, I could show you what rotten luck we had, none of it connected to me— but you get only so many chances. That is, if you were a star on television, you only get so many chances. Meg Ryan was on a soap. Julianne Moore, too. Hilary Swank did a bit part on *my* show. But they weren't well known when they started making movies. I wonder if they have any juice here. I would love a glass of fresh-squeezed orange juice.'

He looked around with the expectation of someone who usually had a person at his beck and call, but then life on set was like that, in Tess's limited exposure to it. For the leads, it was a magical world of enabling elves. Makeup people appeared to touch up the actors' faces, food kept arriving, transportation was arranged. The theory seemed to be that the actors shouldn't expend any energy on activities beyond their performances.

'What do you do with your downtime? Here in Baltimore, I mean.'

'Read, mainly. I like science fiction.' He sounded a little defensive, but Tess was charmed.

In most actor interviews she had read, the oh-so-serious thespians were always claiming to be reading Faulkner or Pynchon, or the cool book of the moment. She never believed those actors, but she had a hunch Johnny Tampa was telling the truth.

'Have you made any friends on set?'

'I like the guys in the present-day scenes—but I'm not with them that much. Actually, it's not a bad thing for my character—I'm isolated, the way he is, cut off from old friends and family, in a strange place. It's good for my character,' he said, making the point a second time, as if trying to convince Tess—and himself. Tess couldn't help noticing, however, that he omitted any mention of Selene, with whom he had the bulk of his scenes.

'Do the cast and crew interact much? Socially, I mean.'

He looked wary. 'Some. There was a party when we came back this summer, after shooting the pilot in the spring. Sometimes, on a Friday night, there will be something impromptu. But the crew works too hard to socialize much, and most of the cast is pretty settled. Plus, they're East Coast-based, mostly from New York, and they go running home the first chance they get.'

On a personal level, Tess liked him for not taking her up on the opportunity to gossip about Selene. But it wasn't helping her job at all. Maybe she could kill two birds with one stone—or one little lie.

'Selene suggested to me that you had something going with Greer.'

His eyebrows shot up—no Botox in that forehead. 'Something going with . . . that's *stupid.*

Why would Selene say that? Greer was engaged. And fifteen years younger than I am.'

More like twenty, Tess thought.

'But she knew something about the steel industry. Said her old man had worked in it, that she could help me fill in some things about what it was like.'

'That was—' Tess had been on the verge of saying, *That was Alicia's father, Greer's father was a teamster*. But she didn't want to stop Johnny, now that he was beginning to open up. 'That was nice of her. Did you learn about her family and come to her, or did she volunteer to help you?'

'It just came up one day, during the lunch break. She began bringing me books, even went to the library and printed out some newspaper articles on Beth Steel.' Tess resented the local shorthand for Bethlehem Steel in Johnny's mouth. 'She helped me a lot. Flip and Ben—look, no knock on them, they're great writers, and they've given me an amazing opportunity—but all they know is Hollywood, and the kind of jobs people have there. They don't know what other people do most of the day, if they don't do it on a movie set. Oh, they think they do. They think that lawyers spend all their time in court making big speeches. They think doctors rush from emergency to emergency, in between banging nurses in the supply closet, and that reporters run around thrusting microphones in people's faces.'

He had a point. True, every job needed to be dramatized in a film or a television show, but the real nature of work was something missing in much of what Tess watched, which had always puzzled her. She was fascinated by what other

276

people did, how they spent their days. This may have been the consequence of an adult life spent as a professional observer—first as a reporter, now as an investigator.

Now that Johnny had gotten going, he was hard to stop. 'I needed to know what this guy did with his days. Mann is like Dorothy, in *The Wizard of Oz*. It's not logical for him to want to go back to modern-day Baltimore—his industry is dying, there's enormous pressure on his family, his job is drudgery. But it's home, it's what he knows, and not even Betsy Patterson, the beautiful belle of nineteenth-century Baltimore, is reason enough to stay.' He finished off his orange juice. 'It was better. When they said good-bye in episode eight. And I'm not saying that just because they're building up Selene's part. That's the show I signed up to make. Now that they're dicking with it—'

Two women with strollers—hip moms, in stylish clothes and fresh makeup, their children tricked out like the accessories they were—had stopped on the sidewalk outside Bonaparte Bread and were peering inside the restaurant, their attention obviously focused on Johnny Tampa. They pointed at him, laughing and nodding, as if the plate glass that separated them was just another television screen, as if he couldn't see them. He appeared— not oblivious, exactly, but resigned to such gawking.

'So Greer helped you, out of the goodness of her heart. And was there anything Greer wanted from you?'

He wasn't dumb, not by a long shot. 'She didn't come on to me. Trust me, I know all the ways that women hit on guys.'

'Yet her boyfriend thought she was cheating on him.'

'He probably just didn't buy the long hours she was working. Most civilians don't have a clue as to what we do. But all that girl did was work. She was driven.'

'So her boyfriend comes by the office, confronts her—maybe over the ring, maybe over his belief that she's two-timed him. But, if Greer was the eager little beaver everyone says she was, wouldn't his late-night visit have affirmed that? He found her working late. How does that escalate into him beating her to death?'

Tampa rubbed his jaw, where there was a faint red mark and the beaded scab of a fresh scratch, left by a woman's fingernail. He had been quick to wade into the fight yesterday, heedless of what many would consider his most valuable asset. He had, in fact, lived up to Tess's teenage version of him, at least for that moment.

'You know what? I don't know. It's beyond me, why people do what they do. Hey—that friend of yours, the scary chick—does she have a boyfriend?'

And in that instant, any remnant of her crush was vanquished. Not out of jealousy over his interest in Whitney, but in his indifference to the story behind the death of someone he had known.

'Call her,' Tess said, sincere in her hope that he would. Because Whitney would swallow Johnny Tampa whole and spit out the bones, assuming there were any bones left in that doughy body.

Speak of the preppy devil—here was Whitney, Selene in tow, almost literally. She was dragging Selene by the elbow, piloting her into the bakery,

278

as insistent as a tugboat guiding an ocean liner.

'You are going to eat something if I have to stand over you with a knife,' she hissed at the girl. 'Sugar-free gum is *not* a food group.'

Johnny brightened, presumably at the sight of Whitney, then frowned when he realized she was here in her professional capacity as bodyguard/nutrition counselor.

'I eat,' Selene protested feebly. 'I eat a lot when I'm on set. I just have a very high metabolism. And it was my idea to come here, remember?'

Whitney brought two croissants, almond and chocolate, over to the adjoining table, then went back to the counter to fetch a large glass of fresh-squeezed orange juice. Tess had assumed that Selene would poke the croissants and break them into ever-smaller flakes, but she dutifully forked up bite after bite, finishing the chocolate one and making it halfway through the almond under Whitney's approving gaze. Tess found herself hoping that Whitney might actually feed Selene, zooming pieces of croissant into her mouth. *'Here comes the Escalade. Here comes the Bentley. Here comes the Prius.'* But such drastic mea-sures were not needed, although Selene promptly excused herself to the restroom when she was finished.

'I should probably follow her, but I'm exhausted,' Whitney said. 'She tried to sneak out twice last night.'

'She did? You should have called me at home.'

'I let you sleep, knowing you had this meeting with what's-his-name. St. Pete, Tampa, whatever.'

Johnny, nonplussed in Whitney's presence, simply nodded, smiling inanely.

'Besides, I don't think she's bulimic. And she's

279

probably telling the truth about her metabolism. Oh, if she let herself go, she might become a size four verging on six, but she doesn't have to worry about her weight.'

'Actually, she does,' Johnny said. 'A size six is way too big for a woman who wants to play romantic leads. Sorry, but that's how it is.'

'Hmmmmph,' Whitney said, reaching into Selene's bag and extracting her iPhone. 'Might as well search her incoming and outgoing calls while she's in there. Jesus, I can't believe how many people she has in her address book. Oh, wait—I can check her e-mails, too. God, I love Mac.'

'That's so . . . rude,' Johnny said, genuinely offended on Selene's behalf. 'Maybe illegal.'

'I don't read anything, or listen to voice mail. I just check the senders. You know what I found under her bed this morning, when I was looking for alcohol?'

'Alcohol?' Tess asked, reaching for the iPhone and running her own check. Several calls from Ben—but nothing *to* him.

'No, not a drop, not even a can of malt liquor. I found two books—Edith Hamilton's Greek mythology and a copy of *Kristin Lavransdatter.*'

'You might have sparked the interest in Hamilton,' Tess said. 'When you told her that her name was from the goddess of the moon, as opposed to a Mormon soap opera.'

'Yeah, but *Kristin Lavransdatter*? And it was the third volume, to boot, *The Cross*. Could she possibly have read volumes one and two?'

'Maybe she thought Lavransdatter was Kirsten Dunst's name before she changed it,' Tess offered.

'Just because she's an actor doesn't mean she's

stupid,' Johnny said with surprising heat. 'Okay, well—Selene isn't a raging intellectual. But you shouldn't mock her for reading. Maybe that's why the books were under the bed in the first place, because she thought you would make fun of her. For all Selene knows, this Lard-butter, or however you say it, is one of those books everyone has read, and she's embarrassed not to know it.'

Whitney nodded. 'And maybe monkeys will fly out my—'

Tess interrupted, hoping to placate Johnny. 'At the very least, it could be for a film. The author was a Nobel Prize winner. Maybe someone's interested in adapting it.'

'It's already been adapted,' Johnny said. 'By Liv Ullmann, back in the 1990s. But, you're right, that wouldn't rule out a Hollywood version, although I haven't heard anything about that on the grapevine.'

Johnny was blushing furiously, his gaze downcast. His crush on Whitney must be really bad, Tess reasoned, if he couldn't even make eye contact. Selene came trip-trapping back to the table in her ridiculously high heels, and Johnny muttered: 'Gotta go.'

'God, he's so jealous of me he can't stand it,' Selene said cheerfully. 'He's even jealous that I had a stalker and he didn't, that I was in most of the photographs and he wasn't.'

A shred of conversation, a piece of unfinished business, came back to Tess. 'The photograph at the memorial—was that one of the stalker's?'

'I *told* you that,' Selene said, stroking her hair, oblivious to the fact that she was leaving little flakes of pastry behind. 'I said it was the guy.'

281

'You said—oh, never mind. Was Greer in all the other photos as well? The ones taken by the dead man, Wilbur R. Grace?'

'Don't be ridic. I mean, Greer was in some, but so was Ben. And Flip and Lottie. But I was in most of them. At least—I was in all the ones I saw. I don't know, maybe there were others, but who's going to be silly enough to stalk Greer?'

Chapter 29

The not-*the*-Meyerhoffs Meyerhoffs lived in Baltimore Highlands, a county neighborhood that people found mostly by accident, taking a wrong turn en route to the Harbor Tunnel. The streets here were named for states, but the pattern was maddeningly indecipherable to Tess—Louisiana led to Tennessee, then Alabama, which was followed, of course, by Pennsylvania, then Michigan and Florida. The Meyerhoffs lived in a brick semidetached on the bottom rung, Delaware Avenue, just north of the thruway to the tunnel, where traffic was a dull, roaring constant.

Before venturing here, Tess had run a quick computer check on Jeanette Meyerhoff. Or, more correctly, paid a premium to have her own ad hoc hacker search the court files and police records. Her suspicion was that a woman who felt comfortable starting a fight at a memorial service might be prone to other crimes of impulse. She was at once gratified and unnerved by how correct her hunch was. Jeanette had a pretty lengthy arrest record—public intoxication, resisting arrest, a string of assault charges. And three of her four sons had amassed similar records, with one currently serving real time down in Jessup, on a drug distro charge.

Yet the only paper on John 'JJ' Meyerhoff was a warrant issued three years ago for failure to appear in traffic court. Based on public records, JJ was the white sheep of his family.

*   *   *

'He was the sweetest of my boys,' Jeanette Meyerhoff said, pouring Tess a generic grape soda. She had been surprisingly affable, almost eager to talk, when Tess showed up at the door. Perhaps it was the sheer novelty of finding someone who wanted to hear JJ's side of the relationship with Greer.

'I know—that's not saying much. We're scrappers. But JJ was my baby. And *smart*. Not book smart, although he did good enough in school, but handy. When Mr. Meyerhoff stepped out ten years ago, it was JJ who kept the roof over our heads. And by that, I mean he got up there and patched the damn thing. Patched the roof, caulked the windows. He put this kitchen in hisself.'

There was nothing extraordinary about the kitchen in which they sat, a clean and simple space, but Tess supposed that was an achievement of a kind.

'He and Greer were high school sweethearts, right?'

'Yeah, but she wasn't Greer then, but Gina. The Greer thing is some made-up name she gave

283

herself, after she moved away. But even in high school her family thought she was too good for him.'

'Greer's—Gina's—father was a teamster, right?'

'Who told you that? He drove a bread truck for H and S.' But Greer had claimed to be the daughter of a teamster when she first inquired about a job with the production. The girl had been scheming from jump. 'They were always full of themselves, the Sadowskis, living west of the boulevard, over toward Linthicum.'

Baltimore was full of such arbitrary geographic distinctions. East or west of the boulevard, above or below the avenue, north or south of the water tower.

'How did they get back together, then?'

'Well, Miss Hoity-Toity had gone out to Hollywood, but her father got sick. Emphysema. And her mother said she had to come home, help her through, because she had to take a second job to pay for everything, and her old man couldn't be left alone. JJ saw Greer at the Checkers on Belle Grove and it started all over again. He was *crazy* for her.'

She paused, as if regretting her choice of words. 'I mean to say, he loved her no matter what she did. She could feed him a shit sandwich, and he would ask for a chaser of piss. He thought the sun and the moon rose in her. He proposed, she said yes. Then she got her promotion and had less and less time for him. I could see the writing on the wall, even if JJ couldn't.'

Mrs. Meyerhoff had put out a package of Hydrox cookies with the grape soda, and Tess had to concentrate fiercely not to wolf down the entire package. Hydrox had disappeared from the snack food chain at least a de-cade ago, but such items often lived on in the tiny groceries and delis of Baltimore. Those corner stores were like archaeological trea-sure troves of discontinued food items. Every now and then, she unearthed a dusty bottle of Wink from deep in the cooler of such places, and it felt as thrilling as if she had found evidence of the Hanging Gardens of Babylon.

'You said she was cheating on him.'

Mrs. Meyerhoff examined the backs of her hands. They were sinewy, with knobby, ringless fingers. Had it hurt, watching her beloved youngest son purchase a ring for someone else, while her own hands went bare?

'I didn't have stone-cold proof,' she admitted. 'But I kept telling JJ, add it up. There was a man who called their apartment at all hours, demanding to talk to Greer.'

'Did he hang up when JJ answered?'

'No, but he wouldn't give his name. Sometimes Greer took the calls, sometimes she didn't, and she would say to him, "Don't call me here." She started working longer and longer hours.'

'I think the long hours were legitimate,' Tess said. 'The one thing that everyone agrees on is that she was truly a hard worker.'

'What I think,' Mrs. Meyerhoff said, sliding a Pall Mall out of its maroon pack, 'is that she had set her cap for that boss of hers.'

'Flip? He's married. Happily, I hear.' And seemingly oblivious to Greer, but it didn't seem polite to mention that. Tess didn't want to tell a grieving mother that the woman who had been such a prize to her son was nothing but a factotum to her boss.

'Yes, but that girl had patience to burn. I'll give her that. When Greer wanted something, she found a way to get it.'

'Greer told people at work that she broke up with JJ. Her mother said it was the other way around, and you say it was all because he thought she was cheating. What happened?'

'I don't really know. We can't know now, can we? A few weeks ago, they had a fight. You know how it goes—she was late, he complained that he had waited for her for over an hour, and next thing you know, he's saying, Well, if you feel that way, maybe you don't want to marry me, and she says, Okay I won't. He didn't think it was permanent. I guess that's why he went to see her that night. She wasn't taking his calls, she had changed the locks at their apartment. It was like—how do I put this? It was like she tricked him into breaking up with her, just so she could keep the ring. She was a greedy girl.'

Tess sipped her grape soda, ate another Hydrox. Mindful of the fact that Mrs. Meyerhoff had a short fuse, she searched carefully for the right words. 'All these things—the breakup, Greer's refusal to speak to him, the disagreement over the ring—they tend to support the police's version of events. He went to see her, maybe with the best intentions of the world, but she angered him, and well. . . .'

Mrs. Meyerhoff nodded. 'I know. And then he gets out of his car when the police pull him over, doesn't stop when they yell at him—I know what it *looks* like. But what if the reason he was crazy is

286

that he had just heard Greer was dead? I know the police thought I was lying, but he really did go off fishing. It's what he did when he felt bad. He woke me up that night, asking me to call in sick for him the next morning, and he headed out. I *saw* him, Miss Monaghan. He didn't have no blood on his clothes or hands, and he didn't leave no bloody clothes behind. He was upset—she had told him there was no way she would get back with him and she wouldn't give the ring back either, because the breakup had been his idea, even if she agreed to it. He drove west, spent a couple of days in the woods, sorting out his thoughts, then headed home. He might not have done it.'

Her tone was that of a woman trying to persuade herself. Four sons, and this was the fate of the 'good' one, the one who had tended to her in his father's absence. Tess was beginning to understand why Mrs. Meyerhoff had crashed the funeral service. One mother had lost a daughter, and it was a tragedy. Mrs. Meyerhoff had lost a son, but that was supposed to be justice. And maybe it was, but didn't that make it only harder to grieve? Tess could see how Mrs. Meyerhoff had become fixated on the ring, for which she was stuck with the payments. The ring was the closest thing she had to a legitimate grievance.

'Look, if you really want to pursue the thing about the ring—I think you might have some standing. You might not get it back, but if Greer's mother insists on keeping it, there may be some way to make her take over the payments. I have a lawyer friend who owes me a favor. He'd do it pro bono.' It felt good, volunteering the services of her aunt's husband, who had never been shy about

287

volunteering *her* for things.

'It's all mute,' Mrs. Meyerhoff said, and Tess needed a second to catch the Bawlmer malaprop. In some ways, the phrase was more elegant than the one Mrs. Meyerhoff actually wanted. All the parties to the dispute had been silenced. 'There ain't no ring. It wasn't on Greer's body when they found her. Police say JJ took it. If that's so, where is it?'

'He would have thrown it away,' Tess said. 'He couldn't hold on to it, much less try to return it or hock it. The ring would have been key to convicting him. And the murder weapon is missing, too, so that's consistent.'

'Yeah,' Mrs. Meyerhoff said, sighing and exhaling at the same time. 'It all fits. And if it were one of my other boys, I'd say, "I knew this day was coming." Do you think my temper is something they inherited? Were my boys doomed to be the way they are because of how I am?'

It was a big question, far too large to be answered in a kitchen on Delaware Avenue, over grape soda and Hydrox. Perhaps too large to be answered anywhere, under any circumstances.

*   *   *

Leaving Mrs. Meyerhoff's house, Tess decided to call Tull.

'Have you closed Greer's murder officially yet?'

'No,' he said. 'We have to be careful on these things, not rush, even when the outcome seems likely.'

'So when will JJ Meyerhoff's things be released? Will his mother get his truck? How does that work?' She wasn't sure if killers got to keep their property, or if their possessions passed to the state.

'Eventually.'

'Did you go over the truck pretty carefully?'

'Of course we did.'

'And you didn't find the ring, much less the murder weapon. Right?'

'How do you know the ring was missing? We held that back.'

'The two mothers had . . . words at the funeral. So, no ring? Are you sure?'

'Look, Tess, this is the least of my problems right now.' A pause. 'I mean, it's not that I have problems, it's just I don't have time for this kind of trivia.'

Tull was an interesting case. Face-to-face, he could lie to anyone, about anything. It was the nature of his job after all. But on the phone, without his handsome stone face to carry his game, his words sometimes betrayed him.

'What's going wrong? I thought the case was a dunker.'

'It is.'

She didn't say anything, waiting him out. Then, when he didn't crack, she added: 'You owe me. The last time I tried to tell you something important, you blew me off, and someone I loved almost got killed.'

That was a sore point and it seemed to anger Tull—because it was true. 'I don't owe you shit. It doesn't work that way. You come in here, solve a couple of my open ones, and maybe then I'll be in your debt. But I'm not accountable to you, or your Hollywood bosses. I know they want this to be all wrapped up. I do, too. But there's . . . a complication.'

'About the ring?'

'Not about the fucking ring!' A pause. 'Okay, I'm sorry, it's just you call me in the middle of the shit storm of shit storms, and you have to promise me that this goes no further. I know you got friends at the newspaper—'

'Not too many at this point.'

'Yeah, well if I read this in the paper tomorrow, you'll never be able to get back in my good graces. The deputy, who brought Meyerhoff down? He's got a bad habit of shooting too fast. Third time he's shot someone in two years, although he's never killed anyone before. I still like Meyerhoff for the Sadowski death, but now we have to wait for Garrett County to investigate his shooting before I can close this out. That's all.'

'That's a lot,' Tess said. 'Look—pull his clothes. Go through all the pockets again. It's not like it was the Hope diamond. It could have gotten stuck in a pocket, snagged on a thread.'

'It would make my life . . . more interesting if we could find it,' Tull admitted.

Good, they were on the same page. The presence of the ring in JJ Meyerhoff's effects was the one thing that could persuade police that he *didn't* kill Greer, just had a very ill-timed confrontation with her the night she died. *No blood on his clothes*, his mother had said, although she could be lying. And breaking up with the love of your life was reason enough to disappear for a few days—assuming one was very young.

Chapter 30

Ben stared at his screen, pretending to write. 'So you've deigned to join us today,' Lottie had said when he arrived at eleven. 'I've already completed a third of the script,' he had lied, smoothly and automatically. 'Besides, I thought you would be grateful for the company.' Lottie blushed, and he almost felt bad, reminding her of the scare she had experienced Friday night, stupid prank though it appeared to be.

Now, after eight grinding long hours, he was just trying to wait everyone out, get a few moments alone. As the evening wore on, he realized Lottie was waiting for *him,* hoping to walk out together. Even when he logged long hours on a script, he seldom burned the midnight oil in the office, preferring to work in his hotel room. But that was back when there was a chance that Selene might visit. No, there was no reason to be there—and every reason to be here.

'Lloyd,' he said, trying to sound casual, 'why don't you walk Ms. MacKenzie to her car, then head home yourself. There's no reason for you to be staying this late.'

'But the script supervisor asked for my help.' Lloyd said this as if it were on a par with being asked to storm SS headquarters and rescue a POW general. 'We have to get ready for the minipub for one-oh-eight, and Flip is way behind.'

'Well, take a break at least. Walk Ms. MacKenzie to her car—'

'I don't *need* an escort,' Lottie said.

291

'—and then go to Nasu Blanca and get me some takeout.' How much time would that give him? Hell, he should have thought of some place farther afield, sent Lloyd on a true scavenger hunt for dinner, but now he was stuck. 'I want the edamame, the spicy tuna tempura roll, and the Kobe beef hamburger. But what I really want is one of those teas you brought the other day. What did you call it, half and half?'

'I got that over in East Baltimore, near where we was on location for the cemetery. I don't know no place around here that serves it. You find those at Chinese joints, mostly.'

'Don't haze him,' Lottie snapped. 'Fetching your dinner is enough.'

'Okay, dinner from Nasu Blanca, but get me an espresso from Vaccaro's, too. I'm going to be working late and need some legal stimulants.'

He watched them leave the parking lot from his office window, then went into the open area where the assistants worked. It was hard to believe that someone had been killed here, not even a week ago. But the police had finished what they needed to do, returning the scattered papers in cardboard boxes that Lloyd was supposed to sort and file, poor kid. No wonder he was excited to be working on the minipub, something actually of consequence to the movie.

Greer's desk had been left unoccupied for the time being, although that bit of respect would probably disappear the moment Flip found a new assistant. Lottie had suggested—tentatively, deferentially, because it was Flip—that he make it through the final weeks without one, which would be good for the budget, but Flip had said he couldn't possibly cope without a personal assistant, and Lottie had acquiesced, as she always did with Flip. Ben began opening Greer's desk drawers, but they were all empty. Of course—Greer's desk had been plundered the night she was killed, its contents scattered far and wide, along with papers from several filing cabinets. Those, too, were among the papers that Lloyd would have to sort. Hey, maybe Ben should give the kid a head start, begin working on those papers now. He could chalk it up to the procrastination of a blocked writer. And him being such an all-a-round good guy.

The first cardboard box was filled with the very archival stuff where all the trouble had begun—scripts and stories and correspondence from their early years. Ben had thought Flip was insanely egotistical to think that USC, where they had attended grad school, would want these papers, but he hadn't seen any reason to object when Flip asked Greer, then just an intern, to start organizing them.

He moved on to the second box, but it seemed to be connected to the production itself—call sheets, beat sheets, Flip's schedule, memos, phone logs . . . *phone logs*. As Lloyd had been instructed on his first day of work, Lottie's system required that every call be recorded with date, time, and a brief description, even if it was something as innocuous as 'Mrs. Flip for Flip. RE: Jewish holidays.' He turned back to July. Yes, in that final month, the poor guy had called constantly, first for Alicia, who had been expert in dodging such kooks, but then it had been Greer who started taking his messages for Flip. Ben wondered that

293

Greer hadn't been tempted to tamper with these records, but the guy's death had been a suicide, straight up, and both girls had readily told the police that the guy was a nut job who called the office, trying to get face time with Flip. Actually, it was Ben he wanted. But he hadn't known that, and Greer hadn't told him. That one small lie—a lie he had never asked anyone to tell, a lie he wouldn't have thought to use to cover his own ass, because he didn't know it needed covering—had changed everything.

But the thing that gnawed at Ben was that he really couldn't remember if he had ever met the guy. The guy said he had, and there was the envelope, stuck among Ben's old papers. And he had sent a photocopy of a photograph, as if that proved anything—twenty-year-old Ben, looking bored and sweaty on the set of Phil Tumulty Sr.'s last Baltimore-based film, an ill-advised attempt to reconnect with the light, whimsical touch he had before he started making megabucks pictures like *The Beast* and *Gunsmoke: The Movie*. Flip had been pissed that Ben wanted to work for his old man, but what other connection did Ben have if he wanted a P.A. job? Flip was the one who met all the big guys, as a little kid, who could drop names like Steve and Barry and Penny and Rob and Francis and Marty. Ben knew one guy, and that guy was Phil Sr., the father of his best friend. So what if Flip hated his dad? It was Ben's foot in the door.

And the job had proved educational in a way Ben never could have predicted. Working on *The Last Pagoda,* he had found out what it was like to be part of a big, fat, stinking flop where everyone was utterly deluded about what they were doing, where everyone kept insisting it was great, genius, a return to form. God, in hindsight, it had been so obviously snake-bit. Start with the title. Locals might have understood that the pagoda was a well-known Baltimore landmark, but everyone else thought the movie was some thirteenth-century shogun shit. As for the script—even at the age of twenty, Ben could see that Phil Sr. had lost touch with everything in his work that a mere ten years earlier had made it original and fun. The question that had plagued him, even at twenty, but now, especially, at thirty-five, was: *But does he know? Does he know that he's squandered his magic?* He had wondered the same things about other directors he once loved. Because if they could lose their instincts about their work—couldn't anyone? Even Ben?

Where was the fucking letter? Goddammit, Greer, where did you hide it, you thieving, scheming cunt?

He returned to the phone logs, going forward now. The strange happenings around the set had started after the suicide of Wilbur Grace. He didn't want to connect the two things—he still believed that the production was simply having a run of bad luck—but someone else had been in Greer's apartment. Someone else *knew*.

'Got your food,' Lloyd said, coming through the door, then stopping short, a frightened look on his face when he saw Ben rooting through the boxes. 'Hey—I know I'm supposed to go through those things, but I thought it was okay to help on the script first, do the boxes in my downtime. Is that okay? I was just trying to be helpful.'

Greer had said those very words: *I was just trying*

295

to be helpful. Ben stared absently at Lloyd, then shook his head. 'I was procrastinating. The script's not coming. I think I'm going to be here all night.'

'The security guard that the building hired leaves at eleven,' Lloyd said. 'But I'll stay, if you like. Lottie says no one's supposed to be alone here anymore, not if the building won't change the security code.'

'I can't keep you that long. Tell you what—I'll eat my dinner, see if I get a second wind. If I'm still not feeling it, we'll both go. Sometimes, part of doing a job is knowing when to stop for a while.'

'I've got a lot to do,' Lloyd protested. 'I really need to stay until I finish.'

You're killing me, Lloyd. But what the hell, he could always come back.

'Tomorrow, Lloyd. Tomorrow and tomorrow and tomorrow. One day, we'll all be dead and none of this will matter anyway.'

'Okay. Can I grab my knapsack? I left it in Flip's office.'

'Enjoying the big man's digs while he was out today?'

Lloyd's discomfiture was almost comic. 'Well, he has a computer, and Greer's is password protected and it was easier for me to work there until an IT guy could come in, and Lottie said it was okay—'

'Whoa, settle down. I was just teasing. Do whatever you have to do, and we'll both head out when I've finished my dinner. You want some?'

Lloyd made a face. 'That weird-ass hamburger? No, thank you. I grabbed a sub from Mustang's.' Again, he looked guilty. 'I hope that was okay, getting something while I was out—'

'Don't sweat it, Lloyd.' Ben wished his own

296

conscience could be weighed down by something so inconsequential as a sub.

Chapter 31

A soft rain had started, a gloomy harbinger of the days to come. It always seemed to rain on her days off, not that it really affected Alicia, given that her primary day-off activity was smoking. Still, she objected on principle; the weather didn't know that smoking was her only hobby. Oh, she did other things, too. Read—and smoked. Watched television—and smoked. Sat at the computer, paging through home decor sites, a cigarette burning almost constantly. Ran errands, smoking on the drive to and from. Some nights, when she tired of her own company, she would walk down to one of the local bars, buy a draft—and smoke. Maryland was one of the last holdouts, with smoking still permitted in its bars and restaurants, although that was said to be changing by next year. Until then—she was going to smoke every chance she got.

She looked at the piece of paper on the coffee table. Was it really so valuable? Without Greer, could anyone swear to its—what was that word, the one used for the antiques and rare objects that she studied covetously in the windows down at Gaines McHale? *Provenance*. Greer, who thought she was so clever, had been stupid to remove it from the envelope, but then—if she hadn't opened the envelope, she never would have known what she had. What if the envelope had been sealed, after all those years? That wouldn't have buttressed anyone's position. Perhaps that was why Greer had gotten rid of the envelope. Plus, it would have been too bulky to hide in her choice spot, especially with that other sheet, which Alicia had left where she found it. She had debated that with herself, leaving the other document behind, but she decided to take only what she needed.

When she drove down to the production offices Friday night, her only thought was to be helpful. As she had told Mr. Sybert, she *knew* Greer, and if she thought things through, she would figure out her hiding place eventually. Greer couldn't destroy the document, because that would end her power. So she had to put it someplace where it was unlikely to be discovered, but also in a location where, if it should be found, Greer couldn't be blamed. That was Greer's MO, avoiding blame, and she had to know that what she was doing was illegal. You couldn't hide documents, because lawyers might want them, much less then swear they never existed. Greer had been willing to risk perjury, and for what? A job in the writers' office, a job as Flip's assistant, maybe a shot as a script supervisor or associate producer down the road.

Greer thought so small.

Alicia didn't. And even as she told herself that she was just trying to help Mr. Sybert out, once she had the document, she couldn't ignore its value. Oh, she would give Mr. Sybert a chance to make his best offer, but shouldn't Ben and Flip have a chance, perhaps even Tumulty Sr.? He had the real deep pockets. He would probably be willing to put up a lot of money to bail out his own son—and avoid being tainted by the implication that he was

298

somehow involved. Then there were her other . . . *clients,* as she liked to think of them. Was this item of use to them? Possibly, but that was harder to gauge. No, she wouldn't bring them into this negotiation, and she didn't owe it to them to do so. She had been paid to do specific things, create disruptions on the set, and she had. That account was in good standing. She was a freelance worker, not exclusive to anyone.

How much should she ask for? And—not to be a total geek, but she had to think everything through—what would be the tax implications? She should probably set it up as a contract, with her providing unspecified services to Tumulty's production company. Quarterly payments for, say, up to five years. Too much? Not enough? A million dollars sounded like a lot, but it wasn't enough to support her for the rest of her life, even if she checked out as early as her parents had. Maybe she should ask for a yearly stipend, some phantom job in Tumulty's production company?

The phone rang, and she jumped, stabbing out her cigarette as if she had just been caught by one of the nuns, smoking in the girls' room at St. Ursula's. But it was just the contractor, pointing out the obvious: He couldn't work on the deck tomorrow if the rain continued. *No shit, Sherlock.* Well, that suited her anyway. She had meetings set up for tomorrow morning, and it would be better if no one was there.

'Of course,' she said. 'But it would be nice if you could get it installed in time for the Christmas holidays.'

'You use your deck at Christmas?'

Shit, didn't anyone understand sarcasm

299

anymore? She wanted to slam the phone down on him, but her contractor was one man she never risked offending. He was too much in demand. Instead, she told him to get to the job when he could—and she would pay the balance when the work was done. That should get results. Money was the universal language.

Speaking of which—she really should give Mr. Sybert a chance to counter before she approached Tumulty Sr. She didn't think he could be competitive, but she owed him the courtesy of making his case, the sad old schlub. She felt almost guilty, taking his money all these weeks, and giving him nothing in return but the information on the e-mailed call sheets and memos, and the code to the security door, which he had never even used.

Instead, Alicia had used it. It seemed as if an eternity passed in that split second while she waited for the front door to buzz Friday night— *could they have changed it, after all?*—but once in the building, it couldn't have been simpler to set off the homemade smoke bomb, then hide in a ladies' room on the first floor. She had stayed there, in fact, until almost two in the morning, which had been unnerving. And wouldn't it have been a bitch if Lottie had remembered to lock the office door after all that?

But, of course, Lottie didn't. Because Lottie would have thought it through, even as she fled, and worried that firefighters would break the door down if she locked it. Careful Lottie, prudent Lottie, always two steps ahead of everyone. It had been a bonus, getting one over on Lottie with that smoke bomb, tricking her to leave the office with the door unlocked. Okay, Lottie had been in the

300

right to fire Alicia, but she couldn't possibly have known that at the time. No one could prove that Alicia had given those things to Wilbur Grace. God, imagine what Lottie would have done if she had figured out that Alicia had *sold* him the things he wanted. But all they had were Greer's meticulous telephone logs, showing that he had called for Alicia several times. They could prove the connection, nothing more. It was easier, in the end, to cop to being naïve, instead of admitting to being greedy.

She felt a pang for Greer, strange to say, even though she had sacrificed Alicia so willingly, screwed her the first chance she got. Two local girls from similar backgrounds—they should have been friends, not competitors. They had their moments of solidarity, laughing behind Lottie's— or Ben's or Flip's—back. You couldn't work next to someone, day in and day out, and not feel *something*. Poor, stupid Greer, who thought she was the winner because she got Alicia's shit job, only to be killed by her crazy-jealous boyfriend. At least she had a boyfriend. Alicia was in a two-year dating slump, although that was in part because she couldn't respect anyone who was attracted to the current Alicia, the loser at the video store. She wondered if she might find someone to her liking, once she was rich. She wondered if she could ever know if a man loved her for herself, or her money.

She decided that was a dilemma she could tolerate.

*   *   *

'Tess.'

Her name surprised her out of sleep, and she realized that part of the reason was that Lloyd so seldom used her name. But here he was, standing at her bedside, whispering her name, which seemed counterproductive. He either wanted her to wake up or not, she thought crankily, glancing at her clock. Almost 1 A.M.

'What?'

'Tess, I fucked up awful bad. *Awful* bad. I broke something.'

She struggled to a sitting position. 'Lloyd, I know I always said I would kill you if you broke one of my commemorative plates, but I was kidding.'

'No, I broke something at the office, and I thought I could fix it, and no one would have to know, but I can't—and, oh shit, they're going to fire me, Tess, and it's all my fault, but I don't know what to do.'

She followed him groggily to the kitchen, aware that Lloyd must believe himself to be in dire straits if he was coming to her for help. His inclination had always been to bluff his way through.

There on the table were the contents of Crow's toolbox, a tube of superglue—and an Emmy. Tess rubbed her eyes. The Emmy was still there, although it looked intact to her eyes—the globe aloft in the woman's upraised arms, both pointy wings still capable of putting someone's eyes out.

'Is that Flip's?'

Lloyd nodded. 'I . . . broke it. I didn't mean to, but I was in his office and I just couldn't help myself. I picked it up and then I heard someone coming, or thought I did, and I kinda dropped it and this band popped off, the one with his name

302

attached.'

'And you brought it home?' That error in judgment struck Tess as potentially more problematic than dropping the thing. 'If the band popped off, I'm sure someone can put it back on. Someone had to put it on in the first place, right?'

'Yeah, but I can't get the band back on with the piece of paper folded up inside, the way it was.'

'Piece of . . . paper?' She held out her hand. 'Give it to me.'

'Don't unfold it,' Lloyd said. 'It's like a piece of organic-ami.' She knew he meant origami. 'If you unfold it, we'll never get it back together. I think it's the certificate or something.'

Ignoring Lloyd's anxiety, Tess carefully unfolded the piece of paper. It was a photocopy, yellowed from age, but the creases seemed relatively new. It may be old, but it hadn't been folded until recently.

But what was it? What did it signify? As far as Tess could tell, it was nothing more than a list, almost like something from an IQ test in which one was asked to explain the relationship between a series of items.

Small Catholic college   Small Catholic college
(Catholic colleges traditionally have strong basketball programs.)

Priests   Priests
(Priests tend to be found at Catholic colleges.)

Nuns   Nuns
(Nuns are often found in proximity to priests.)

The two columns continued in this baffling vein—similarities conceded, but always with a duh-obvious rationalization. There was a handwritten note at the bottom, in a rather fussy hand:

This document was one of the key pieces of evidence presented in *Zervitz v. Hollywood Pictures,* where a judgment of a million dollars was awarded to the plaintiff. I am working on my own list but have been advised that I need the letter about which we spoke to proceed. Yours, Wilbur R. 'Bob' Grace.

Tess examined the base of the Emmy. Perhaps the band had popped off with such ease because it had been removed recently and not replaced as it should be. What had Ben said about Greer? *She loves to buff Flip's Emmy. She just took it to a local jeweler to have it all shined up.*

'You're getting fingerprints on it,' Lloyd said frantically. 'We need to fold it up and put it back the way it was, and I gotta get to the office before everyone else tomorrow, even Lottie.'

'I don't think so,' Tess said. 'In fact, I think you've done a good thing, finding this.'

'Yeah? What is it?'

'Possibly the MacMuffin.'

'MacGuffin,' Lloyd said.

TUESDAY

Chapter 32

While Tess often lamented the colliding spheres that had made her sometimes rowing coach and erstwhile employer into her uncle, there were advantages to having Tyner Gray in the family. After all, few other lawyers would manage to get the details on *Zervitz v. Hollywood Pictures* while she was on the water, her first rowing session since she collided with Hollywood a mere eight days ago. And fewer still would then meet at the boathouse to brief her—and not charge her a dime for any of it.

'You could have found most of what you needed to know from the *Beacon-Light* archives,' Tyner scolded her. It was his style to be perpetually disappointed in her, but Tess had come to realize it was how he expressed affection. 'But I hunted down the judge and got an overview.'

'And?' Tess asked, hosing down her shell, taking care to avoid Tyner. She wouldn't have minded splashing him, but the water was hell on his wheelchair.

'There was this Kevin Bacon movie, *The Air Up There,* about a basketball coach who goes to Africa to recruit players. Think what's-his-name.'

'Manute Bol.' Tess had seen the impossibly tall, impossibly thin Sudanese native play for the Washington team years ago, so long ago it was still known as the Bullets. 'Was that movie even successful?'

'A movie doesn't have to be successful to be plagiarized. Zervitz, a local man, said he gave

Barry Levinson's assistant a two-page treatment for a college basketball film. Later, Levinson's literary agent happened to be one of the producers on *The Air Up There,* along with her husband. They never proved that anyone saw Zervitz's treatment, other than Levinson's assistant, who swore she didn't pass it along. The credited writer even produced notebooks that purportedly showed he started working on the idea before any of this happened. But a local jury awarded the guy a million bucks, and the Hollywood Pictures people decided not to appeal it.'

'So they *did* steal it,' Tess said.

'Don't be unsophisticated, Tess. No one will ever know exactly what happened to that two-page treatment, and the defendants may have decided it was cheaper, in the end, to pay the guy off. The plaintiff had expert witnesses saying it was too similar, it had to be stolen. But there also is a school of thought that writers, working independently, can produce strikingly similar stories, especially if they're working in a conventional vein.'

'"Nuns are often found in proximity to priests,"' Tess said, quoting from the document she had found last night.

'Yes, the list you saw was part of the defense, taken from the case file, a side-by-side comparison of the two projects.'

Tess was now in sync with Tyner, her mind speeding along a parallel track. 'Wilbur R. Grace showed the list to someone—presumably Greer—because he thought he had a similar claim against *Mann of Steel.* But he mentioned a letter that he had to have as well. Greer had the letter that

Grace wanted, but instead of giving it to him, she used it to leverage her position in the production. This is what Ben has been looking for, but who else? Who else wants that letter, now that Grace is dead? And where is it?'

'Maybe Greer was playing more than one person. Aren't there a lot of people who would be upset to see *Mann of Steel* undone by a legal claim?'

Tess thought about that. Flip and Ben would be devastated, of course. They believed this was their chance to have a commercial success. Lottie, too, would be disappointed. The local crews wanted the show as well, in hopes that it would provide steady work.

And then there was one person who would be thrilled to see it all fall apart—Selene. But Selene didn't have the power to give Greer anything she wanted.

'Thanks, unc,' she said, raising her shell over her head, preparatory to putting it away. She used the nickname because she knew he found it doubly infuriating. Tyner didn't want to be called uncle, and he found 'unc' loathsome. 'You're a gem.'

'I can't believe that you think that was even an adequate washing,' he said. 'You know better than that, Tess. Why bother to hose it off at all if you're not going to do the job right?'

'Love you!' she called out from under the shell. One half-assed wash job wouldn't destroy her scull, and she was keen to talk to Ben, find out what he knew about Wilbur R. Grace.

* * *

Ben wasn't at the office when Tess arrived at nine, but almost everyone else was—including several Baltimore detectives. Tess, who had told Lloyd to let her keep the Emmy for now, worried that its absence had already been noted, prompting Lottie or Flip to report a burglary to the police. Tess should have remembered how jumpy everyone was about any breach of security at the production office.

'Is this about Flip's Emmy?' she asked. 'Because I have it, but there's a reason—'

'Flip's Emmy?' Lottie asked blankly. 'No—God, no. I wish, it's just—' And with that, tough little Lottie broke down and began to cry, while Flip tried to comfort her, although Flip's idea of comforting someone seemed to consist of soft punches to the shoulder.

'Johnny Tampa,' Lloyd said. 'He was kidnapped.'

'Kidnapped?'

'Grabbed right out in front of his condo this morning,' Flip said. 'His driver saw the whole thing as he was arriving. Two guys came out of nowhere, dragged him into a car.'

'Has there been a ransom demand?'

Flip shook his head. 'Not yet.'

'And Selene?'

'Safe and sound. Thanks to your detail, no one can get close to her. We told her to stay in the condo until we hear something. We've had to suspend shooting, of course. When the West Coast wakes up, they're going to ream me about this.'

Tess turned to the nearest detective. 'How are you handling this? Do you have to call the feds in because it's a kidnapping?'

'We're keeping them out of it for now. This happened only an hour ago, and there's been no communication. It seems that Tampa went to a bar last night and flirted with a local, pissed off her husband. This could be related. But that makes it more of a mobile beat-down than a kidnapping.'

This didn't sound like the Johnny Tampa whom Tess had observed over the past week. Lottie, too, looked surprised, but Flip was nodding.

'I was there. He invited me out last night, after we finished, and I thought I should go, in the interest of, you know, male bonding. We went to this place in Fells Point, near where he lives, and he was chatting up a woman in there, and it clearly bugged the guy she was with.'

It was bugging Tess, too—but not for the same reasons. 'Flip, I think we should both go check on Selene. You know how high-strung she is. You don't want her flaking out because she feels vulnerable. Let's go over there and assure her that everything is being done to find Johnny, and that we're ready to order extra security for her.'

'God, the budget—' Lottie began, then caught Tess's gaze. In that moment, Tess could tell, Lottie decided she could trust her, that Tess was not another local trying to shake her down at every opportunity. She also seemed to get that Tess had an insight into this that no one else had. 'No, you're right, of course. I'll stay here, wait for updates. You go take care of Selene.'

*   *   *

Flip didn't speak a word on the short drive to Selene's condo, just sat in the front seat of Tess's car, twisting the brim of his Natty Boh hat. He broke his silence only after Tess parked.

'Maybe this project *is* cursed,' he said. 'Maybe I've been stupid not to heed the warnings. A murder, and now a kidnapping. What next?'

'Flip, you've got problems we haven't even discussed yet, but I think Johnny Tampa's disappearance is the least of them.'

In her living room, Selene was stretched out on the sofa, watching television and toying with her iPhone, a kid enjoying an unexpected snow day. Whitney was in Selene's closet, a walk-in the size of the guest bedroom at Tess's house, going through Selene's clothes.

'Hey, I got your voice mail about what's going on. I'm sorting,' she said, pointing to the various piles around her. 'Dirty and clean—Miss Waites seems a little confused about how laundry works. Then, we further subdivide into "whore" and "not whore." Yes, in case you're wondering—I'm bored out of my mind. I'd be cataloging her books—if she owned more than two.'

'Well, if we're lucky, Miss Talbot's Boarding School for Spoiled Actresses may be able to close down today.'

'I don't see how—' Flip began.

'Trust us,' Tess said, leading him back to the living room, Whitney trailing. Selene was smiling at something on her phone's screen, although the smile disappeared when Whitney snatched the phone away from her. In fact, this time Selene actually dared to grab for the phone, but Whitney swatted her away. Selene then tried to climb Whitney, reaching for the phone the whole time, but Whitney simply tossed the iPhone to Tess.

' "Whassup?" ' Tess read. 'Would it have been so hard to write it as two words? Who's this from? Oh, it's from *Pete*. Should I answer him?'

Selene was a scrapper. She leaped off Whitney and tried to charge Tess, but Whitney caught her by the arm and held her fast.

U R BUSTED, Tess typed back, once she figured out how to make the iPhone's keyboard appear. Then, to Selene: 'So where is Johnny while he's pretending to be kidnapped?'

'Shut up!' Selene yelled, putting her hands over her ears. 'Shut up, shut up, shut up!'

'Selene, you know I went through your phone the other night. That's how I found out about you and Ben. And that's why Whitney has been checking your phone at every opportunity, to see who else calls you on a regular basis. And, thanks to the wonders of the iPhone, she's also had easy access to your e-mail.'

'Ben?' Flip squeaked. 'What about Selene and Ben?'

Tess didn't have time for that side trip. 'Whitney noticed that a large volume of your e-mail came from someone named Pete. I didn't think about it twice, until I remembered that Whitney called Johnny "St. Pete" at breakfast the other morning. Apparently, Johnny thinks that's too funny, the joke about his real name being St. Petersburg but he shortened it to Tampa. He uses it every chance he gets. So this guy—the man who says he hates you, and you say you hate him—has been in constant contact with you. What's that about?'

Selene burst into tears. *Damn, she's good,* Tess thought.

'Oh, stop it, Selene. It's clear that you and

313

Johnny were in on this together, but once you got a security detail, more of the dirty work fell to Johnny. We know why you want out of *Mann of Steel,* but what's Johnny's angle? This is supposed to be his big comeback.'

Selene, realizing her tears were having no effect, not even on Flip—who still seemed stuck on the reference to Ben—slouched her way over to one of the overstuffed chairs. 'Derek wanted Johnny for the other lead in that movie he's developing, the one about the gay chaplains in World War I. They share a manager, and he asked Flip and Ben to work around Johnny's schedule if he got a movie, and they said no, they had to have him in first position. It was unfair, if you think about it. They wanted it both ways—they were cutting Johnny's part to build up mine, but they still insisted he was the lead. The linchpin.'

A part of Tess's mind registered the correct use of *linchpin*. The Selene she knew—or thought she knew—would have said clothespin. Oh, what a fine actress she was. *Actor.*

'What about Greer's murder? Do you know anything about that?'

'No,' Selene said. 'It was just that Johnny couldn't make waves. He's been out of work too long to risk a reputation as difficult. Whereas for me—the crazier I am, the higher my quote goes, the more in demand I am. So we agreed that I would be the difficult one, make life hell for everybody.'

'What was in it for you?'

'Derek's company has the rights to a biopic of Sigrid Undset, the Nobel Prize winner. That and the biopic of Debbie Harry of Blondie, but I heard

314

she didn't think I could play her. Which pisses me off, given how hard I've been practicing.'

Well, that cleared up one mystery—the presence of *Kristin Lavransdatter* beneath Selene's bed. And, having heard Selene's version of 'Call Me,' Tess could understand Deborah Harry's reluctance.

'So the little fires, the disgruntled steelworkers, the angry community activist—that was all you?'

'Only the first two,' Selene said. 'The production managed to piss off the neighborhood lady on its own. That was pure lagniappe.'

This from a girl who had pretended not to know the difference between crawfish and mussels.

'But how did you—' Flip began.

'After you fired Alicia, Johnny went to her, asked for her help. She was happy to do it. She was pissed at being fired. She had an in with the local steelworkers, her dad being one and all. Plus, we paid her, and Alicia liked money.'

Alicia. Everyone had been focused on the suicide as the seminal incident, but Alicia had been fired subsequent to Wilbur Grace's suicide. Tess had a sudden memory of the decking material stacked in Alicia's backyard, the shelter magazines in the bathroom. *When I have time, I don't have money; when I have money, I don't have time.* Tess had assumed Alicia had run out of funds. But, no, she was just too busy with her two full-time jobs, video store clerk and set gremlin, to work on her house.

'Did she arrange the abduction of Johnny Tampa?'

'We set that up with some friends of Derek. After the smoke bomb Friday—not one that we planned, by the way, and Alicia said it wasn't her—

315

and the fight at the funeral, we thought it could tip the balance. Who could blame Johnny if he didn't want to come back to Baltimore for season two? He'd be traumatized.'

'Selene,' Tess said, still using the slow, patient voice that she had always used with the girl, although she realized now it was far from necessary. 'The things you've done—they're not practical jokes. You're in felony territory. Arson, making a false report.'

'I didn't report anything,' she pointed out. 'Johnny's driver did, and he was utterly sincere. He saw two guys grab Johnny. It's not our fault if he inferred something was going on.'

Tess sighed, even as part of her mind registered Selene's correct usage of *inferred*. 'Look, you're a smart girl, smarter than any of us knew. Maybe I can make this go away, but only if everything ends now. Where's Johnny?'

Selene gave Flip one last through-the-lashes look, one last trembling pout, but he wouldn't even meet her gaze. 'He's up in Philadelphia, playing cards and hanging out,' she said. 'The plan is for him to take the train home tonight and be found wandering in East Baltimore.'

'You were right,' Tess said to Flip, who looked absolutely stricken. 'It was Selene and Johnny all along, with the help of one disgruntled employee.'

'Who cares?' Flip said. 'It was one thing for Selene to be such a bitch—'

'Hey!' Selene objected. She probably wasn't used to being called that, at least not to her face.

Flip didn't care. 'But Johnny fucking Tampa. No one wanted to hire him when we picked him up. He only has heat because of this project. That guy is a fuckin' backstabber.' He looked as if he wanted to shake Selene. 'Do you two morons realize this wasn't just about you? That Ben and Lottie and I have careers, too? Not to mention the crew, which worked sixteen-, eighteen-hour days? Or the money—Jesus fuckin' Christ, the money. We're spending twenty-five million dollars, just to make eight episodes. Didn't any of that matter?'

Selene shrugged, lifting her tiny shoulders ever so slightly, making her shoulder blades stand out like bony, immature wings—not that anyone in this room would mistake her for an angel.

'You know what?' Whitney said. 'I liked you better when I thought you were stupid.'

*   *   *

It took much of the afternoon and pretty much all Tess's accumulated credits with various local law enforcement agencies to clean up Selene and Johnny's mess. The U.S. attorney's office, mindful of the fact that one of its own had once ruthlessly hounded Tess not so long ago, decided to ignore the whole thing. After all, the FBI hadn't been brought into it officially. The police and firefighters also calmed down, especially after Flip promised generous donations to their fraternal organizations. Tull got on the phone, too, largely to be assured that Selene and Johnny's reign of terror hadn't extended to Greer's murder.

'No,' Tess told him. 'One thing that they were clear on was that they had nothing to do with the incidents at the production office, not even Friday's smoke bomb. Didn't fit their strategy, which was to make the production look like a

317

public nuisance. Hey—did you find Greer's engagement ring?'

'No,' Tull said.

'Have you closed the case?'

'Getting there.'

She wanted to argue, although today's events made it more likely that JJ Meyerhoff had killed Greer. Selene had been genuinely mystified when Tess asked if Greer might have information that could harm *Mann of Steel*. 'By the way, there was a local girl tangled up in this mess, but I'd like to give her a bye. You see a problem there?'

'No, but then—none of this is my problem, thank God. Look, if there's no charges, there's no story. The problems go away, the production finishes up, and everyone goes back to fuckin' California. Looks like you actually managed to do what they wanted all along, protect them from the local media—and themselves.'

Tess hung up the phone. It was going on 3 P.M. and she hadn't found time to talk to Flip about his broken Emmy. It seemed almost too much. Maybe she should track down Ben, arrange to meet with him, confront him with the information she had about *Zervitz*.

Only—where was Ben? He had never shown up at the office, and no one had heard from him.

'He doesn't always come in or call,' Lloyd said when Tess asked if he knew where Ben was. 'He likes to write at Starbucks. But we have a deal—he always answers my messages, because I call only if it's important, shit-hit-the-fan time.'

'Call him now.'

'But, Tess—'

'Lloyd, the shit has hit.'

318

He did as he was told, sighing and shrugging. Somehow, it was more appealing on Lloyd than it had been on Selene. But then, Selene had been playing a part. Lloyd really was a peevish adolescent, sure that all the adults around him were idiots.

'He ain't answering,' he said, puzzled. 'But the phone's not off. If it was off, it wouldn't ring at all, just send me straight to voice mail. Let me try a text.'

The text, too, went unanswered.

'He should be calling back,' Lloyd said. 'He knows I only call if he's in trouble.'

'Work was called off,' Tess said.

'Ben might not know,' Lloyd pointed out. 'He don't check e-mail either.'

But maybe Ben did know the secret of the Emmy and what it held. Maybe Ben had the mystery letter all along. Tess was suddenly very tired of Hollywood people and their machinations. She decided to call Alicia Farmer, tell her that the jig was up, that Tess had protected her out of homegirl loyalty, misplaced as it might have been. Johnny and Selene reminded her of Tom and Daisy Buchanan, although she would never have described them as careless. They had been meticulous in the way they had tried to smash up things. True, local girl Alicia might have been a little money hungry, but she hadn't stood a chance with those slicksters.

Tess tried the video store first, only to be told that Alicia hadn't come in today.

'Didn't come in, or wasn't scheduled to come in?'

'Didn't show for her shift, which started at noon.

Boss is pissed.'

'Is this typical? Alicia not showing up?'

Impossible to know over the phone, but Tess sensed she had just been shunted off with a shrug for the third time that day.

'Not my problem. Although, I guess it is, because now I have to work to close and—'

Tess was not unsympathetic to the Charm City Video employee's plight, but she didn't have time for the rest of the story. She hung up, grabbed her keys and her purse, and raced out.

*   *   *

When she reached Alicia's house twenty-five long minutes later, she was relieved to hear footsteps heading to the door promptly upon her knock.

And surprised to be greeted by a very pale, drawn-looking man, circles under his eyes and a tremor in his limbs.

'Hey,' Ben Marcus said, his voice thin and flat. 'There's a guy just behind me, with a gun in my back, and he would like you to come inside, too, or he's going to kill me.'

Ben must have seen in Tess's face that she was quickly running through the possible options, wondering what would happen if she simply ran or began to scream. Or produced the gun from her own purse.

'He's already killed Alicia,' Ben said. 'He really doesn't have a lot to lose.'

Chapter 33

Alicia's body was on the floor of her den, facedown. Tess didn't know from forensics—she had never even seen an episode of *CSI*—but she was reliably sure that Alicia had been there for several hours, possibly overnight. She had been shot from behind, in the base of the head, presumably after turning her back on the man who now sat in one of the club chairs, a gun pointed at Ben.

Thoughts zinged through Tess's head like so many errant pinballs, and she managed to keep one ball in play longer than usual, banging it against various pockets of memory: *whap, whap, whap. Who, who, who.*

'You can't be Wilbur R. Grace,' she said at last to the man. 'But I think you must be connected to him.'

'He was my brother-in-law for thirty years and my best friend since I could remember,' said the man. How old? Fifties was the best Tess could do. Thin brown hair. Two eyes, yes, although you'd be hard-pressed to put a color to them. It was a face made to be forgotten. A local man, judging by his accent, the kind of man her Uncle Donald knew from his work in various state bureaucracies.

'And he killed himself, and you blame . . . ?'

Ben, who usually thrummed with excess energy, looked catatonic. How long had he been here? Since last morning? Since last night? Lloyd said he had been at the office with him until eleven. The older man, by contrast, looked fresh, composed.

321

'He hung himself in despair,' the man said, 'after Greer Sadowski reversed herself and claimed she had no memory of finding his treatment for our movie, *The Duchess of Windsor Hills*.'

'Ah,' Tess said, smiling more broadly than this weak bit of local wordplay deserved. Windsor Hills was a neighborhood in Northwest Baltimore; the woman who had persuaded the Prince of Wales to forsake the British crown was a Baltimore girl, Wallis Warfield Simpson. 'Very clever.'

'*We* thought so,' the man said defensively, unsure if he was being mocked. Perhaps he had been ridiculed a lot, or felt that way. 'You see, the Duke of Windsor was something of a Nazi sympathizer. If he hadn't married Simpson, he would have become king, and who knows what kind of world we would be living in now?'

'You have something there,' Tess said, falling back on one of her generically truthful phrases. *You have something there. That's an idea.*

'It was my concept, although Bob was the one who fleshed it out. He was the writer. Also the cinematographer. But the ideas often started with me, some offhand observation I might make. That's how we worked.'

'Sure,' said Tess, trying not to look at the body on the floor. *One shot, two shots, three shots, a dollar. Once you're in for capital murder, stand up and holler.* 'I bet.'

'*Don't* patronize me,' the man said, now pointing his gun at Tess. It was a small thing, not at all formidable, but at this range, it didn't have to be.

'I'm not,' Tess said. 'I'm piecing together what I

know. You had an idea, one similar to *Mann of Steel,* and you believe that someone from the production saw that idea—'

'I *know,'* the man said. 'I did it. I walked right up to this gentleman on the set of *The Last Pagoda* and handed him our idea, in a sealed envelope. I have a photo in my scrapbook, of me on set, and you can see this Ben Marcus right there in the background. That's a much more definitive link than anything that Zervitz put up, and he won a million dollars.'

He slapped a fabric-covered album on the coffee table with his left hand, holding fast to his gun with the right. So that was the scrapbook, the repository of his dreams.

'Over the years, we forgot about it, figured out no one ever saw it. But then this *Mann of Steel* show comes to town, and once Bob reads the pilot script, he's sure it's our story. Our idea was stolen and passed on to the son, but it's still ours.'

'Phil Tumulty doesn't send Flip birthday cards, much less give him ideas,' Ben put in, wan but defiant. 'If Phil Tumulty had a great idea—and he hasn't had one for years—he'd keep it for himself.'

'Shut up,' the man said, swinging the gun back to Ben. 'Shut up. You're the one who took our idea, you're the one who gave it to Flip. Phil Tumulty never saw it *because you took it.* Say it. Admit it.'

Ben straightened up, although it took him some effort. 'I would—if I did. But I honestly don't remember. If I ever read your scenario, it was, what? Fifteen years ago? Do you think I sat on it all this time, while developing other shows, thinking, Boy, this *Duchess of Wind-sor Hills* is my golden ticket? I don't remember it. Maybe I read it, maybe I didn't. But . . . I . . . didn't . . . remember . . . it, so how could I steal it?'

The man stood up, shaking all over, and Tess believed that he would have pistol-whipped Ben if it hadn't required stepping over Alicia's body to get to him. He was enough of an amateur to be squeamish. Good to know.

'There's time travel, same as ours,' he said, holding up the index finger of his left hand. 'A regular guy—factory worker in ours—involved with a royal woman.' Middle finger out, followed quickly by his ring finger, which had a slender gold band. 'And, finally, there was the concept of the alterna-history, how things change if you disrupt even one tiny thing. You had Napoleon, we had Nazis, but it was basically the same.'

'Maybe,' Ben said. 'Possibly. If I ever saw it— only I didn't.'

That was enough to goad the man into standing up, crab-walking past Alicia's body, and smacking Ben with the pistol. Ben's nose started to gush blood, and he whimpered. Tess tried to get her hand inside her bag where her Beretta waited, safe and serene, but she wasn't quick enough.

'Is that what everyone has been looking for, this letter written years ago? Is that the proof you needed to bring your claim against the production?'

'It's not proof—' an unrepentant Ben began nasally, hands clapped over his bloody nose, and while Tess was impressed by how ballsy he was, she tried to cram a world of meaning into one stern look. *Shut UP.*

'We didn't keep a copy. Bob didn't even have a

computer then. People didn't, in 1992, and we didn't think to photocopy it. We thought we were dealing with an honorable man. He kept calling the office, asking for a meeting with Flip Tumulty, sure he would do the right thing if he knew. The girls kept putting him off, although this one'—he gestured at Alicia's body—'didn't mind selling him the pilot script, so he could start working on the comparison chart that our lawyer recommended. But after that, she stopped taking his calls, made the other girl deal with him.'

Alicia had sold Wilbur 'Bob' Grace the scripts, then taken Selene's and Johnny's money to wreak havoc on the set. Whatever one thought of her ethics, she was certainly entrepreneurial.

'So who found the letter, after all?' Tess asked.

'Ms. Sadowski. She called Bob, all excited, said she had found what he wanted. Then, two days later—she denied it all, said she was mistaken. I knew she was lying. But Bob gave up, and Alicia got fired, so she didn't have access to Flip anymore. I had to get to the other one, don't you see? I knew she had it, that she couldn't destroy it. And once I got into her apartment, I was more sure than ever it was at the office, but I couldn't go back there. . . .'

Back there. Tess's mind registered that. He had been to the office and Greer's apartment. But it had all been for naught.

'Alicia found it, Friday night,' Ben said. 'She was the one who planted the smoke bomb, then hid in the building until the firefighters left. Then she went into the office and found it. The only thing I can't figure out is where, because I've been looking for it since Greer died.'

325

'The base of Flip's Emmy.' Tess gave him a sad look, aware of the irony. 'Lloyd dropped it just last night, and the band popped off, and I remembered how you said—'

'That Greer was always buffing Flip's Emmy, that she had just brought it back from being shined up. Damn. I can't believe Alicia figured that out and I didn't.'

The man with the gun had grown impatient, or perhaps he felt frustrated that even a firearm couldn't guarantee him center stage. 'It was my property, with Bob gone. She had no right to sell it. But I came here this morning, and she said she was going to meet with Ben next, see what he was willing to pay, and that she would get back to me.' He was waving his hands as he spoke, getting more and more worked up. Tess didn't think that was to anyone's benefit. '*Get back to me.* Do you know how many times I've heard that? Do you know how many times I said that, back when I had a job? *I'll get back to you.* It always means they won't, that you'll have to call and call, and ask to speak to their supervisors.'

Tess gave him a chance to catch his breath, then asked: 'Can I see it?'

'What?'

'The letter, the one you say you gave to Ben.'

'It's not a matter of saying. I have photographic proof.' He gestured again to the scrapbook lying on the coffee table in front of Ben, then opened it with his left hand. He was being very disciplined about maintaining his grasp on his gun, much to her disappointment.

Tess looked. There indeed was a young Ben, in the background of a photo, which had been

326

carefully labeled. GEORGE ON THE SET OF *THE LAST PAGODA,* SUMMER 1992.

'You're George?' she asked. Fifteen years had worn much differently on this man than they had on Ben. Harder. Was it just that the trip from twenty to thirty-five was less fraught than the journey from early forty-something to late fifty-what-ever? Or had this man weathered a much tougher fifteen years than Ben?

'I'd prefer to be called Mr. Sybert. I deserve that courtesy.'

'Okay, Mr. Sybert.'

Ben looked stricken, as if knowing the man's name put them at greater risk. *It's not* Reservoir Dogs *and he's not Mr. Brown,* Tess yearned to tell him. *For one thing, you're not tied to that old sofa. For another, you still have both your ears.* There was a dead body at their feet and the man had already revealed his relationship to Wilbur Grace. His name was small potatoes.

'So you came here this morning, thinking you were going to be given this letter?'

'Yes.'

'And you just happened to have a gun with you?'

Mr. Sybert hesitated, working through the implications of Tess's question.

'None of this matters, Mr. Sybert,' she assured him. 'I'm not a police officer, and this isn't a confession. I'm merely curious. I want to know your side of things. Did you come here, knowing you would use violence if Alicia didn't give you what you wanted? Or was it more like the night at the production office, where you lost control and killed Greer when she refused to listen to you?'

'I didn't kill that girl,' he said tentatively, as if

327

testing a story out. 'She was dead when I got there. I started to search for things, but I got scared and left.'

'Here, though . . .' Tess was making a considerable effort not to throw up when she looked at the body between them. Judging by Ben's face and the sickly dairy smell that lingered in the room, he had lost that battle sometime earlier.

'I pulled the gun, but only to get what I wanted.' He was still trying out his story, thinking as he spoke. 'It was an accident?'

'I can see how that might happen,' she lied. Again, one didn't have to be a regular viewer of *CSI* to wonder how a person got shot in the back of the head, accidentally. The silence in the room stretched out, uncomfortable, possibly lethal. Tess knew that she could get to her gun and get a shot off. But Ben was so nearby. She couldn't be sure that Mr. Sybert wouldn't shoot him, if only by accident. And—she tried to suppress the thought, but there it was, flickering at first, then bright as neon: *She didn't want to kill this man, if she could avoid it*. Yes, she knew he had shot Alicia, and probably in the most cowardly fashion possible. She didn't believe his story about Greer, either. Yet she couldn't help thinking that if she kept calm, if she continued to show him respect, all three of them might leave here alive.

'A friend of mine explained the basics of the Zervitz case to me,' Tess said, more to Ben than to Sybert, as if she had all the time in the world. 'The thing that sticks in my head is that they never proved the producers of the film saw the original treatment. They just proved that they *might* have, that it was reasonable to infer that from the similarities. Expert witnesses for both sides then argued whether the film clearly plagiarized the two-page scenario. The plaintiff's witness said yes, the defense's witness said no, and the jury decided they believed the plaintiff.'

'Home court advantage,' Ben muttered. Tess wished he would stop being so damn feisty. She had a hunch that simple acknowledgment could go far in this situation.

'Well, let me be the judge. Literally. Mr. Sybert, would you show me the letter—'

'No,' he said, patting his breast pocket with his left hand. 'I don't intend to let anyone else touch this.'

'Then read it to me, Mr. Sybert. Go through it, a paragraph at a time, and then we'll let Ben counter how his idea was different. After all, with me you'll have—what did Ben call it—home-court advantage. And I always root for the home team.'

She was charmed in spite of herself by how conscientiously Mr. Sybert managed to remove the letter and his reading glasses from his pocket, all the while keeping a firm grip on the gun. Ah, too bad, she had hoped he might put it down for this recitation.

'Let the record reflect,' he began 'that the letter is dated June 19, 1992. Now that I have it in my possession, I can have someone test it, however they do that, prove that it was written when it says it was, but you can see'—he flipped it quickly, too quickly for Tess to see anything, not that it mattered—'that it was written on a typewriter, just as I told you. That typewriter is still in Bob's house by the way, so we'll be able to match it.'

'Noted for the record,' Tess said, in what she hoped was a judicious tone.

'For fuck's sake,' Ben said. Tess tried another stern look, but Ben was impervious. Luckily, Mr. Sybert had started to read.

' "Dear Mr. Tumulty: As you may recall, we met a few years ago, when you were filming *Pit Beef*. I was the photographer who came to the set with my brother-in-law, George, and talked to you about the old Westview movie theater, how weird it was to see Barry Levinson use that as a nightclub in *Tin Men*. Anyway, I am a filmmaker, too, and although I usually work from classic texts, my brother-in-law, George, had a terrific idea the other day: What if Wallis War-field Simpson, a Baltimore girl as you well know, didn't marry King Edward, but instead settled in Windsor Hills with a nice Baltimore boy who worked in a factory?" '

He looked up at Tess expectantly. 'Okay,' she said. 'I see the royal angle. You had the would-be Duchess of Windsor settle for a Baltimore boy—'

'A factory worker,' Mr. Sybert clarified.

'Ben has a steelworker romancing Napoleon's future sister-in-law. I'll give you that point. It's suspiciously similar.'

'Don't I get to speak?' Ben asked.

'Keep it brief,' Tess admonished.

'Okay, two things: Betsy Patterson's marriage to Jerome Bonaparte didn't last. And, two, our original plan was for Mann to leave Patterson in the nineteenth century, let her pursue her destiny. That's in the bible. It's the network that wanted them to marry and time-travel together.'

Tess pretended to think about this. 'I see what you're saying,' she said. 'Still, this round goes to

Mr. Sybert.'

The man's chest seemed to expand. Someone was listening to him, drinking in every word with rapt attention. Attention must be paid, as Mrs. Loman had tried to tell us. Mr. Sybert resumed reading.

'"Now, as many people know, Edward was thought to be a Nazi sympathizer. But if Wallis Warfield Simpson had married someone else and Edward had not, in fact, given up the throne, could that have affected the outcome of World War II? In our alternative version of history, Mrs. Simpson's decision to marry a Baltimore man has that catastrophic effect, and the present day shows us a world controlled by the Nazis. The resistance's only hope is to send an emissary back into the past and get Mrs. Simpson to make a different romantic choice."'

'That's a direct steal from the *Terminator*,' Ben said. 'I can't believe you're calling me a plagiarist when you're ripping off James Cameron right and left.'

'Ours is an homage,' Mr. Sybert replied. 'Besides, that's our very next line— Think *Terminator*, by way of Robert Harris. See, the fact that you mentioned that movie proves that you read Bob's letter.'

'Or proves that there's no such thing as an original idea, so it's actually reasonable to believe I developed my show without ever seeing your stupid letter.'

Stupid was a mistake. Tess saw the man's cheeks redden while his chest, swollen with pride just a few seconds ago, started heaving.

'I agree with Mr. Sybert,' she said quickly.

'There's a difference between conscious tribute and ripping off someone's idea without acknowledgment. And it is awfully coincidental that you cited the same movie, Ben.'

'A person would have to be a moron not to see—' he began, then finally—*finally*—caught the look in Tess's eye and seemed to realize exactly who, in this scenario, was being moronic. 'Okay, I concede this round, too. I mean, I'm not admitting that I did anything, but I can see that a jury might find it suspect. But then I always knew that a jury might not believe me. That's why I panicked when Greer showed me the letter, stuck in a bunch of school crap that Flip asked her to sort. My conscience is clear on this score, and I haven't been able to say that very often in my life. I think the local jury was crazy to find for the plaintiff in that other case, but I could see that these guys had an even better case. I told Greer I would get her a paid job if she could make the letter disappear.'

'And that's when she became Flip's assistant,' Tess said, still trying to work out the timeline.

'No, that was a few weeks later, after Alicia was fired for letting go of the pilot script. Remember, Greer was an unpaid intern at first, going through boxes of crap, same as Lloyd is doing now. God knows what *he'll* find on me, given enough time. When she came back for the second favor, I saw I was never going to be free of her.'

'So *you* killed her,' Mr. Sybert said.

'What the fuck are you talking about? I wasn't even there that night.' Ben's confusion was genuine, but Tess realized that Mr. Sybert was sophisticated enough to realize that a defense attorney could offer conflicting theories if he were

332

tried in Greer's death—the boyfriend did it, the blackmailed writer did it. But Mr. Sybert was still going to have to explain how Alicia had ended up dead at his feet.

'This is about money,' she said. 'Plain and simple. Mr. Grace's idea was used, and he was entitled to payment. Mr. Sybert, as his heir—'

'Well, my wife, Marie, is his heir, but she's helpless about money matters,' he said. The warm, wry affection inspired by his wife was so normal, so endearing that Tess almost forgot the gun in his hand, the one, maybe two people he had killed.

'What if we paid you a half million and gave your brother-in-law a created-by credit?'

'No fucking way,' Ben fumed, but Tess could tell he was playing along now, that he realized he shouldn't cave too easily. 'I could have optioned the last three Pulitzer Prize winners for that kind of money. And I've got the created-by credit on this. You're taking money out of my pocket.'

'Well,' Tess said, 'that's how damages work. Someone has been hurt. Someone has to make up for that. And I know from the background checks that I performed on the production that you have that much cash in your Fidelity account alone. You could probably run up to the local branch right now and get a cashier's check in that amount. I'll stay here, for insurance as they say.'

'It's almost five now,' Mr. Sybert objected, 'and he'd never make it in time, not in rush hour.'

'Not even if he took Northern Parkway to Perring, then took that back way over to Providence Road?'

'Oh, I know a better shortcut than that,' Mr. Sybert said.

'No way. How would you go?'

And that was all it took, the Achilles' heel of the born, bread-and-buttered Baltimorean, his—or her—certainty of the city's geography, the parochial pride in knowing the best shortcuts. Mr. Sybert put his gun down on the coffee table, ready to show Tess on the back of one of Alicia's magazines how to drive to Towson in rush hour— and she head-butted him, threw herself into his soft, round stomach so hard that she tipped over the chair in which he was sitting.

There was much thrashing of limbs and grunting on both their parts, more than Tess had anticipated. He was stronger than he looked, but then—he would have to be. After all, she was now certain that he had beaten a woman to death, which required considerable stamina and commitment. All Tess could do was hope that Ben Marcus had seen enough goddamn movies to realize he should grab the gun left on the table.

In fact, Ben had the posture down—legs braced, if a little quivery, both hands holding the gun. Yes, he had the posture down, but not, thank God, the patter. In fact, Ben didn't utter a single syllable in the endless two minutes it took for Tess to retrieve her own gun and call 911.

Not that Mr. Sybert was fighting anymore, either. He sat placidly on the floor, reading and rereading his brother-in-law's letter. He wasn't smiling—he wasn't so crazy that he couldn't realize how much trouble he was in—but the letter clearly brought him some comfort. He had proof, and someone had finally listened to him. On some level, he believed himself vindicated.

'He was really so very clever,' he said when the

sirens began echoing down Walther Avenue. 'My brother-in-law, I mean. Bob. He could have made a beautiful movie, as good as anything you'd see in Hollywood, if only someone had given him a chance.'

'I suppose,' Tess said, as kindly as she could to a man who had killed two women, 'that it really does come down to who you know.'

Ben opened his mouth, as if to contradict her, then stopped. His instincts were good. If he had said something argumentative or tried a bit of snappy banter just now, Tess might have pistol-whipped him, too.

LAST LOOKS

JANUARY

Chapter 34

The *Mann of Steel* premiere—really, more a one-time showing for the Baltimore-based crew and their families, as the real premiere was to be in Los Angeles two days later—was held at the Senator Theater. The grand old movie house had screened many of Baltimore's homegrown projects and had its own Grauman-style sidewalk devoted to the various productions. The squares didn't come cheap, and Tess knew that Lottie had wanted to forgo the tradition. But Flip was keen to have one, even if it did end up in what Ben called the 'Tumulty ghetto,' just beyond the area devoted to his father's work.

There was even a red carpet of sorts, although no real stars to walk it. Selene Waites was in Prague, working on an independent film, while Johnny Tampa refused to attend when the production—Lottie again—balked at sending him *four* first-class tickets—one for him, one for his mother, one for the newly minted Mrs. Tampa, and one for *her* mother. Lottie was willing to go as high as three but drew the line at Tampa's mother-in-law. The new Mrs. Tampa, a former Miss Hawaiian Tropic Tan, had been met and married in a whirlwind courtship over the Christmas holidays. But the courtship was not so heady, according to gossip, that Johnny had neglected a prenup.

Good old Johnny, Tess thought, studying one of the posters outside the theater, where Johnny had been given the benefit of a much tighter jawline than he had in real life. *He thinks everything through.*

A local television reporter tried to catch Tess's eye when she stopped, but she managed to get inside before he could approach her. She and Ben had agreed not to talk publicly about what happened in Alicia Farmer's house, and George Sybert was remaining silent as well. As far as the public knew, a city man had killed a city woman in some sort of personal dispute, then agreed to a plea bargain that the beleaguered state's attorney's office was happy to make. Some details couldn't be kept back—George Sybert's name, the fact that he had been fired from the school district a few months earlier and was increasingly desperate to provide for his invalid wife—but those facts only confused the situation more. A deal had been struck, and there would be no jail-house interviews about stolen scenarios and *The Duchess of Windsor Hills,* no accusations of plagiarism.

And no charge against Sybert for the murder of Greer Sadowski. That one remained on JJ Meyerhoff's scorecard. Sybert could not be shaken in his story: He went to the office that night to confront Greer, and she was already dead. Yes, he was the one who had opened drawers, but he hadn't taken her ring, didn't even remember seeing a ring. Tess had been scouring pawnshops and less-than-meticulous antique dealers all fall and into the winter, looking for the simple pear-shaped diamond she remembered, but nothing had shown up. She had even asked Marie Sybert if she had received the gift of a ring last fall, but the poor woman had denied it, and Tess didn't have the heart to press her. Marie Sybert had enough worries, with her brother dead and her husband in prison.

Tess understood the police indifference to breaking Sybert's story down. There was no percentage in letting citizens know that they had killed the wrong suspect while the real killer had remained at large, only to kill again. She understood—the first rule of bureaucracy is 'Cover your ass,' as her father might say—but she didn't have to like it. The only consolation was that the decision had been made far above Tull's head, and she believed that this particular closed case would remain forever open to the conscientious detective. If he got a chance to clear Meyerhoff, he would. Would a ring in a pawnshop prove anything? Only if someone at the store could swear that it was Sybert who had brought it in. Even then, that might not be enough. She was chasing her own MacGuffin, but it seemed more productive than trying to persuade Sybert to confess. Still, she kept visiting him, in hopes he might come clean.

'I wish you had killed me that night,' George Sybert said the last time that Tess saw him, a week before Christmas. 'My life insurance would have been sufficient to take care of Marie.'

'Are you sure?' Tess asked.

'Oh yes, I know all the ins and outs of my policies.'

'No, I mean—are you sure that you'd like to be dead?'

'Marie would be better off.'

'Does Marie think so?'

His eyes moistened, and Tess had to remind herself that this disarmingly devoted husband had killed two women. The problem with George Sybert—the problem with most of humankind—was that the only pain that mattered to him was his own. He mourned his brother-in-law and best friend. He would go to any lengths to take care of his Marie. But what about Greer? What about Alicia? Neither one deserved to be dead.

Boy meets girl. Bob Grace gets to Alicia, then Greer gets to him, promising him the document he thinks will prove everything. *Boy loses girl.* Greer recants, and Bob Grace, despairing of seeing his dream realized, kills himself. His brother-in-law takes over his quest. *Boy gets girl.* George Sybert kills Greer, then Alicia.

'Popcorn?' Crow asked.

'Of course,' Tess said.

Tess, Crow, and Lloyd had been given reserved seats, far better than Lloyd's status would normally confer, just two rows behind the producers. Ben motioned Tess to join him in the aisle.

'Can you keep a secret?' Ben asked.

'I would think that my track record speaks for itself.'

The old Ben might have had a comeback for that. The new one said:

'We're getting a pickup, even before the first episode airs. It's not exactly the vote of confidence it seems—they just don't have enough in the production pipeline, so they're using the pickup to create heat for the show. You know—*a show so good we didn't even wait for ratings.* That kind of crap. But they were really excited by the reaction at T.C.A.'

'T.C.A.?'

'The television critics. They meet twice a year,

preview stuff. We got great buzz.'

'Congratulations. So *Mann of Steel* returns to Baltimore. I'll try to keep the glorious news to myself.'

Ben glanced over his shoulder to see who was nearby. 'That's the thing—we're not coming back here. The network gave us an early pickup, in part, so we could figure out a way to work around everyone's schedule. Johnny's going to do his film this winter, while we've agreed to keep Selene light during the season so she can go make her vanity biopic. But the trade-off is we have to do it closer to home, probably Vancouver. It simplifies things, especially now that Johnny's new wife has decided she wants to live in Hawaii part of the year. Besides, the Maryland Film Commission's budget was slashed. No more givebacks.'

'So everyone gets what they want, and Baltimore is left empty-handed?'

'Most of Baltimore. How many people live here? Six hundred thousand or so? Well, five hundred ninety thousand, nine hundred ninety-nine get bupkes. But if Lloyd settles down, earns his GED? Flip and I are committed to paying his way through school. USC, NYU, community college, a technical school if that's what he wants—he gets in, we pay. And we'll do whatever we can to find him work when he gets out.'

Tess was stunned—happily, for once. 'That could be a lot of money, four years of college.'

'Yeah, it's about what I make a month, since we negotiated our new deal.' The man who had once called her an asshole waited, clearly expecting Tess to say something cutting or sarcastic, but she was at a loss.

'Well . . . thanks. That's huge.'

Ben seemed a little disappointed that rudeness had failed her for once. 'The movie's starting. We should go back to our seats.'

'It's a television show.'

'Well, we call it the movie sometimes.'

'And actresses are actors. Sorry, I've been out of the loop.'

Before the screening of the pilot, Flip took the stage and made a little speech, thanking the crew and the city, hitting all the right self-deprecatory notes. Tess remembered him at Greer's memorial service, how well he had spoken there, too. Yes, Flip had the knack of saying the right words in the right way, but did he ever mean any of them? Here he was, praising his father's hometown to the skies, knowing that he wouldn't be returning. He had gotten what he needed out of the city and was moving on. The people who were laughing appreciatively at his jokes and witticisms would have to find new gigs, perhaps move to other cities for work.

Flip returned to his seat to enthusiastic applause, and *Mann of Steel* began with a bright, peppy credit sequence that made Baltimore look like the Disney version of a working-class town. Tess watched, absorbed in spite of herself. It was actually pretty good. But as the show wore on, she couldn't help noticing that something had changed. *She* had changed. Aware now of what happened behind the camera, she couldn't stop breaking down the effects required by each scene. There was Mann in the union office, but all Tess could focus on was pudgy, vain Johnny Tampa and the view through the window, which she now knew to be translights, computer digitized images lighted for daytime. She watched Selene float into the frame, and she thought about how the camera must have rolled along a track to create that giddy, gliding sensation. She listened to the sounds of a modern port, knowing much of it had been overlaid later, in a studio. She saw the moon rise and wondered if that had been easier or more difficult to capture than a sunrise, or if some stupid local girl had blundered into that shot as well.

And then, just like that, it was over.

With the crew present, the credits were one of the indisputable highlights, applause and shouts greeting each name. Even Tess found herself applauding one small line of type—*based on a short story by Bob Grace*. With eight episodes this season and a pickup for next, that credit was better than an annuity for Marie Sybert, Bob's heir. That had been Flip's idea, but it hadn't been done out of kindness, or even a belief that George Sybert had a legitimate claim. It was simply the cheapest way to buy Sybert's silence, to end any embarrassing talk of theft and plagiarism. More important to Flip, it kept his father out of things. For the thing that bugged Flip the most, Ben had told Tess, was not the possibility that someone would think his idea was stolen, but that it had been offered to his father first.

Lloyd's credit—assistant to Mr. Marcus—was at the very end, one of a long list. Tess and Crow hooted, pumping their fists, while Lloyd pretended to be profoundly humiliated. Or maybe he wasn't pretending. Tess noticed that others in the crew had cheered, too, and felt encouraged. Maybe

Lloyd had found his place in the world, a place where he could succeed.

'It's so much better than I thought it would be,' she whispered to Crow as the lights came up.

'Well,' he said, gathering up the debris at their feet, 'based on everything you ever told me, it would have to be.'

'No, I mean it's good, really good. When I could forget how they did things—and when I could forget that the leads were played by two people I loathe—it was really affecting, and surprisingly funny. They got Baltimore right. Sort of.'

She wondered if she would ever be able to watch a television show or a film in the same way again, now that she knew too much. She wondered if it was even possible to know too much about something—or someone—that you had once loved. And she had loved movies, once upon a time, not even a decade ago, when it was unthinkable not to be in line at the multiplex every weekend, when it was urgent and essential to see movies the very night they opened. In college, she had once driven to a Philadelphia art house, a distance of more than a hundred miles, to see— well, what was it that she had driven almost two hours to see? A German film, possibly Herzog, maybe Wenders. *The American Friend*? *Aguirre, The Wrath of God*? That was it—*Aguirre*, a film in which a character clutched something secret and vital in his hand, yet died without ever revealing what it was. Tess had left the theater almost in a swoon, so dazed and rapt by Herzog's images that she forgot to get a cheese steak on her way out of town.

Yet here was Lloyd, who knew far more about

what happened behind the scenes than she did, and it was still magical for him. In fact, the movies might just save Lloyd's life.

'Dinner?' Crow asked.

'Sure,' Tess said. 'Lloyd's choice. It's his night, after all.' So what if he picked some lowbrow franchise? A little grease was probably good for the stomach and the soul.

She glanced back at Flip and Ben, surrounded by well-wishers and sycophants, all those little moths beating their wings against the bright promise embodied in the two friends' careers. Tess could all but read their thoughts: *If only they had a contact, an in, a friend of a friend of a friend. If only they could tell someone of their amazing ideas, they would be rich beyond their wildest dreams.*

Someone—an older man, the kind of person who seldom attracted a second glance, whether alone or in a crowd—appeared to be thrusting an envelope toward Ben, but he was much too slick for that now. He raised his hands, as if to surrender—then shoved them back into his pockets and quickly walked away, motioning Flip to follow. The man rescued his envelope from the theater's sticky floor and watched them go, his face still weary with hope.

AUTHOR'S NOTE

I put these things at the end for a reason, so be forewarned: You might read something here that will spoil part of the story for you.

This is a work of fiction. Seriously. Yes, I am married to a television producer, David Simon, one of those behind HBO's *The Wire*. But *The Wire,* during its six years in Baltimore, had little drama behind the scenes. The actors were down-to-earth; the crew worked hard; the only real drama queen along the way was the former mayor of Baltimore. In order to write this novel, I had to create my own show—not just the concept, but its cast and crew, its behind-the-scene problems and interpersonal relationships—wholly from scratch. The only true thing in this book is that people in television work harder than most of us can ever imagine.

In that light this book is dedicated to the memory of Bob Colesberry, an executive producer on *The Wire* for seasons one and two. No one ever worked harder on filmmaking, or loved it more. Bob died just as season three was beginning to prep. I don't want to pretend to a greater friendship with him than I had, but I will be forever grateful to Bob because (a) he was always up for a good meal and (b) he helped keep my significant other happy and relatively sane. (David once described their working relationship, which dates back to *The Corner,* as one of the most successful shotgun marriages in history.) Nina K. Noble continues in that latter capacity, bless her and all the other Nobles—David, Nick, and Jason. Ditto, Joe Chappelle. William F. Zorzi Jr. and George Pelecanos also were sources of ballast, and while I wouldn't say that Ed Burns keeps David sane, he does help him to stay grounded and makes the work better in every way. It's impossible to name everyone in our extended *Wire* family, which included virtually every department head and actor, but I do want to give a shout-out to Karen Thorson and John Chimples. Last but never least, I am indebted to Laura Schweigman, David's assistant. 'The *good* Laura,' as we often call her, is sweet, conscientious, and supercapable. She was kind enough to take time, in the middle of her sixteen-hour days, to explain to me the inner workings of a production office.

While I'm on the subject of family—Ethan Simon is the best son that any hardworking father ever had and the best company his stepmom has ever known; Ethan's mom, Kayle Tucker Simon, could make a claim to being Ms. Incredible, given her flexibility in the face of unending chaos.

As for *my* sanity—to the extent that I have any, I credit the staff of Spoons and Todd Bauer. I also owe props to Linda Perlstein and John Miller, good neighbors and good friends. Besides, John let me use his iPhone to see just how quickly a novice could learn to navigate the device without any instruction.

Two names in this text appear here because of donations made, respectively, to Health Care for the Homeless and the Parks & People Foundation's Ella Thompson Fund. Thank you, gentlemen, for your generosity to two causes that mean so much to my house-hold. You know who

351

you are.

Finally, partial spoiler here: *Zervitz v. Hollywood Pictures* was a real lawsuit and is presented here in a factual light, based on my own reporting during my years at the *Sun*. I never wrote about the case, but I read the entire court file and interviewed several of the principals. Any errors—whether they involve the production of a television show, legal issues, the tenancy rate or security systems at Tide Point, or even the regular presence of a Kobe beef hamburger on the menu at Nasu Blanca—are my own, the consequence of oversight, manipulation, or downright wishful thinking.